THE MONSTE

Hidden beneath the streets of London
ment known as The Monster Club, whe.. ...
different kind of Bloody Mary and ghouls tear into their gruesome repasts.
Here, along with the usual monsters – vampires, werewolves, ghouls, and
some of Dr Frankenstein's more freakish creations – you'll find other,
less familiar ones. You'll meet the frightening Fly-by-Night, the hideous
shaddy, the horrible mock, and the dreaded shadmock, perhaps the most
terrible of all.

When Donald McCloud offers a starving man a meal, he unexpectedly
discovers that the man is a vampire – and he's the main course! Accompa-
nying the vampire, Eramus, to The Monster Club, Donald encounters a
whole host of strange monsters, who, in a series of five linked stories,
recount to Donald their monstrous exploits. But as Donald is regaled with
these tales of monsters and their unfortunate human victims, it gradually
dawns on him that as the only human in a club full of bloodthirsty monsters, he might be in a bit of a predicament. . . .

First published as a paperback original in 1976, R. Chetwynd-Hayes's
The Monster Club was adapted for a 1981 film starring Vincent Price, John
Carradine and Donald Pleasence, and both book and film have gone on
to become cult classics. Told in a wry, tongue-in-cheek style, the tales
in *The Monster Club* are simultaneously horrific, comical, and curiously
moving. This edition is the first in more than twenty years and features a
new introduction by Stephen Jones and a reproduction of John Bolton's
painting from the comic book adaptation of the film.

R. CHETWYND-HAYES

THE MONSTER CLUB

With a new introduction by

STEPHEN JONES

VALANCOURT BOOKS

Richmond, Virginia

2013

The Monster Club by R. Chetwynd-Hayes
Originally published London: New English Library, 1976
First Valancourt Books edition, October 2013

The Publisher is grateful to Mr John Bolton for his kind
permission to reproduce his painting for the cover of this edition.

Published by Valancourt Books, Richmond, Virginia
Publisher & Editor: JAMES D. JENKINS
20th Century Series Editor: SIMON STERN, University of Toronto
http://www.valancourtbooks.com

ISBN 978-1-939140-76-0
Also available as an electronic book

All Valancourt Books publications are printed on acid free
paper that meets all ANSI standards for archival quality paper.

Cover painting by John Bolton
Set in Dante MT 11/13.2

'Shadmocks Only Whistle': An Introduction to
The Monster Club

RONALD CHETWYND-HAYES came relatively late to writing fiction. His first book was not published until 1959, when he was about to enter his forties. Yet in a career that spanned the four decades until his death in 2001, he published thirteen novels, edited twenty four anthologies and was the author of more than 200 short stories, collected in twenty-five volumes and reprinted in numerous languages around the world.

Despite his aristocratic name, Ronald Henry Glynn Chetwynd-Hayes was born at 7 Swan Street in the West London suburb of Isleworth on May 30, 1919. The son of Henry (a movie-theatre manager) and Maisie, his mother tragically died at a young age and Ronald was fostered during his early years before going to live with his grandmother and then his aunt, Doris Cleghorn.

He left school in 1933 and for the next six years worked in a number of dead-end jobs, mainly as an errand boy for a butcher or hardware store. The young Chetwynd-Hayes also appeared as a schoolboy extra in a number of pre-War British movies, including *A Yank at Oxford* (1938) and *Goodbye, Mr. Chips* (1939), and he developed a life-long devotion to the moving pictures.

'I haunted the cinemas and fantasized film stories, with myself playing the leading roles,' he remembered. 'I cannot count the number of times I rescued Fay Wray from the clutches of King Kong!'

In 1939, at the outbreak of World War II, he followed his Quartermaster Sergeant father into the Army, rising to the rank of Sergeant in the Middlesex Regiment. He was one of thousands of soldiers successfully evacuated from Dunkirk, only to return to the beaches of France on D-Day.

Once his Army service was over, Ronald joined the furniture department of Harrods' world-famous store in London's Knightsbridge as a trainee buyer. Four and a half years later he moved to the Peerless Built-in Furniture Emporium in fashionable Berkeley Street as a showroom manager. He also discovered that he had a brother, Len, who he never knew existed. The pair of siblings became close friends and quickly made up for lost time.

Ronald lived in a basement flat in Richmond for many years until his Aunt Doris died, when he moved into her house at Hampton Hill. Throughout this period he read voraciously and, soon convinced that he could do better himself, he began writing his own stories – everything from romances to his favourite genre, historical fiction. Despite infrequent success – he sold his first story, 'The Orator', to *The Lady* magazine in 1953 – along the way he garnered numerous rejection slips from periodicals and book publishers.

'I used to try to write the great novel,' he once lamented. 'Try to be another Brontë. But, of course, nobody wanted to publish it. Then when I looked on the bookstalls and saw all these supernatural titles, I thought that was obviously the market to aim for. I'd always been interested in the supernatural anyway.'

In fact, his first published work was a science fiction novel, *The Man from the Bomb*, which appeared from John Spencer's Badger Books imprint in 1959. 'I sent that all over the place,' he recalled. 'Badger offered to take it, so I let them have it. They paid me £25 for the novel and all rights to it. The layout and printing were terrible, but I was so delighted to see a book of mine in print, I was inclined to overlook those defects.'

With a published book finally under his belt, the author followed it in 1964 with a novel from Sidgwick and Jackson about reincarnation, *The Dark Man* (later repackaged in America as a romantic Gothic under the title *And Love Survived*). But only after it was rejected by nineteen other publishers.

By the late 1960s and early '70s he had started selling short stories to such anthology series as the infamous *Pan Book of Horror Stories* and the *Fontana Book of Great Horror Stories* and the *Fontana Book of Great Ghost Stories*. He then decided to put his own collection together, and *The Unbidden* appeared from Tandem Books in 1971.

The next few years were highly productive for Ronald. Not only was he turning out multiple collections with titles like *Cold Terror*, *Terror by Night*, *The Elemental*, *The Night Ghouls and Other Grisly Tales* and *Tales of Fear and Fantasy*, but in 1973 he had also taken over editorship of *The Fontana Book of Great Ghost Stories* from Robert Aickman.

'In those days, everything to do with the supernatural sold,' he explained. 'At one time I had six volumes with my name on them in bookshops.'

Now hailed as 'Britain's Prince of Chill', Ronald's highly original tales of terror and the supernatural invariably combined horror and humour in equal measure, giving them a style that was uniquely the author's own. 'I've always got this terrible urge to send the whole thing up,' he admitted. 'It just slips in, I have never been able to stop it.'

Not only was he happy to write about such genre standards as ghosts, demons, ghouls, vampires and werewolves, but he delighted in making up his own bizarre monster variations that managed to stretch the imaginations of both author and reader alike – the Wind-Billie, the Mudadora, the Slippity-Slop, the Gale-Wuggle, the Cumberloo, and Ronald's own personal favourite (and mine), the Jumpity-Jim.

This ability to create new creatures is perhaps never more evident than in his most famous book, *The Monster Club*, in which he set out 'The Basic Rules of Monsterdom':

Vampire – sup; Werewolves – hunt; Ghouls – tear; Shaddies – lick; Maddies – yawn; Mocks – blow; Shadmocks – only whistle.

Published as a paperback original in March 1976 by New English Library in Britain, the volume was quickly reprinted in a number of foreign editions around the world.

The Monster Club consists of five original stories linked by a Prologue, four 'Interludes' and an Epilogue set in the titular establishment, situated somewhere off Swallow Street in London.

The book was moderately successful at the time, but Ronald was soon back at work on his novels and compiling various collections and anthologies, and *The Monster Club* only received its first hardcover edition, from Severn House Publishers, in 1992.

Twenty years earlier, while still selling furniture in London's West End, Ronald had been approached by film producer Milton Subotsky, who had wanted to make a film of some of his stories under the Amicus Productions banner. 'We'd just been taken over and I'd got the sack,' he recalled, 'so it was marvellous. I became a freelance writer on the strength of it. It terrified me – I suddenly realized I had to live on my own wits – but it was something I wanted to do. Look at the book I turned out as a result of that!'

Following the successful anthology format the company had established with such portmanteau films as *Dr. Terror's House of Horrors* (1965) and *Torture Garden* (1967), Amicus adapted four of the author's stories – 'The Gate Crasher', 'An Act of Kindness', 'The Elemental' and 'The Door' – in *From Beyond the Grave* (1973), featuring an all-star cast that included Peter Cushing, Donald Pleasence and Diana Dors.

In 1980 Ronald was again contacted by Subotsky, who by this time had a new production company, Sword & Sorcery, and wanted to make a horror film for children, based around Ronald's collection of linked stories, *The Monster Club*.

'Milton Subotsky was the kindest man I ever met,' observed the author, 'but he should never have made a film. His idea of humour was silly. He had to crack a walnut with a sledgehammer. In *The Monster Club*, he had that business where Richard Johnson gets up out of his coffin and says, "I was wearing a stake-proof vest", then turns to his wife and says, "Look, ketchup!" They could have made it much funnier.'

Filmed at Shepperton Studios and various locations around Hertfordshire by director Roy Ward Baker, Ronald visited the set during shooting and met the stars of the film, horror veterans Vincent Price and John Carradine (who was reputedly a replacement for Christopher Lee). 'Poor old John Carradine played me in the film,' explained the author. 'That was Milton's idea of a joke because I had put him into the book as "Lintom Busotsky", an anagram of his name.

'When I saw Carradine he was seventy-four years old and crippled with arthritis. At the preview, a lady came up to me and said, "I'm so sorry you suffer from arthritis." I said, "I don't, that's John Carradine!"'

Released in 1981 by ITC Entertainment Group, with an impressive supporting cast that included Donald Pleasence (again), Stuart Whitman, Britt Ekland, Simon Ward, Patrick Magee and Anthony

Steel, scriptwriters Edward and Valerie Abraham adapted three of the author's stories, of which only two – 'The Humgoo' and 'The Shadmock' – were included in the original book. ('My Mother Married a Vampire' was in fact taken from a 1978 collection by the author.)

'Vincent Price played a vampire in *The Monster Club*,' recalled Ronald about the linking story, 'and he was good. He was such a nice man, and he would tell me some wonderful stories about Hollywood.'

ITC was so confident about the success of the film that they commissioned a thirty-page comic book adaptation, scripted by Dez Skinn and illustrated by John Bolton, to distribute as a promotional item (the cover of which graces this particular edition), while New English Library issued a film tie-in paperback with a scene from the movie on the front.

Unfortunately, back in the early 1980s critics and audiences didn't know what to make of a horror film specifically targeted at children (today it constitutes a hugely successful sub-genre known as 'young adult') – especially one that included some already-outdated songs (from B. A. Robertson, The Pretty Things and UB40, amongst others) and a cartoon stripper who peeled off all her flesh!

In the end, *The Monster Club* was poorly distributed in the UK and was eventually released directly to television in America. However, over the years its reputation has continued to grow, and a recent DVD release has only cemented its position as a cult favourite amongst some viewers.

After eventually breaking into the booming paperback market of the early 1970s, Ronald began a long and successful relationship with publishing company William Kimber in 1978 with the publication of his first hardcover collection, *The Cradle Demon and Other Stories of Fantasy and Horror*, which he also considered to be his best.

Over the next ten years (until the imprint disappeared and he was forced to find another publisher for his work), Ronald produced a further twelve original collections for Kimber, which were aimed principally at the library market in Britain.

These books proved to be extremely popular, and Ronald was always proud of the fact that each year he was one of the highest earners of the annual Public Lending Right (PLR), based on the number of times an author's books are loaned out from libraries in the UK.

In 1989 both the Horror Writers of America and the British Fantasy Society presented Ronald with Lifetime Achievement Awards, and he was the Special Guest at the 1997 World Fantasy Convention in London.

When, due to failing health, Ronald's stream of imaginative fiction began to dry up in the late 1990s, it was my honour to help him compile some new volumes of his fiction, which were produced in handsome hardcover editions that quickly sold out of their modest print runs.

In May 2000 he moved into a care home in Teddington, where he died of bronchial pneumonia on March 20th the following year at the age of 81.

Ronald often stated that he was writing for posterity and that he hoped his stories would continue to appear to entertain new generations after his death: 'I'm writing for the future. I hope in a hundred years' time some editor will find one of my old books and decide it will fill up a gap. And so I shall live again. In that respect, I suppose being a writer is very much like being a vampire . . .'

With this welcome reissue of *The Monster Club*, the inimitable Ronald Chetwynd-Hayes and his fiction certainly live again. My hope is that readers familiar with the book will rediscover its pleasures, while those who are coming upon his work here for the first time will enjoy it enough to seek out more of his titles.

As Ronald himself would have said: Happy Shuddering, and may black angels keep watch around your bed.

STEPHEN JONES
London

September 25, 2013

STEPHEN JONES is a prolific editor of horror anthologies and the author of *Basil Copper: A Life in Books* (2008), which won the British Fantasy Award. His books have previously received the Hugo Award, several Bram Stoker Awards, and the World Fantasy Award. He has edited several collections of the stories of R. Chetwynd-Hayes, including *The Vampire Stories of R. Chetwynd-Hayes*, *Phantoms and Fiends*, and *Frights and Fancies*.

THE MONSTER CLUB

CONTENTS

AUTHOR'S NOTE

I would like to stress that the Monsteral Table which can be found on page 54 is only intended as a rough guide to the breeding habits of modern monsters. Interbreeding between primates, secondaries and hybrids is not common, but not unknown. For example, if a *shadmock* should mate with a *vampire*, their issue will be known as a *shadvam*. A *mock* to a *ghoul* would produce a *mocgoo*, and so on.

In the third story I have crossed a *ghoul* with a *human* – or in monsteral parlance a *hume* – and begat a *humgoo*.

Doubtless if the serious student of monstrumology keeps his eyes open, he will discover many strange mixtures walking about in our public places or strap-hanging in the underground.

The basic rules of Monsterdom

Vampires – sup; Werewolves – hunt; Ghouls – tear; Shaddies – lick;
Maddies – yawn; Mocks – blow; Shadmocks – only whistle.

Prologue

Donald McCloud, despite his Scottish name, had a heart as big as the world, and in consequence a bank account much smaller than it should have been. He could not pass a match-seller without buying most of his stock. Collectors for charity gravitated into his orbit like wasps to a jar of honey: clergymen with belfries in need of repairs came to his door with outstretched hands, and begging letters formed a large part of his daily mail. Therefore when the little man in the dirty raincoat fainted in the Charing Cross Road, he was the first, if not the only person, from the passing crowd, to offer assistance. He ran forward, knelt down on the damp pavement and turned the little man over.

A man with a much smaller heart might well have been revolted by what he saw. The little face was merely a skull covered with dead-white skin, the lank hair looked like greasy cotton, and the large, yellow teeth were chattering in a most alarming fashion.

'How do you feel?' Donald enquired when the pale blue eyes opened and gave him a cold stare. A hoarse whisper seeped out from behind the yellow teeth.

'Famished.'

'Oh, dear!' Donald thought of restaurants, cafés, Lyons' tea shops, then he looked at the skeleton scarecrow on the pavement and thought again. 'Look, you must come to my place.'

'Famished,' the little man repeated. 'Need nourishment.'

'Yes, I can see you do. We'll take a taxi, then I'll get you a meal.'

'Me mouth's dry.' The little man, assisted by Donald got shakily to his feet and eyed the passers-by hungrily. 'Me stomach's empty.'

'Disgraceful!' Donald glared at the prosperous looking man who was staring at the little starveling with total disbelief. 'You talk about an affluent society and here is a man who is near starvation.'

'Famished,' the little man insisted. 'Haven't had a sup for two weeks.'

'Taxi!' Donald's voice rang out like a clarion call. 'Emergency, taxi . . .'

Donald helped the little man up the stairs and into his top floor flat, where he seated him in an armchair, before repairing with all haste to the kitchen. He heated up some hot-pot left over from yesterday, and opened a tin of creamed rice which had been strongly recommended on a television commercial only the week before. He then arranged this makeshift meal tastefully on a nice pink formica tray and carried it into the sitting-room. The little man watched his approach with something less than enthusiasm.

'Now,' Donald said heartily, 'set to . . . er . . . what shall I call you?'

'Eramus.' The little man was looking at the steaming hot-pot with marked distaste. 'I don't think I could eat that.'

Donald nodded with understanding sympathy. 'Naturally, when you have gone without food for such a long time, you will have to be careful. Sip some of the gravy and that will get your digestive juices working again.'

'I don't think you get the picture, guv,' Eramus said. 'I can't keep solids down. This is not my scene, see.'

'You mean,' Donald frowned, 'you have to live on slops?'

Eramus appeared to be a little embarrassed.

'Sort of. You could say I have to live off a special kind of slops. Red slops.'

'You mean . . . ?'

Eramus nodded very slowly. 'That's right, guv. I'm a vampire.'

Donald regained consciousness some twenty minutes later and found that Eramus had thoughtfully put a wet towel round his head and poured a glass of whisky down his throat. There was also a slight soreness on the left hand side of his neck, and when he tentatively explored the area of discomfort he discovered two minute punctures. Eramus was apologetic.

'I hope you didn't mind, guv, but I only moistened me lips. Well, just a swig. After all, you did invite me up for nourishment.'

'I do think you might have asked,' Donald complained, as he clambered unsteadily to his feet, then staggered to the nearest chair. 'I mean to say, it's rather bad form to help yourself.'

'The trouble is, guv,' Eramus did his best to explain, 'I find most people are backward in coming forward, when they're asked to part with a drop of the red stuff. Greediness really, because most of 'em have got more than they need.'

'I'm of the opinion,' Donald stated with deep sincerity, 'that being a vampire is not a nice profession. In fact, if you will forgive me for saying so, it's disgusting.'

'You don't have to tell *me*, guv,' Eramus exclaimed with much shaking of head. 'It's bloody horrible. There's no profit in being a vampire these days. I mean to say, put yourself in my place. Imagine a diet of blood, night after night, year after year. And don't think it's easy to come by. People are educated now. Not like when I first started in this game.'

'Educated!' Donald expressed his surprise. 'In what way?'

'Horror films.' Eramus made a rude noise and screwed up his face into an expression of profound displeasure. 'They shouldn't be allowed. A gross betrayal of professional secrets. Taking the blood out of our mouths.' He leaned forward and emphasised his indignation with shaking forefinger. 'Do you realise that every Tom, Dick and Harry now knows that two pieces of crossed wood is poison to us? And that business of running water. A very good friend of mine was lured into a shower bath by a wench who ought to have had her arse tanned. Another thing – whenever I kip down in me wooden overcoat, I can never be certain some knowall won't get cracking with a sharp stake during me rest period.'

Donald's kind heart was greatly distressed by this account of the tribulations suffered by a persecuted minority group, and he signified his sympathy by a deep sigh.

'I can quite understand your difficulties. On the other hand, blood is one of the few commodities that is not taxed these days, and naturally people are rather keen to hang on to it. I can't help feeling that there is an excellent opening for a manufacturer who is prepared to can blood and sell it to you people at a handsome profit. Possibly some kind of supermarket would be in order. Then you could stroll round with a wire basket and purchase your needs.'

Eramus tried to smile, but due possibly to lack of practice, did not quite make it.

'That's a great idea, guv, and I'd like to say it's a treat to find someone who can see our point of view. Most people go all toffee-nosed whenever they find out my line of business. I appreciate your kindness, and so will my friends, whatever their afflictions.'

'We have all got our crosses to bear,' Donald remarked sententiously. Eramus flinched.

'Please, guv, I'd rather you didn't use that word.'

'I do beg your pardon. Now, about . . . your immediate needs . . .'

'S'alright, guv.' Eramus waved his hand. 'The little refresher you so kindly donated 'as set me on my feet, so to speak, and I'll be able to get round to the club. There I'll be able to have my weekly ration.'

'Club!' Donald was aware of a certain lively curiosity. 'I was not aware that . . .'

'Oh, yes,' Eramus nodded, 'we drop-outs have to be united, or we'd have been wiped out years ago. We've got what you might call, a varied membership. Apart from my lot, there's werewolves, snakemen, waspwomen, stranded hadel-monsters, ghouls, both common and king, a few of old Baron Frankenstein's not-so-successful experiments, one fly-by-night that got grounded by a broken wing, a Jumpity-Jim that's been looking for a virginal bare back for the past twenty years, and a thing from outer space that got left behind from a reconnoitring party back in '57.'

'Goodness gracious!' Donald could not help shuddering, although he knew this could be interpreted as an impolite act towards his guest. 'You must have . . . some jolly times.'

'We have some rare old get togethers,' Eramus agreed, 'specially around Christmas time. Tell you what, how would you like to come round sometime?'

'I don't know.' Donald displayed reluctance, although he felt a certain fearful interest. 'Surely I wouldn't fit in. I mean, I'm not . . .'

'Not a monster?' Eramus made a hollow, and what Donald could only think of as a churchyard chuckle. 'But you are, guv. See it from our point of view. You eat meat and veg, apple pie and cream, you sleep at night, and walk about when the sun is blazing 'ot and does a lot of other unnatural things. There again, you've no horns that I can see, or scales, pointed ears, fur, gills, fangs, snout, tail, talons, tusks – I'd say, begging your pardon, you're the biggest monster of us all. Let me take you along as a guest, and if you like, I'll put you up to the committee as a prospective member.'

Donald experienced all the gratification that comes to one who is on the outside, and has been invited to come in.

'That's really awfully kind of you. But won't it be too much bother?'

Eramus emitted a kind of bubbling chuckle.

'Bother! How you carry on, guv. You'll be a feather in my cap, as the saying goes. Devil, love a duck, you'll be doing me a favour.'

'If you put it that way,' Donald found his curiosity out-voting his reluctance, 'I can't very well refuse.'

'Then get your hat and coat,' Eramus instructed, 'and we'll be on our way.'

'What – now?'

'No time like the present.' Eramus got to his feet and rubbed his hands in joyful anticipation. 'The night is short and we vamps have to live for the moment. There's a flipping parson round my way, that I'd be willing to swear has his tabs on me. Hurry up, I'm famished again.'

The Monster Club was situated in Swallow Street, tucked unobtrusively between an oyster bar and a curry restaurant, and reached by means of a flight of ill-lit steps which ran down into a deep basement. Donald followed his host through a gloomy passage, round two or three corners, in and out of several doorways, and at length into a small, brightly lit reception hall. A tall, extremely thin man with a corpselike face, who looked as if he might be Eramus's elder brother, stood behind a counter. He was staring at a notice board, which announced in large red lettering:

> In this club all members are equal, be they of claw, talon or fang: skin, fur, or scale: from grave, tomb or laboratory: if they slither, walk or crawl: if they breathe, gasp or do neither. No one monster will take precedence over another.
>
> Signed EATM Ghoul (Hon Sec)

'Evening, Theobald,' Eramus greeted this sad looking individual. 'Still on the wagon?'

Theobald nodded mournfully. ''Fraid so. Aint 'ad so much as a nibble all week.' He looked hopefully at Donald, then asked in a low whisper. 'What's all this then? Brought your own dinner?'

'No, this is my guest. Guv, meet my cousin, Theobald. Like the rest of us vamps, he's down on his luck.'

'I am sorry,' Donald commiserated, while gripping a cold, dead hand that seemed reluctant to part company with his own. 'I do hope something turns up for you.'

'Thank you, sir.' Theobald inclined his head, then turned to Eramus. 'Got your ration book, Eramus? The committee has tightened up since the acute blood shortage.'

Eramus produced a very dingy brown book from his breast pocket, and Theobald snipped three coupons from a single page with a pair of nail scissors. In return he handed him a red card.

'Good for four small glasses,' he said.

'Barely enough to keep skin and bone together,' Eramus complained, pushing open a green baize door. 'When I think of the gallons I have donated as a subscription in the past, it makes my fangs rattle.'

But Donald paid him little attention, being more concerned with the scene now before him. It was a large room, looking much like an ordinary, fairly high-class restaurant: tables were covered with snow-white cloths, gilt, high-backed chairs, there was even a small stage at one end, where a three-man band was playing some low, blood-cooling music. The lighting was dim, which from Donald's point of view, was just as well. For the clientele was such as to send the normal guest screaming from the room. He saw the hairy face, beetling brows of the werewolf: the long mournful face and shrouded form of the common or graveyard ghoul: the square head, hulking body of the odd monster turned out by some mad scientist in his mountain laboratory: the solid stone mass of the Golem: the writhing coils of the snake-woman: the slimy tentacles of an awful looking thing, that might well have strayed in from some black lagoon, and lots of other weird looking creatures that could have been related to two or more of the predominate monsters.

The vampire family seemed to provide all the staff. A cigarette girl, attired in a flimsy costume, bared her long eye-teeth in a simpering smile: a waiter, resplendent in black, drooled when his pupil-less eyes alighted on Donald's well-fleshed neck. As for the orchestra leader, he had a pair of fangs that jutted out over his lower lip and dimpled his chin.

The waiter led them to a table situated in one corner, just to the left of the stage. There he handed Donald a menu that was divided into various sections, each catering for the needs and appetites of the different customers. Vampires fared very badly. Under the single item 'Four Glasses Per Person', was the footnote 'Why not have part of your ration clotted and served with ice-cream?'

The ghouls came off best. Under the heading 'Meat Dishes', Donald observed such tasty dishes as 'Pickled Carrion Served With Tombstone Sauce', and, 'Graveyard Stew – A Must For The Mostest'. Werewolves were invited to 'Grind Your Fangs On a Virginal Thighbone', while marine monsters were offered 'Long Dead Sailor In Shipwreck Gravy'. Way at the bottom of the menu was a section headed: 'Human Donators', and this, Donald found, catered for his needs. He could order fish and chips, roast beef and Yorkshire pudding, stewed tripe and onions, and much else that was guaranteed to 'Replenish What Has Been Taken So You May Donate Again'. He was a little uneasy regarding this instruction and drew his host's attention to it. But Eramus dismissed it with a wave of his hand.

'No need to worry, you're a guest. We vamps have come a long way since the days when the old count used to take his nourishment where he found it. You get stuck in to whatever you fancy, and if you care to donate afterwards, that's entirely up to you.'

Donald ordered roast beef which he thought was fairly safe, and hoped the chef would not get careless and mix his dishes. Eramus had his ration served with strawberry ice-cream, and really one had to admit it did look most appetising. Then he sat back and feasted his eyes on the various celebrities that were dining at nearby tables.

Eramus drew his attention to a large, well built lady with a square head who was entertaining a number of odd looking creatures, who seemed to have been wrongly put together. One had hands sprouting from where his ears should have been. Another had a superabundance of noses; one extremely large organ was flanked on either side by two smaller, and misshapen ones. Yet another had a perpendicular row of ears running down either side

of his decidedly long face. Even as Donald was about to frame
a very intelligent question, the large lady proclaimed in a loud
whisper.

'Really, I cannot be held responsible for my grandfather's mistakes.'

'Baroness Frankenstein,' Eramus whispered. 'The grand-daugh-
ter of the great baron and his home-made bride.'

Donald said, 'Oh!' and watched the baroness with great interest, for he had followed her grandfather's amazing career on late
night cinema from early childhood.

'She has a very kind heart,' Eramus explained, 'and keeps what
you might call a proprietary eye on her grandfather's little mishaps. She dines 'em here twice a year.'

Donald would have asked some very pertinent questions, had
they not been interrupted by the arrival of one of the more strange-
looking creatures that had aroused his curiosity from the moment
he had entered the dining-room. Eramus made the introduction.

'Guv, this is Manfred the werevamp.'

There was a mutual exchange of courtesies and Manfred lowered himself into a chair and accepted an offer of a Bloody Mary,
while Donald examined his really alarming appearance. He saw a
long, deadly white and not unhandsome face, which was enhanced
by the vampire's long eye-teeth, but here his resemblance to the
blood-drinkers ended. The long matted hair, the taloned hands and,
in particular, the fur covered tail which had to be pushed through
a special hole in the chairback when he sat down – all proclaimed
descent from a werewolf. The large, brown eyes were sad as he
downed the Bloody Mary in a single gulp, and Donald suspected
he had been over-indulging for some time.

'Manfred has a problem,' Eramus confided, 'which is only to be
expected if you think about it.'

'I am sorry,' said Donald, his compassion instantly aroused.
'What exactly is his problem?'

'Well, it's like this,' Eramus began, then with an unexpected
delicacy nodded to Manfred. 'You tell him, Manfred.'

'Briefly,' the werevamp spoke in a low, cultured voice, 'my
mother was a vampire of a very good family, descended from the
famous Count, no less. But my father was a werewolf of frankly

– and I'm no snob – of proletarian stock. In consequence, I have a split personality. One half of me wants to genteelly suck, while the other demands I chew like a common beast. It really is too much, and sometimes I think it would be well if I went for a long walk in the bright sunlight.'

'Now, now,' Eramus admonished, 'that's no way to carry on. Try to look on the bright side. After all you have the best of two worlds. When there's a blood shortage, you can raise the old hackles and go hunting.'

'That's all very well,' Manfred shook his head, 'but don't you realise that the werewolf side of me only manifests during the period of the full moon? For the rest of the time I am a humvamp.'

'Satan's knee-breeches!' Eramus swore. 'That's grim. In fact it's the grimmest thing I have ever heard.'

'It certainly is. Half the time I don't know if I want to suck 'em or kick 'em.'

They were interrupted by a ghoul who asked if they could kindly direct him to the gentlemen's cloakroom. Manfred watched the retreating figure with some envy.

'At least he's got a trade,' he complained.

Donald's curiosity would not be denied, and at the risk of offending the afflicted creature opposite by a display of bad taste, he asked, 'Forgive me, but I was not aware that – how shall I put it? – different species could – eh – marry. Could you tell me how your father and mother . . . well, got together?'

'It's a long and sad story,' Manfred said, wiping a tear-bright eye on the back of a hairy hand.

'That it is,' Eramus nodded grimly. 'It's a story that I guarantee would make a statue weep. He's an orphan you know.'

'Oh, dear.'

'Yep.' Eramus nodded again, but this time with gloomy satisfaction. 'His father was shot to death with a silver bullet by a little perisher who had been to see *The Werewolf of Hackney Wick*. And his poor mother . . . You tell him, Manfred.'

'A mad parson with a tent peg and a coal hammer.'

'Which only bears out what my old dad used to tell me,' Eramus stated. 'Son, he said, keep well away from parsons and boy scouts.'

A long silence followed this profound statement, and Donald

used it to run his eye round the neighbouring tables and marvel afresh that such a collection of monsters could exist in modern, swinging London, and not be detected. Then he remembered some of the faces he had seen on the underground, and marvelled no more. Baroness Frankenstein was graciously listening to some anecdote being related by one of her grandfather's mishaps, and once interrupted to say: 'I understand the Baron's favourite expression was – "back to the drawing board".'

He was abruptly brought back to his immediate surroundings by Manfred suddenly asking: 'Would you care to hear the story of my lamented parents?'

'If it would not be too painful.'

Manfred sighed and displayed the feigned reluctance of the practised raconteur.

'You don't want to be bored by my family misfortunes.'

'Indeed I do,' Donald said, then realised that this was not perhaps the most tactful of answers. 'I would love to hear your story – so long as it does not cause you pain or embarrassment.'

'Spit it out,' Eramus invited, 'and don't balls about.'

The werevamp sighed. 'Very well, if you insist. But do you think before I begin . . .'

Eramus waved to the long-toothed waiter.

'Two Bloody Marys. Tomato juice for the human donator.'

'I will,' stated Manfred, after he had sipped from his glass, 'tell the story in the third person. This will make it more interesting, and after all, it is my father's story, not mine.'

And so, surrounded by members of the unique Monster Club, Donald sat back, nursed his drink and listened to the story.

The Werewolf and the Vampire

George Hardcastle's downfall undoubtedly originated in his love for dogs. He could not pass one without stopping and patting its head. A flea-bitten mongrel had only to turn the corner of the street and he was whistling, calling out: 'Come on, boy. Come on then,' and behaving in the altogether outrageous fashion that is peculiar to the devoted animal lover.

Tragedy may still have been averted had he not decided to spend a day in the Greensand Hills. Here in the region of Clandon Down, where dwarf oaks, pale birches and dark firs spread up in a long sweep to the northern heights, was a vast hiding place where many forms of often invisible life, lurked in the dense undergrowth. But George, like many before him, knew nothing about this, and tramped happily up the slope, aware only that the air was fresh, the silence absolute and he was young.

The howl of what he supposed to be a dog brought him to an immediate standstill and for a while he listened, trying to determine from which direction the sound came. Afterwards he had reason to remember that none of the conditions laid down by legend and superstition prevailed. It was mid-afternoon and in consequence there was not, so far as he was aware, a full moon. The sun was sending golden spears of light through the thick foliage and all around was a warm, almost overpowering atmosphere, tainted with the aroma of decaying undergrowth. The setting was so commonplace and he was such an ordinary young man – not very bright perhaps, but gifted with good health and clean boyish good looks, the kind of Saxon comeliness that goes with a clear skin and blond hair.

The howl rang out again, a long, drawn-out cry of canine anguish, and now it was easily located. Way over to his left, somewhere in the midst of, or just beyond a curtain of, saplings and low, thick bushes. Without thought of danger, George turned off the beaten track and plunged into the dim twilight that held perpetual domain during the summer months under the interlocked higher branches. Imagination supplied a mental picture of a gin-trap and a tortured animal that was lost in a maze of pain. Pity lent speed to his feet and made him ignore the stinging offshoots that whipped at his face and hands, while brambles tore his trousers and coiled round his ankles. The howl came again, now a little to his right, but this time it was followed by a deep throated growl, and if George had not been the person he was, he might have paid heed to this warning note of danger.

For some fifteen minutes, he ran first in one direction, then another, finally coming to rest under a giant oak which stood in a small clearing. For the first time fear came to him in the surrounding gloom. It did not seem possible that one could get lost in an English wood, but here, in the semi-light, he conceived the ridiculous notion that night left its guardians in the wood during the day, which would at any moment move in and smother him with shadows.

He moved away from the protection of the oak tree and began to walk in the direction he thought he had come, when the growl erupted from a few yards to his left. Pity fled like a leaf before a raging wind, and stark terror fired his brain with blind, unreasoning panic. He ran, fell, got up and ran again, and from behind came the sound of a heavy body crashing through undergrowth, the rasp of laboured breathing, the bestial growl of some enraged being. Reason had gone, coherent thought had been replaced by an animal instinct for survival; he knew that whatever ran behind him was closing the gap.

Soon, and he dare not turn his head, it was but a few feet away. There was snuffling, whining, terribly eager growling, and suddenly he shrieked as a fierce, burning pain seared his right thigh. Then he was down on the ground and the agony rose up to become a scarlet flame, until it was blotted out by a merciful darkness.

An hour passed, perhaps more, before George Hardcastle returned to consciousness. He lay quite still and tried to remember why he should be lying on the ground in a dense wood, while a dull ache held mastery over his right leg. Then memory sent its first cold tentacles shuddering across his brain and he dared to sit up and face reality.

The light had faded: night was slowly reinforcing its advance guard, but he was still able to see the dead man who lay but a few feet away. He shrank back with a little muffled cry and tried to dispel this vision of a purple face and bulging eyes, by the simple act of closing his own. But this was not a wise action for the image of that awful countenance was etched upon his brain, and the memory was even more macabre than the reality. He opened his eyes again, and there it was: a man in late middle life, with grey, close cropped hair, a long moustache and yellow teeth, that were bared in a death grin. The purple face suggested he had died of a sudden heart attack.

The next hour was a dimly remembered nightmare. George dragged himself through the undergrowth and by sheer good fortune emerged out on to one of the main paths.

He was found next morning by a team of boy scouts.

Police and an army of enthusiastic volunteers scoured the woods, but no trace of a ferocious wild beast was found. But they did find the dead man, and he proved to be a farm worker who had a reputation locally of being a person of solitary habits. An autopsy revealed he had died of a heart attack, and it was assumed that this had been the result of his efforts in trying to assist the injured boy.

The entire episode assumed the proportions of a nine-day wonder, and then was forgotten.

Mrs Hardcastle prided herself on being a mother who, while combating illness, did not pamper it. She had George back on his feet within three weeks and despatched him on prolonged walks. Being an obedient youth he followed these instructions to the letter, and so, on one overcast day, found himself at Hampton Court. As the first drops of rain were caressing his face, he decided to make a long-desired tour of the staterooms. He wandered from room to room, examined pictures, admired four-poster beds, then listened to a guide who was explaining the finer points to a crowd of tourists. By the time he had reached the Queen's Audience Room, he felt tired, so seated himself on one of the convenient window-seats. For some while he sat looking out at the rain-drenched gardens, then with a yawn, he turned and gave a quick glance along the long corridor that ran through a series of open doorways.

Suddenly his attention was captured by a figure approaching over the long carpet. It was that of a girl in a black dress; she was a beautiful study in black and white. Black hair, white face and hands, black dress. Not that there was anything sinister about her, for as she drew nearer he could see the look of indescribable sadness in the large, black eyes, and the almost timid way she looked round each room. Her appearance was outstanding, so vivid, like a black and white photograph that had come to life.

She entered the Queen's Audience Room and now he could hear the light tread of her feet, the whisper of her dress, and even those small sounds seemed unreal. She walked round the room, looking earnestly at the pictures, then as though arrested by a sudden sound, she stopped. Suddenly the lovely eyes came round and stared straight at George.

They held an expression of alarmed surprise, that gradually changed to one of dawning wonderment. For a moment George could only suppose she recognised him, although how he had come to forget her, was beyond his comprehension. She glided towards him, and as she came a small smile parted her lips. She sank down on the far end of the seat and watched him with those dark, wondering eyes.

She said: 'Hullo. I'm Carola.'

No girl had made such an obvious advance towards George before, and shyness, not to mention shock, robbed him of speech. Carola seemed to be reassured by his reticence, for her smile deepened and when she spoke her voice held a gentle bantering tone.

'What's the matter? Cat got your tongue?'

This impertinent probe succeeded in freeing him from the chains of shyness and he ventured to make a similar retort.

'I can speak when I want to.'

'That's better. I recognised the link at once. We have certain family connections, really. Don't you think so?'

This question was enough to dry up his powers of communication for some time, but presently he was able to breathe one word. 'Family!'

'Yes.' She nodded and her hair trembled like black silk in sunlight. 'We must be at least distantly related in the allegorical sense. But don't let's talk about that. I am so pleased to be able to walk about in daylight. It is so dreary at night, and besides, I'm not really myself then.'

George came to the conclusion that this beautiful creature was at least slightly mad, and therefore made a mundane, but what he thought must be a safe remark.

'Isn't it awful weather?'

She frowned slightly and he got the impression he had committed a breach of good taste.

'Don't be so silly. You know it's lovely weather. Lots of beautiful cloud.'

He decided this must be a joke. There could be no other interpretation. He capped it by another.

'Yes, and soon the awful sun will come out.'

She flinched as though he had hit her, and there was the threat of tears in the lovely eyes.

'You beast. How could you say a dreadful thing like that? There won't be any sun, the weather forecast said so. I thought you were nice, but all you want to do is frighten me.'

And she dabbed her eyes with a black lace handkerchief, while George tried to find his way out of a mental labyrinth where every word seemed to have a double meaning.

'I am sorry. But I didn't mean . . .'

She stifled a tiny sob. 'How would you like it if I said – silver bullets?'

He scratched his head, wrinkled his brow and then made a wry grimace.

'I wouldn't know what you meant, but I wouldn't mind.'

She replaced the lace handkerchief in a small handbag, then got up and walked quickly away. George watched her retreating figure until it disappeared round the corner in the direction of the long gallery. He muttered: 'Potty. Stark raving potty.'

On reflection he decided it was a great pity that her behaviour was so erratic, because he would have dearly liked to have known her better. In fact, when he remembered the black hair and white face, he was aware of a deep disappointment, a sense of loss, and he had to subdue an urge to run after her. He remained seated in the window bay and when he looked out on to the gardens, he saw the rain had ceased, but thick cloud banks were billowing across the sky. He smiled gently and murmured, 'Lovely clouds – horrible sunshine.'

George was half way across Anne Boleyn's courtyard when a light touch on his shoulder made him turn, and there was Carola of the white face and black hair, with a sad smile parting her lips.

'Look,' she said, 'I'm sorry I got into a huff back there, but I can't bear to be teased about – well, you know what. But you are one of us, and we mustn't quarrel. All forgiven?'

George said, 'Yes, I'm sorry I offended you. But I didn't mean to.' And at that moment he was so happy, so ridiculously elated, he was prepared to apologise for breathing.

'Good.' She sighed and took hold of his arm as though it were the most natural action in the world. 'We'll forget all about it. But, please, don't joke about such things again.'

'No. Absolutely not.' George had not the slightest idea what it was he must not joke about, but made a mental note to avoid mention of the weather and silver bullets.

'You must come and meet my parents,' Carola insisted, 'they'll be awfully pleased to see you. I bet they won't believe their noses.'

This remark was in the nature of a setback, but George's newly found happiness enabled him to ignore it – pretend it must be a slip of the tongue.

'That's very kind of you, but won't it be a bit sudden? I mean, are you sure it will be convenient?'

She laughed, a lovely little silver sound and, if possible, his happiness increased.

'You are a funny boy. They'll be tickled pink, and so they should be. For the first time for years, we won't have to be careful of what we say in front of a visitor.'

George had a little mental conference and came to the conclusion that this was meant to be a compliment. So he said cheerfully, 'I don't mind what people say. I like them to be natural.'

Carola thought that was a very funny remark and tightened her grip on his arm, while laughing in a most enchanting fashion.

'You have a most wonderful sense of humour. Wait until I tell daddy that one. I like them to be natural . . .'

And she collapsed into a fit of helpless laughter in which George joined, although he was rather at a loss to know what he had said

that was so funny. Suddenly the laugh was cut short, was killed by
a gasp of alarm, and Carola was staring at the western sky where
the clouds had taken on a brighter hue. The words came out as a
strangled whisper.

'The sun! Oh, Lucifer, the sun is coming out.'

'Is it?' George looked up and examined the sky with assumed
interest. 'I wouldn't be surprised if you're not right . . .' Then he
stopped and looked down at his lovely companion with concern.
'I'm sorry, you . . . you don't like the sun, do you?'

Her face was a mask of terror and she gave a terrible little cry of
anguish. George's former suspicion of insanity returned, but she
was still appealing – still a flawless pearl on black velvet. He put
his arm round the slim shoulders, and she hid her eyes against his
coat. The muffled, tremulous whisper came to him.

'Please take me home. Quickly.'

He felt great joy in the fact that he was able to bring comfort.

'There's no sign of sunlight. Look, it was only a temporary
break in the clouds.'

Slowly the dark head was raised, and the eyes, so bright with
unshed tears, again looked up at the western sky. Now, George
was rewarded, for her lips parted, the skin round her eyes crin-
kled and her entire face was transformed by a wonderful, glorious
smile.

'Oh, how beautiful! Lovely, lovely, *lovely* clouds. The wind is
up there, you know. A big, fat wind-god, who blows out great bel-
lows of mist, so that we may not be destroyed by demon-sun. And
sometimes he shrieks his rage across the sky; at others he whispers
soft comforting words and tells us to have faith. The bleak night of
loneliness is not without end.'

George was acutely embarrassed, not knowing what to make
of this allegorical outburst. But the love and compassion he had
so far extended to dogs, was now enlarged and channelled towards
the lovely, if strange, young girl by his side.

'Come,' he said, 'let me take you home.'

George pulled open a trellis iron gate and allowed Carola to pre-
cede him up a crazy-paved path, which led to a house that gleamed
with new paint and well-cleaned windows. Such a house could

have been found in any one of a thousand streets in the London suburbs, and brashly proclaimed that here lived a woman who took pride in the crisp whiteness of her curtains, and a man who was no novice in the art of wielding a paint brush. They had barely entered the tiny porch, where the red tiles shone like a pool at sunset, when the door was flung open and a plump, grey-haired woman clasped Carola in her arms.

'Ee, love, me and yer dad were that worried. We thought you'd got caught in a sun-storm.'

Carola kissed her mother gently, on what George noted was another dead-white cheek, then turned and looked back at him with shining eyes.

'Mummy, this . . .' She giggled and shook her head. 'It's silly, but I don't know your name.'

'George. George Hardcastle.'

To say Carola's mother looked alarmed is a gross understatement. For a moment she appeared to be terrified, and clutched her daughter as though they were both confronted by a man-eating tiger. Then Carola laughed softly and whispered into her mother's ear. George watched the elder woman's expression change to one of incredulity and dawning pleasure.

'You don't say so, love? Where on earth did you find him?'

'In the Palace,' Carola announced proudly. 'He was sitting in the Queen's Audience Room.'

Mummy almost ran forward and after clasping the startled George with both hands, kissed him soundly on either cheek. Then she stood back and examined him with obvious pleasure.

'I ought to have known,' she said, nodding her head as though with sincere conviction. 'Been out of touch for too long. But what will you think of me manners? Come in, love. Father will be that pleased. It's not much of a death for him, with just us two women around.'

Again George was aware of a strange slip of the tongue, which he could only assume was a family failing. So he beamed with the affability that is expected from a stranger who is the recipient of sudden hospitality, and allowed himself to be pulled into a newly decorated hall, and relieved of his coat. Then Mummy opened a door and ordered in a shouted whisper: 'Father, put yer tie on,

we've got company.' There was a startled snort, as though someone had been awakened from a fireside sleep, and Mummy turned
a bright smile on George.

'Would you like to go upstairs and wash yer hands, like? Make
yourself comfy, if you get my meaning.'

'No, thank you. Very kind, I'm sure.'

'Well then, you'd best come into parlour.'

The 'parlour' had a very nice paper on the walls, bright pink
lamps, a well stuffed sofa and matching armchairs, a large television set, a low, imitation walnut table, a record player, some awful
coloured prints, and an artificial log electric fire. A stout man with
thinning grey hair struggled up from the sofa, while he completed
the adjustment of a tie that was more eye-catching than tasteful.

'Father,' Mummy looked quickly round the room as though to
seek reassurance that nothing was out of place, 'this is George. A
young man that Carola has brought home, like.' Then she added
in an undertone, 'He's all right. No need to worry.'

Father advanced with outstretched hand and announced in a
loud, very hearty voice: 'Ee, I'm pleased to meet ye, lad. I've always
said it's about time the lass found 'erself a young spark. But the reet
sort is 'ard to come by, and that's a fact.'

Father's hand was unpleasantly cold and flabby, but he radiated
such an air of goodwill, George was inclined to overlook it.

'Now, Father, you're embarrassing our Carola,' Mummy said.
And indeed the girl did appear to be somewhat disconcerted, only
her cheeks instead of blushing, had assumed a greyish tinge. 'Now,
George, don't stand around, lad. Sit yerself down and make yerself
at 'ome. We don't stand on ceremony here.'

George found himself on the sofa next to Father, who would
insist on winking, whenever their glances met. In the meanwhile
Mummy expressed solicitous anxiety regarding his well-being.

'Have you supped lately? I know you young doggies don't 'ave
to watch yer diet like we do, so just say what you fancy. I've a nice
piece of 'am in t' fridge, and I can fry that with eggs, in no time at
all.'

George knew that somewhere in that kindly invitation there
had been another slip of the tongue, but he resolutely did not
think about it.

'That's very kind of you, but really . . .'

'Let 'er do a bit of cooking, lad,' Father pleaded. 'She don't get much opportunity, if I can speak without dotting me Is and cross-ing me Ts.'

'If you are sure it will be no trouble.'

Mummy made a strange neighing sound. 'Trouble! 'Ow you carry on. It's time for us to have a glass of something rich, anyway.'

Mother and daughter departed for the kitchen and George was left alone with Father who was watching him with an embarrass-ing interest.

'Been on 'olidays yet, lad?' he enquired.

'No, it's a bit late now . . .'

Father sighed with the satisfaction of a man who is recalling a pleasant memory. 'We 'ad smashing time in Clacton. Ee, the weather was summat greet. Two weeks of thick fog – couldn't see 'and in front of face.'

George said, 'Oh, dear,' then lapsed into silence while he digested this piece of information. Presently he was aware of an elbow nudging his ribs.

'I know it's delicate question, lad, so don't answer if you'd rather not. But – 'ow often do you change?'

George thought it was a very delicate question, and could only think of a very indelicate reason why it had been asked. But his conception of politeness demanded he answer.

'Well . . . every Friday actually. After I've had a bath.'

Father gasped with astonishment. 'As often as that! I'm sur-prised. The last lad I knew in your condition only changed when the moon was full.'

George said, 'Goodness gracious!' and then tried to ask a very pertinent question. 'Why, do I . . .'

Father nodded. 'There's a goodish pong. But don't let it worry you. We can smell it, because we've the reet kind of noses.'

An extremely miserable, not to say self-conscious, young man was presently led across the hall and into the dining-room, where one place was set with knife, fork and spoon, and three with glass and drinking straw. He was too dejected to pay particular heed to this strange and unequal arrangement, and neither was he able to really enjoy the plate of fried eggs and ham that Mummy put down before him, with the remark: 'Here you are, lad, get wrapped round that, and you'll not starve.'

The family shared the contents of a glass jug between them, and as this was thick and red, George could only suppose it to be tomato juice. They all sucked through straws; Carola, as was to be expected, daintily, Mummy with some anxiety, and Father greedily. When he had emptied his glass, he presented it for a refill and said: 'You know Mother, that's as fine a jug of AB as you've ever served up.'

Mummy sighed. 'It's not so bad. Mind you, youngsters don't get what I call top grade nourishment, these days. There's nothing like getting yer teeth stuck into the real thing. This stuff 'as lost the natural goodness.'

Father belched and made a disgusting noise with his straw.

'We must be thankful, Mother. There's many who 'asn't a drop to wet their lips, and be pleased to sup from tin.'

George could not subdue a natural curiosity and the question slipped out before he had time to really think about it.

'Excuse me, but don't you ever eat anything?'

The shocked silence which followed told him he had committed a well nigh unforgivable sin. Father dropped his glass and Carola said, 'Oh, George,' in a very reproachful voice, while Mummy creased her brow into a very deep frown.

'George, haven't you ever been taught manners?'

It was easy to see she spoke more in sorrow than anger, and although the exact nature of his transgression was not quite clear to George, he instantly apologised.

'I am very sorry, but . . .'

'I should think so, indeed.' Mummy continued to speak gently but firmly. 'I never expected to hear a question like that at my table. After all, you wouldn't like it if I were to ask who or what you chewed up on one of your moonlight strolls. Well, I've said me piece, and now we'll forget that certain words were ever said. Have some chocolate pudding.'

Even while George smarted under this rebuke, he was aware that once again, not so much a slip of the tongue, as a sentence that demanded thought had been inserted between an admonishment and a pardon. There was also a growing feeling of resentment. It seemed that whatever he said to this remarkable family, gave offence, and his supply of apologies was running low. He waited until Mummy had served him with a generous helping of chocolate pudding, and then replenished the three glasses from the jug, before he relieved his mind.

'I don't chew anyone.'

Mummy gave Father an eloquent glance, and he cleared his throat.

'Listen, lad, there are some things you don't mention in front of ladies. What you do in change period is between you and black man. So let's change subject.'

Like all peace-loving people George sometimes reached a point where war, or to be more precise, attack seemed to be the only course of action. Father's little tirade brought him to such a point. He flung down his knife and fork and voiced his complaints.

'Look here, I'm fed up. If I mention the weather, I'm ticked off. If I ask why you never eat, I'm in trouble. I've been asked when I change, told that I stink. Now, after being accused of chewing people, I'm told I mustn't mention it. Now, I'll tell you something. I think you're all round the bend.'

Carola burst into tears and ran from the room: Father swore, or rather he said, 'Satan's necktie,' which was presumably the same thing, and Mummy looked very concerned.

'Just a minute, son,' she raised a white, rather wrinkled fore-finger, 'you're trying to tell us you don't know the score?'

'I haven't the slightest idea what you're talking about,' George retorted.

Mummy and Father looked at each other for some little while, then as though prompted by a single thought, they both spoke in unison.

'He's a just bittener.'

'Someone should tell 'im,' Mummy stated, after she had watched the, by now, very frightened George for an entire minute. 'It should come from a man.'

'If 'e 'ad gumption he were born with, 'e'd know,' Father said, his face becoming quite grey with embarrassment. 'Hell's bells, my dad didn't 'ave to tell me I were vampire.'

'Yes, but you can see he's none too bright,' Mummy pointed

out. 'We can't all 'ave your brains. No doubt the lad has 'eart, and I say 'eart is better than brains any day. Been bitten lately, lad?'

George could only nod and look longingly at the door.

'Big long thing, with a wet snout, I wouldn't be surprised. It's a werewolf you are, son. You can't deceive the noses of we vamps: yer glands are beginning to play up – give out a bit of smell, see? I should think . . . What's the state of the moon, Father?'

'Seven eighths.'

Mummy nodded with grim relish. 'I should think you're due for a change round about Friday night. Got any open space round your way?'

'There's . . .' George took a deep breath, 'there's Clapham Common.'

'Well, I should go for a run round there. Make sure you cover your face up. Normal people go all funny like when they first lays eyes on a werewolf. Start yelling their 'eads off, mostly.'

George was on his feet and edging his way towards the door. He was praying for the priceless gift of disbelief. Mummy was again displaying signs of annoyance.

'Now there's no need to carry on like that. You must 'ave known we were all vampires – what did you think we were drinking? Raspberry juice? And let me tell you this. We're the best friends you've got. No one else will want to know you, once full moon is peeping over barn door. So don't get all lawn tennis with us . . .'

But George was gone. Running across the hall, out of the front door, down the crazy-paving path, and finally along the pavement. People turned their heads as he shouted: 'They're mad . . . mad . . . mad . . .'

There came to George – as the moon waxed full – a strange restlessness. It began with insomnia, which rocketed him out of a deep sleep into a strange, instant wakefulness. He became aware of an urge to go for long moonlit walks; and when he had surrendered to this temptation, an overwhelming need to run, leap, roll over and over down a grassy bank, anything that would enable him to break down the hated walls of human convention – and express. A great joy – greater than he had ever known – came to him when he leaped and danced on the common, and could only be released by a shrill, doglike howl that rose up from the sleeping suburbs and went out, swift as a beam of light, to the face of mother-moon.

This joy had to be paid for. When the sun sent its first enquiring rays in through George's window, sanity returned and demanded a reckoning. He examined his face and hands with fearful expectancy. So far as he was aware there had been no terrible change, as yet. But these were early days – or was it nights? Sometimes he would fling himself down on his bed and cry out his great desire for disbelief.

'It can't happen. Mad people are sending me mad.'

The growing strangeness of his behaviour could not go undetected. He was becoming withdrawn, apt to start at every sound and betrayed a certain distrust of strangers by an eerie widening of his eyes, and later, the baring of his teeth in a mirthless grin. His mother commented on these peculiarities in forcible language.

'I think you're going up the pole. Honest I do. The milkman told me yesterday, he saw you snarling at Mrs Redfern's dog.'

'It jumped out at me,' George explained. 'You might have done the same.'

Mrs Hardcastle shook her head. 'No. I can honestly say I've never snarled at a dog in my life. You never inherited snarling from me.'

'I'm all right.' George pleaded for reassurance. 'I'm not turning into – anything.'

'Well, you should know.' George could not help thinking that his mother was regarding him with academic interest, rather than concern. 'Do you go out at nights after I'm asleep?'

He found it impossible to lie convincingly, so he countered one question with another. 'Why should I do that?'

'Don't ask me. But some nut has been seen prancing round the common at three o'clock in the morning. I just wondered.'

The physical change came gradually. One night he woke with a severe pain in his right hand and lay still for a while, not daring to examine it. Then he switched on the bedside lamp with his left hand and after further hesitation, brought its right counterpart out from the sheets. A thick down had spread over the entire palm and he found the fingers would not straighten. They had curved and the nails were thicker and longer than he remembered. After a while the fear – the loathing – went away, and it seemed most natural for him to have claws for fingers and hair-covered hands. Next morning his right hand was as normal as his left, and at that period he was still able to dismiss, even if with little conviction, the episode as a bad dream.

But one night there was a dream – a nightmare of the blackest kind, where fantasy blended with fact and George was unable to distinguish one from the other. He was running over the common, bounding with long, graceful leaps, and there was a wonderful joy in his heart and a limitless freedom in his head. He was in a black and white world. Black grass, white tinted trees, grey sky, white moon. But with all the joy, all the freedom, there was a subtle, ever-present knowledge, that this was an unnatural experience, that he should be utilising all his senses to dispel. Once his brain, that part which was still unoccupied territory, screamed: 'Wake up,' but he was awake, for did not the black grass crunch beneath his feet, and the night breeze ruffled his fur? A large cat was running in front, trying to escape – up trees – across the roofs – round bushes – he finally trapped it in a hole. Shrieks – scratching claws – warm blood – tearing teeth . . . It was good. He was fulfilled.

Next morning when he awoke in his own bed, it could have been dismissed as a mad dream, were it not for the scratches on his face and hands and the blood in his hair. He thought of psychiatrists, asylums, priests, religion, and at last came to the only possible conclusion. There was, so far as he knew, only one set of people on earth who could explain and understand.

Mummy let George in. Father shook him firmly by the hand. Carola kissed him gently and put an arm round his shoulders when he started to cry.

'We don't ask to be what we are,' she whispered. 'We keep more horror than we give away.'

'We all 'ave our place in the great graveyard,' Father said. 'You hunt, we sup, ghouls tear, shaddies lick, mocks blow, and fortunately shadmocks can only whistle.'

'Will I always be – what I am?' George asked.

They all nodded. Mummy grimly, Father knowingly, Carola sadly.

'Until the moon leaves the sky,' they all chanted.

'Or you are struck in the heart by a silver bullet,' Carola whispered, 'fired by one who has only thought about sin. Or maybe when you are very, very old, the heart may give out after a transformation . . .'

'Don't be morbid,' Mummy ordered. 'Poor lad's got enough on plate without you adding to it. Make him a nice cup of tea. And you can mix us a jug of something rich while you're about it. Don't be too 'eavy handed on the O group.'

They sat round the artificial log fire, drinking tea, absorbing nourishment, three giving, one receiving advice, and there was a measure of cosiness.

'All "M's" should keep away from churches, parsons and boy scouts,' Father said.

'Run from a cross and fly from a prayer,' intoned Mummy.

'Two can run better than one,' Carola observed shyly.

Next day George told his mother he intended to leave home and set up house for himself. Mrs Hardcastle did not argue as strongly as she might have had a few weeks earlier. What with one thing and another, there was a distinct feeling that the George, who was standing so grim and white faced in the kitchen doorway, was not the one she had started out with. She said, 'Right, then. I'd say it's about time,' and helped him to pack.

Father, who knew someone in the building line, found George a four-roomed cottage that was situated on the edge of a churchyard, and this he furnished with a few odds and ends that the family were willing to part with. The end product was by no means as elegant or deceptive as the house at Hampton Court, but it was somewhere for George to come back to after his midnight run.

He found the old legends had been embellished, for he experienced no urge to rend or even bite. There was no reason why he should; the body was well fed and the animal kingdom only hunts when goaded by hunger. It was sufficient for him to run, leap, chase his tail by moonlight, and sometimes howl with the pure joy of living. And it is pleasant to record that his joy grew day by day.

For obvious reasons the wedding took place in a registry office, and it seemed that the dark gods smiled down upon the union, for there was a thick fog that lasted from dawn to sunset. The

wedding-supper and the reception which followed were, of necessity, simple affairs. There was a wedding cake for those that could
eat it: a beautiful, three-tier structure, covered with pink icing,
and studded with what George hoped were glacé cherries. He of
course had invited no guests, for there was much that might have
alarmed or embarrassed the uninitiated. Three ghouls in starched,
white shrouds, sat gnawing something that was best left unde-
scribed. The bride and her family sipped a basic beverage from red
goblets, and as the bridegroom was due for a turn, he snarled when
asked to pass the salt. Then there was Uncle Deitmark, a vampire
of the old school, who kept demanding a trussed-up victim, so that
he could take his nourishment direct from the neck.

But finally the happy couple were allowed to depart, and Mummy
and Father wept as they threw the traditional coffin nails after the
departing hearse. 'Ee, it were champion,' Father exclaimed, wiping
his eyes on the back of his hand. 'Best blood-up I've seen for many
a day. You did 'em proud, Mother.'

'I believe in giving the young 'uns a good send off,' Mummy
said. 'Now they must open their own vein, as the saying goes.'

Carola and George watched the moon come up over the church
steeple, which was a little dangerous for it threw the cross into
strong relief, but on that one night they would have defied the very
pope of Rome himself.

'We are no longer alone,' Carola whispered. 'We love and are
loved, and that surely has transformed us from monsters into gods.'

'If happiness can transform a tumbledown cottage into paradise,' George said, running his as yet uncurved fingers through her
hair, 'then I guess we are gods.'

But he forgot that every paradise must have its snake, and their
particular serpent was disguised in the rotund shape of the Reverend John Cole. This worthy cleric had an allegorical nose for
smelling out hypothetical evil, and it was not long before he was
considering the inhabitants of the house by the churchyard with a
speculative eye.

He called when George was out and invited Carola to join the
young wives' altar dressing committee. She turned grey and begged
to be excused. Mr Cole then suggested she partake in a brief read-
ing from holy scripture, and Carola shrank from the proffered

Bible, even as a rabbit recoils from a hooded cobra. Then the Reverend John Cole accidentally dropped his crucifix on to her lap, and she screamed like one who is in great pain, before falling to the floor in a deathlike faint. And the holy minister departed with the great joy that comes to the sadist who knows he is only doing his duty.

Next day George met the Reverend Cole, who was hastening to the death bed of a sinful woman, and laid a not too gentle hand on the flabby arm.

'I understand you frightened my wife, when I was out yesterday.'

The clergyman bared his teeth and although George was now in the shape with which he had been born, they resembled two dogs preparing to fight.

'I'm wondering,' the Reverend Cole said, 'what kind of woman recoils from the good book and screams when the crucifix touches her.'

'Well, it's like this,' George tightened his grip on the black-clad arm, 'we are both allergic to bibles, crosses and nosy parsons. I am apt to burn one, break two, and pulverise three. Am I getting through?'

'And I have a duty before God and man,' John Cole said, looking down at the retaining hand with marked distaste, 'and that is to stamp out evil wherever it be found. And may I add, with whatever means that are at my disposal.'

They parted in mutual hate, and George in his innocence decided to use fear as an offensive weapon, not realising that its wounds strengthen resistance more often than they weaken. One night, when the moon was full, turning the graveyard into a gothic wonderland, the Reverend John Cole met something that robbed him of speech for nigh on twelve hours. It walked on bent hind-legs, and had two very long arms which terminated in talons that seemed hungry for the ecclesiastical throat, and a nightmare face whose predominant feature was a long, slavering snout.

At the same time, Mrs Cole, a very timid lady who had yet to learn of the protective virtues of two pieces of crossed wood, was trying so hard not to scream as a white-faced young woman advanced across the bedroom. The reaction of husband and wife was typical of their individual characters. The Reverend John Cole after the initial cry did not stop running until he was safely barricaded in the church with a processional cross jammed across the doorway. Mrs Cole, being unable to scream, promptly fainted, and hence fared worse than her fleetfooted spouse. John Cole, after his run was a little short of breath: Mary Cole, when she returned to consciousness, was a little short of blood.

Mr Cole was an erratic man who often preached sermons guaranteed to raise the scalps of the most urbane congregation, if that is to say, they took the trouble to listen. The tirade which was poured out from the pulpit on the Sunday after Mrs Cole's loss and Mr Cole's fright, woke three slumbering worshippers, and caused a choirboy to swallow his chewing-gum.

'The devil has planted his emissaries in our midst,' the vicar proclaimed. 'Aye, do they dwell in the church precincts and do appear to the God-fearing in their bestial form.'

The chewing-gum bereft choirboy giggled, and Mr Cole's wrath rose and erupted into admonishing words.

'Laugh not. I say to you of little faith, laugh not. For did I not come face to face – aye, but a few yards from where you now sit – with a fearsome beast that did drool and nuzzle, and I feared that my windpipe might soon lie upon my shirt-front. But, and this be the truth, which did turn my bowels to water, there was the certain knowledge that I was in the presence of a creature that is without precedence in Satan's hierarchy – the one – the only – the black angel of hell – the dreaded werewolf.'

At least ten people in the congregation thought their vicar had at last turned the corner and become stark raving mad. Twenty more did not understand what he was talking about, and one old lady assumed she was listening to a brilliant interpretation of Revelation, chapter XIII, verses 1 to 3. The remainder of the congregation had not been listening, but noted the vicar was in fine fettle, roaring and pounding the pulpit with his customary gusto. His next disclosure suffered roughly the same reception.

'My dear wife – my helpmeet, who has walked by my side these past twenty years – was visited in her chamber by a female of the species . . .' Mr Cole nodded bitterly. 'A vampire, an unclean thing that has crept from its foul grave, and did take from my dear one, that which she could ill afford to lose . . .'

Ignorance, inattention, Mr Cole's words fell on very stony ground and no one believed – save Willie Mitcham. Willie did believe in vampires, werewolves and, in fact, also accepted the existence of banshees, demons, poltergeists, ghosts of every description, monsters of every shape and form, and the long wriggly thing, which as everyone knows, has yet to be named. As Willie was only twelve years of age, he naturally revelled in his belief, and moreover made himself an expert on demonology. To his father's secret delectation and his mother's openly expressed horror, he had an entire cupboard filled with literature that dwelt on every aspect of the subject. He knew, for example, that the only sure way of getting a banshee off your back is to spit three times into an open grave, bow three times to the moon, then chant in a loud voice:

> Go to the north, go to the south,
> Go to the devil, but shut your mouth.
> Scream not by day, or howl by night,
> But gibber alone by candlelight.

He also knew, for had not the facts been advertised by printed page, television set and cinema screen, that the only sure way of killing a vampire is to drive a sharp pointed object through its heart between the hours of sunrise and sunset. He was also joyfully aware of the fatal consequences that attend the arrival of a silver bullet in a werewolf's hairy chest. So it was that Willie listened to the Reverend John Cole with ears that heard and understood, and he wanted so desperately to shout out the simple and time honoured cures, the withal, the ways and means, the full, glorious and gory details. But his mother nudged him in the ribs and told him to stop fidgeting, so he could only sit and seethe with well-nigh uncontrollable impatience.

One bright morning in early March the total population of the graveyard cottage was increased by one. The newly risen sun peeped in through the neatly curtained windows and gazed down upon, what it is to be hoped, was the first baby werevamp. It was like all newly born infants, small, wrinkled, extremely ugly, and favoured its mother in so far as it had been born with two prominent eye-teeth. Instead of crying it made a harsh hissing sound, not unlike that of an infant king-cobra, and was apt to bite anything that moved.

'Isn't he sweet?' Carola sighed, then waved a finger at her offspring, who promptly curled back an upper lip and made a hissing snarl. 'Yes he is . . . he's a sweet 'ickle diddums . . . he's mummy's 'ickle diddums . . .'

'I think he's going to be awfully clever,' George stated after a while. 'What with that broad forehead and those dark eyes, one can see there is a great potential for intelligence. He's got your mouth, darling.'

'Not yet he hasn't,' Carola retorted, 'but he soon will have, if I'm not careful. I suppose he's in his humvamp period now, but when the moon is full, he'll have sweet little hairy talons, and a dinky-winky little tail.'

Events proved her to be absolutely correct.

The Reverend John Cole allowed several weeks to pass before he made an official call on the young parents. During this time he reinforced his courage, of which it must be confessed he had an abundance; sought advice from his superiors, who were not at all helpful, and tried to convince anyone who would listen of the danger in their midst. His congregation shrank, people crossed the road whenever he came into view, and he was constantly badgered by a wretched little boy, who poured out a torrent of nauseating information. But at last the vicar was as ready for the fatal encounter as he ever would be, and so, armed with a crucifix, faith and a small bottle of whisky, he went forth to do battle. From his bedroom window that overlooked the vicarage, Willie Mitcham watched the black figure as it trudged along the road. He flung the window open and shouted: 'Yer daft coot. It's a full moon.'

No one answered Mr Cole's thunderous assault on the front door. This was not surprising as Carola was paying Mrs Cole another visit, and George was chasing a very disturbed sheep across a stretch of open moorland. Baby had not yet reached the age when answering doors would be numbered among his accomplishments. At last the reverend gentleman opened the door and after crossing himself with great fervour, entered the cottage.

He found himself in the living-room, a cosy little den with

whitewashed walls, two ancient chairs, a folding table, and some very nice rugs on the floor. There was also a banked up fire, and a beautiful old ceiling oil-lamp that George had cleverly adapted for electricity. Mr Cole called out: 'Anyone there?' and receiving no answer, sank down into one of the chairs to wait. Presently, the chair being comfortable, the room warm, the clergyman felt his caution dissolve into a hazy atmosphere of well-being. His head nodded, his eyelids flickered, his mouth fell open and in no time at all, a series of gentle snores filled the room with their even cadence.

It is right to say Mr Cole fell asleep reluctantly, and while he slept he displayed a certain amount of dignity. But he awoke with a shriek and began to thresh about in a most undignified manner. There was a searing pain in his right ankle, and when he moved something soft and rather heavy flopped over his right foot and at the same time made a strange hissing sound. The vicar screamed again and kicked out with all his strength, and that which clung to his ankle went hurling across the room and landed on a rug near the window. It hissed, yelped, then turning over, began to crawl back towards the near prostrate clergyman. He tried to close his eyes, but they insisted in remaining open and so permitted him to see something that a person with a depraved sense of humour might have called a baby. A tiny, little white – oh, so white – face, which had two microscopic fangs jutting out over the lower lip. But for the rest it was very hairy; had two wee claws, and a proudly erect, minute tail, that was at this particular moment in time, lashing angrily from side to side. Its little hind legs acted as projectors and enabled the hair-covered torso to leap along at quite an amazing speed. There was also a smear of Mr Cole's blood round the mouth; and the eyes held an expression that suggested the ecclesiastial fluid was appealing to the taste-buds, and their owner could hardly wait to get back to the fount of nourishment.

Mr Cole released three long drawn out screams, then, remembering that legs have a decided and basic purpose, leaped for the door. It was truly an awe-inspiring sight to see a portly clergyman who had more than reached the years of discretion, running between graves, leaping over tombstones, and sprinting along paths. Baby-werevamp squatted on his hind legs and looked as wistfully as his visage permitted after the swiftly retreating cleric. After a while, baby set up a prolonged howl, and thumped the floor with clenched claws. His distress was understandable. He had just seen a well-filled feeding bottle go running out of the door.

Willie Mitcham had at last got through. One of the stupid, blind, not to mention thick-headed adults had been finally shocked into seeing the light. When Willie found the Reverend John Cole entangled in a hawthorn bush, he also stumbled on a man who was willing to listen to advice from any source. He had also retreated from the frontiers of sanity, and was therefore in a position to be driven, rather than to command.

'I saw 'im.' Willie was possibly the happiest boy in the world at that moment. 'I saw 'im with his 'orrible fangs and he went leaping towards the moors.'

Mr Cole said, 'Ah!' and began to count his fingers.

'And I saw 'er,' Willie went on. 'She went to your house and drifted up to the main bedroom window. Just like in the film *The Mark of the Vampire*.'

'Destroy all evil,' the Reverend Cole shouted. 'Root it out. Cut into . . .'

'Its 'eart,' Willie breathed. 'The way to kill a vampire is drive a stake through its 'eart. And a werewolf must be shot with a silver bullet fired by 'im who has only thought about sin.'

'From what authority do you quote this information?' the vicar demanded.

'Me 'orror comics,' Willie explained. 'They give all the details, and if you go and see the *Vampire of 'Ackney Wick*, you'll see a 'oly father cut off the vampire's 'ead and put a sprig of garlic in its mouth.'

'Where are these documents?' the clergyman enquired.

Mr and Mrs Mitcham were surprised and perhaps a little alarmed when their small son conducted the vicar through the kitchen and after a perfunctory: 'It's all right, mum, parson wants to see me 'orror comics,' led the frozen-faced clergyman upstairs to the attic.

It was there that Mr Cole's education was completed. Assisted by lurid pictures and sensational text, he learned of the conception, habits, hobbies and disposal procedures of vampires, werewolves and other breathing or non-breathing creatures that had attended the same school.

'Where do we get . . . ?' he began.

'A tent peg and mum's coal 'ammer will do fine,' Willie was quick to give expert advice.

'But a silver bullet,' the vicar shook his head. 'I cannot believe there is a great demand . . .'

'Two of grandad's silver collar studs melted down with a soldering iron, and a cartridge from dad's old .22 rifle. Mr Cole; please say we can do it. I promise never to miss Sunday school again, if you'll say we can do it.'

The Reverend John Cole did not consider the problem very long. A bite from a baby werevamp is a great decision maker.

'Yes,' he nodded, 'we have been chosen. Let us gird up our loins, gather the sinews of battle, and go forth to destroy the evil ones.'

'Coo!' Willie nodded vigorously. 'All that blood. Can I cut 'er 'ead off?'

If anyone had been taking the air at two o'clock next morning, they might have seen an interesting sight. A large clergyman, armed with a crucifix and a coal hammer was creeping across the churchyard, followed by a small boy with a tent peg in one hand and a light hunting rifle in the other.

They came to the cottage and Mr Cole first turned the handle, then pushed the door open with his crucifix. The room beyond was warm and cosy, firelight painted a dancing pattern on the ceiling, the brass lamp twinkled and glittered like a suspended star, and it was as though a brightly designed nest had been carved out of the surrounding darkness. John Cole strode into the room like a black marble angel of doom, and raising his crucifix bellowed: 'I have come to drive out the iniquity, burn out the sin. For, thus saith the Lord, cursed be you who hanker after darkness.'

There was a sigh, a whimper – maybe a hissing whimper. Carola was crouched in one corner, her face whiter than a slab of snow in moonlight, her eyes dark pools of terror, her lips deep, deep red, as though they had been brought to life by a million, blood-tinted kisses, and her hands were pale ghost-moths, beating out their life against the invisible wall of intolerance. The vicar lowered his cross and the whimper grew up and became a cry of despair.

'Why?'

'Where is the foul babe that did bite my ankle?'

Carola's staring eyes never left the crucifix towering over her.

'I took him . . . took him . . . to his grandmother.'

'There is more of your kind? Are you legion? Has the devil's spawn been hatched?'

'We are on the verge of extinction.'

The soul of the Reverend John Cole rejoiced when he saw the deep terror in the lovely eyes, and he tasted the fruits of true happiness when she shrieked. He bunched the front of her dress up between trembling fingers and jerked her first upright, then down across the table. She made a little hissing sound; an instinctive token of defiance, and for a moment the delicate ivory fangs were bared and nipped the clergyman's hand, but that was all. There was no savage fight for existence, no calling on the dark gods; just a token resistance, the shedding of a tiny dribble of blood, then complete surrender. She lay back across the table, her long, black hair brushing the floor, as though this were the inevitable conclusion from which she had been too long withheld. The vicar placed the tip of the tent peg over her heart, and taking the coal hammer from the overjoyed Willie, shouted the traditional words.

'Get thee to hell. Burn for ever and a day. May thy foul carcase be food for jackals, and thy blood drink for pariah dogs.'

The first blow sent the tent peg in three or four inches, and the sound of a snapping rib grated on the clergyman's ear, so that for a moment he turned his head aside in revulsion. Then, as though alarmed lest his resolve weaken, he struck again, and the blood rose up in a scarlet fountain; a cascade of dancing rubies, each one reflecting the room with its starlike lamp, and the dripping, drenched face of a man with a raised coal hammer. The hammer, like the mailed hand of fate, fell again, and the ruby fountain sank low, then collapsed into a weakly gushing pool. Carola released her life in one long, drawn out sigh, then became a black and white study in still life.

'You gotta cut 'er 'ead off,' Willie screamed. 'Ain't no good, unless you cut 'er 'ead off and put a sprig of garlic in 'er mouth.'

But Mr Cole had, at least temporarily, had a surfeit of blood. It matted his hair, clogged his eyes, salted his mouth, drenched his clothes from neck to waist, and transformed his hands into scarlet claws.

Willie was fumbling in his jacket pocket.

'I've got me mum's bread knife here, somewhere. Should go through 'er neck a treat.'

The reverend gentleman wiped a film of red from his eyes and then daintily shook his fingers.

'Truly is it said a little child shall lead them. Had I been more mindful of the Lord's business, I would have brought me a tenon saw.'

He was not more than half way through his appointed task, when the door was flung back and George entered. He was on the turn. He was either about to 'become', or return to 'as was'. His silhouette filled the moonlit doorway, and he became still; a black menace that was no less dangerous because it did not move. Then he glided across the room, round the table and the Reverend John Cole retreated before him.

George gathered up the mutilated remains of his beloved, then raised agony-filled eyes.

'We loved – she and I. Surely, that should have forgiven us much. Death we would have welcomed – for what is death, but a glorious reward for having to live. But this . . .'

He pointed to the jutting tent peg, the half-severed head, then looked up questioningly at the clergyman. Then the Reverend John Cole took up his cross and holding it before him he called out in a voice that had been made harsh by the dust of centuries.

'I am Alpha and Omega saith the Lord, and into the pit which is before the beginning and after the end, shall ye be cast. For you and your kind are a stench and an abomination, and whatever evil is done unto you, shall be deemed good in my sight.'

The face of George Hardcastle became like an effigy carved from rock. Then it seemed to shimmer, the lines dissolved and ran one into the other; the hairline advanced, while the eyes retreated into deep sockets, and the jaw and nose merged and slithered into a long, pointed snout. The werewolf dropped the mangled remains of its mate and advanced upon her killer.

'Satanus Avaunt.'

The Reverend Cole thrust his crucifix forward as though it were a weapon of offence, only to have it wrenched from his grasp and broken by a quick jerk of hair covered wrists. The werewolf tossed the pieces to one side, then with a howl leaped forward and buried his long fangs into the vicar's shoulder.

The two locked figures, one representing good, the other evil, swayed back and forth in the lamplight, and there was no room in either hate-fear filled brain for the image of one small boy, armed with a rifle. The sharp little cracking sound could barely be heard above the grunting, snarling battle that was being raged near the hanging brass lamp, but the result was soon apparent. The werewolf shrieked, before twisting round and staring at the exuberant Willie, as though in dumb reproach. Then it crashed to the floor. When the clergyman had recovered sufficiently to look down, he saw the dead face of George Hardcastle, and had he been a little to the right of the sanity frontier, there might well have been terrible doubts.

'Are you going to finish cutting off 'er head?' Willie enquired.

They put the Reverend John Cole in a quiet house surrounded by a beautiful garden. Willie Mitcham they placed in a home, as a juvenile court decided in its wisdom, that he was in need of care and protection. The remains of George and Carola they buried in the churchyard and said some beautiful words over their graves.

It is a great pity they did not listen to Willie, who after all knew what he was talking about when it came to a certain subject.

One evening, when the moon was full, two gentlemen who were employed in the house surrounded by the beautiful garden, opened the door, behind which resided all that remained of the Reverend John Cole. They both entered the room and prepared to talk. They never did. One dropped dead from pure, cold terror, and the other achieved a state of insanity which had so far not been reached by one of his patients.

The Reverend John Cole had been bitten by a baby werevamp, nipped by a female vampire, and clawed and bitten by a full-blooded, buck werewolf.

Only the good Lord above, and the bad one below, knew what he was.

Monster Club Interlude: 1

A long, thought-filled silence followed the recital of Manfred's story, and Donald could only marvel that such extraordinary events could take place behind the commonplace façades of everyday life. In fact he would have doubted the veracity of the account, were it not for the fearsome appearance of the werevamp, who was at that moment wiping his eyes with a black handkerchief.

'I told you it was a sad story,' Eramus said, while he nodded with grim satisfaction. 'And it is even more depressing by being true. If people knew what was going on under their noses, I doubt if anyone would ever turn a light out.'

Donald said he agreed absolutely, and swore that from then onwards he would keep away from woods and deserted places. Eramus grinned and even the werevamp allowed himself a pale smile.

'Honestly, guv, do you imagine you're safe in a crowd? Don't you realise that there is four monsters to every full bus?'

'I can't believe . . .' Donald began, but Eramus was nodding slowly, like a man who is determined to reveal a grim secret.

'At least four to every full bus. And the underground! Cor strike a light! The rush hour trains are packed with them. The amount of biting, nipping and sucking that goes on down there between the hours of five and seven, it's a wonder anyone comes up in one piece.'

Donald shuddered and made a silent vow that here was yet another place where he would never go. The werevamp noted his disquiet and tried to reassure him.

'Don't let the knowledge you will gain from this establishment worry you unduly. The air is full of dangerous germs, you accept them as the natural order of things. And remember, we do not advertise our condition. Were you to meet me in my humvamp stage, you would only see a man with a very pale face who had a thing about sunlight. Those of us who are unusually gifted only go out on foggy nights and favour broadbrimmed hats and dark glasses. Bear in mind, we have more reason to fear you, than you us.'

'Granted.' Donald tried to put his point of view as tactfully as possible. 'But, all that biting, sucking and so on.'

'Donators rarely know they have donated,' Eramus said with a supercilious smirk. 'A slight weakness, a few days in bed and all is forgotten. Sometimes the newspapers report a mild flu epidemic. Nothing more.'

'But what about those who – ?'

'Join our ranks?' Eramus grinned and rubbed his hands gleefully. 'It's then we send out the resurrection squads. Dig 'em up and get 'em going.'

'I was dug up,' a voice said suddenly.

A little man with a pale face which was enhanced by tapering ears and a pair of white horns that stood up from a mass of bristling hair, had silently seated himself at their table and was now glaring at Donald as though daring him to argue. Instead, the young man's natural kindness made him commiserate.

'That must have been awful for you.'

'No it wasn't.' The little man scowled and shook his head violently. 'The best thing that ever happened to me. I hadn't really lived until I was buried and dug up again. You should try it some time. As a matter of fact if you want to hear an exciting story, you should hear mine. Mind you, it's sad as well.'

'Oh, no!' Eramus groaned. 'Not again? Listen, old son, we've all got our troubles, but we don't go around worrying other mons about them. I've heard your story at least a dozen times.'

'And I, at least two dozen times,' the werevamp added caustically. 'Give it a rest.'

'But your guest hasn't heard it once,' the little man pointed out. 'I am sure he will be interested.'

There was a pregnant silence and Donald realised that he was expected to pronounce judgement.

'I would love to hear his story,' he said, with it must be confessed, more politeness than truth.

'Splendid!' The little man smiled and looked expectantly round the table. 'Do you suppose . . . ?'

Eramus sighed and beckoned to a long-toothed waiter. 'Two OBs and two Bloody-Marys.'

'I,' pronounced the little man after the refreshments had been served, 'am a Mock.'

Donald almost said 'how nice', but checked himself just in time. Instead, he smiled and tried to look wise. The little man appeared to be lost in thought for some time, then he sighed.

'Mother should have told me. I was eighteen before I found out.'

'For hell's sake get on with it,' Eramus ordered. 'We haven't got all night. And make it brief.'

The little man shot him a very nasty look, but after emptying his glass, he took a deep breath and began to relate the story of . . .

The Mock

'Why won't you marry me?' I asked.

Sheila was blonde, beautiful and an intellectual. She believed in always telling the truth, being of the opinion that rose-tinted spectacles were bad for spiritual eyesight. She was very fond of the expression: 'I am being cruel to be kind.'

'You really want to know?' she enquired.

'Yes,' I said.

'Very well. You are so ugly.'

'Oh!' I said.

'I am sure you are much too intelligent to resent being told the truth. Please stop me if I hurt your feelings.'

'No. Please go on.'

'Well, being ugly would not matter all that much. Some ugly men are very attractive. But you are repulsively ugly.'

I said, 'Oh!' again. There wasn't really much else I could say. Sheila gave me a look of concern.

'You must understand, I don't mean to be unkind. I mean I am only telling you this for your own good. If you persist in proposing to girls – well, it's stupid to be modest – as attractive as me – you will only be hurt. Some girls may lack my tact.'

'No, no. I am very . . . grateful.'

'I don't know what makes you so repulsive. Something to do with your ears, possibly. You must admit they are large. Remind me of Dumbo the elephant sometimes. Then you have that awful, white, almost sluglike face. I didn't say anything at the time, but after you kissed me under the mistletoe – remember, last Christmas – I was sick in the bathroom. Then, your touch is so cold and clammy . . . What's the matter? You're not going to be silly about this, are you?'

But like any wounded animal I was running for cover. Hunting for shadows. Looking for a hole. I went home.

'Mother,' I asked, 'Why?'

'What do you mean – why?' She was making a sampler. Just

like those young Victorian ladies made and framed afterwards. Although she had only half embroidered hers, the full text was inscribed in red crayon. It read:

> I must be bad some of the time,
> And evil all the time.
> But I must pretend to be good part of the time,
> And kind all of the time.
> But I must never be good or kind,
> At anytime.

'You really must break the habit of asking questions.' She threaded a length of red wool into a large needle. 'Questions invite answers, and they are always those we do not wish to hear.'

'But, Mother, why am I so ugly? So repulsively ugly?'

She broke the red wool between her strong white teeth, then smiled.

'You are as your ancestors made you. It is possible that there are those who would consider you quite handsome.'

'Who are they?'

'Those who dance by moonlight and howl by night, and blacken innocence by candlelight.'

'You talk in riddles,' I objected.

'That is the only satisfactory way to talk,' she answered.

We sat together and watched the fire as it spluttered in the old fashioned iron grate, and formed itself into dancing, orange shapes, that sent out searing, golden tongues that licked the smooth logs. I dared to ask the forbidden question.

'Who was my father?'

Mother completed the 'e' in 'evil' before answering.

'A wise man knows neither who or what his father was – or is.'

'Then you won't tell me?'

She looked up at the marble mantelpiece clock, then smiled again.

'It's time for tea. Go and put the kettle on.'

As long as I can remember no one came to the house. Certainly none of my friends – if they can be so called – were invited. The house was gloomy, set back in the midst of an unkept garden, and the windows were like dead men's eyes; blank, as though paned with black glass. Daylight seemed to be afraid to enter and there was a perpetual damp, chilly atmosphere, that grew more pronounced as darkness fell. Mother refused to have electricity installed and artificial illumination was provided by oil lamps equipped with frosted globes, and these cast eerie circles of light over ceilings and walls. It was strange, or so it appeared then, how a certain face could materialise anywhere.

I could not have been more than five years of age when I first saw the face of a bearded man looking at me out of the dressing-table mirror. I suppose I was too young to be afraid, and experienced a kind of excited curiosity as I crept out of bed and approached the dressing-table. The face was covered with black, curling hair, save for a little patch round the eyes, and these were blue, small and shining. One closed, then opened in a kind of lewd wink, while a hole appeared in the midst of this hairy nest and toothless gums were bared in an awful grin. Then the face vanished and I went back to bed and forgot all about the incident until a long time afterwards.

I was possibly ten when I saw the same face floating on the bath water. When I put my foot into the water the face elongated and stretched for the entire length of the bath and its grin became a long, oval slit. I was frightened and ran to tell Mother. She only smiled and said: 'Why should you mind being watched? Have you got something to hide?'

There was really no satisfactory answer to such a question, and in future whenever I saw the face, be it in window-pane, mirror, on moonlit wall, or built from planes of mist that drifted across the room, I kept the information to myself. The face became part of my growing up and I often suspected it watched me from places that I never thought about. I remember once glimpsing it in a bucket of water.

I suppose it came as a surprise to learn that no one else saw faces in baths or mirrors, for I had considered such a phenomenon as commonplace. Once, when fired by an urge to communicate with a fellow creature, I mentioned the matter to a school mate, he stared at me with an expression that denoted fear and astonishment.

'You're loony,' he stated. 'Ugly as sin and loony.'

I fought the isolation that cut me off from the rest of the world, ignored the snubs, pretended not to see the look of revulsion that greeted my entry into a room, and actually had the audacity to fall in love. The result I have recorded. From then on I took an unhealthy interest in my appearance.

A round face that was as white as a pound of lard. A pair of large, red-veined ears that looked as if they might flap if given the opportunity: piglike blue eyes and a flattened nose, plus a really awful receding chin, and white, pointed teeth. For the rest, my body was thin and narrow and gave the impression it might blow away in a strong wind, and the hands were so tiny – like little white claws. My black hair would never lie flat, or grow very long. It stood upright on my narrow skull, so that it resembled the bristles on a cheap scrubbing brush. After due reflection I had to admit I was a particularly unappetising sight. I again approached my mother.

'Mother, Sheila Benson is absolutely right. I am repulsively ugly.'

She had completed the fourth line of her sampler. She chuckled.

'Wait until you've cut your horns.'

'Horns!'

'Horns, I said. Horns I mean. Two little white ones. You'll have to hide them. People are so unreasonable when they face the unusual.'

'Mother – you must be joking.'

'I never joke about the ridiculous. Why should you worry about a pair of horns? Bulls have them, so do rams, goats and deceived husbands. You mustn't be so sensitive.'

'Mother – what am I?'

'A mock.'

'A mock? Mother – what is a mock?'

'A polite word for mongrel.'

'Mother – I don't understand. Please explain.'

She finished off the 'e' in 'time', then broke the wool between her teeth.

'It's time for tea. Go and put the kettle on.'

A week later two large boils appeared just above the temples on either side of my head and in view of my mother's warning, I knew what to expect. It was rather like cutting one's wisdom teeth. The boils grew larger and extremely painful and I developed a slight fever. Mother gave me a black draught and put bread poultices on my inflamed protuberances while smiling at my anxiety.

'It's only horn-cutting fever. Nothing to get in a fuss about.'

'But, Mother, I don't *want* horns.'

'Nonsense. You'll find them very useful for punching holes in condensed milk cans.'

The boils broke two days later and two white, bony tips peeped coyly out from their ragged craters. When I examined them in the bathroom mirror, I came to the inevitable conclusion that they did not improve my appearance.

'The worst is over now.' Mother did her best to console me, although she was very phlegmatic about the entire business. 'They'll grow now to a height of about three inches. How lucky you are. They appear to be nice and healthy and shouldn't give you any trouble. I can remember one of your cousins had to have several fillings.'

This was the first time she had ever hinted of the existence of any kind of relative, and I eagerly grabbed this morsel of information.

'If I have a cousin, he must be the child of an uncle.'

Mother sighed and nodded. 'That would be a logical conclusion.'

'Would that uncle be my father's brother or yours?'

'I think we can safely say he was the son of his father and the nephew of his uncle.'

'Mother, why won't you tell me anything?'

She had almost completed her sampler. Only the 'e' and 'm' in 'anytime' were still inscribed in red crayon.

'Because the time is not yet. But now you have cut your horns, it will be the duty of your father to explain the facts of life to you.'

'My father! But . . .'

'No more questions. As you are still poorly, I will pop downstairs and put the kettle on.'

My horns grew apace. White, shiny and pointed, they jutted up from my head like two misplaced tusks. Mother instructed me in the art of plaiting my hair round them, so now I resembled a man who had crawled through a hedge backwards and lost his comb. During the days that followed I detected a measure of regard in her attitude towards me, that had been so woefully lacking before.

Once she kissed my horns and murmured: 'My little pup is growing up. He should be proud.' And I assumed 'he' to be my, as yet,
unknown father. Moreover, as the nights grew longer and the first
cold fingers of frost drew their pattern on the window-panes,
Mother seemed to become younger – almost like a young girl who
is eagerly looking forward to a reunion with her lover. One day in
late November she called me into the front room and handed me
a sheet of paper.

'Now you have come of age, I will want you to do the shopping.
And I mean *real* shopping. Not groceries and rubbish like that. But
essentials.'

I said, 'Yes, Mother. Thank you for your trust,' and tried to read
the list written on the paper, but it was an indecipherable scrawl,
rather like a doctor's prescription. Mother made me fold the paper
up and put it safely away in my breast pocket.

'Now, listen carefully,' she instructed. 'I want you to get the
pushcart out of the old coach house and push it down to the town.
Go past the churchyard and take the first turning on the left and
knock on the first door on the right. You can't miss it – it's painted
red. Got that?'

I nodded and Mother patted my horns.

'Good. A little man will answer the door and you must say to
him in a very distinct voice: "Tomorrow is my father's rising day"
and hand him this list. He will provide all that is necessary.'

I was very breathless by the time I reached the house with the
red door, for the pushcart was very large and there was a steep hill
to climb after one had passed the churchyard. The little man who
answered my knock was almost as ugly as I was. True, his ears were
not so large, but he had a nose of unreasonable proportions, and
his tongue was most definitely too large for his mouth. This caused
him to splutter when he spoke.

'Whash all this then? I don'ts wash to buy anythings.'

I remembered my mother's instructions and spoke loud and
clear.

'Tomorrow is my father's rising day.'

He narrowed his small eyes and stared at me with an expression that I could only suppose to be one of dawning astonishment.
Then he shook his head in pretended disbelief.

'A mock! As I'se leve and breash – a mock! Then youse Daddy's a Shaddy?'

I said: 'Please, sir, I don't know what you're talking about. Mother told me that tomorrow is father's rising day and I was to give you this list.'

The little man took the sheet of paper and after unfolding it, read the contents with evident satisfaction.

'Expert,' he breathed. 'Drasn up by expert. Gos round back and I'se issue supplies.'

It took me some time to load the cart, for there were six very large, sealed cans, two plastic sacks of something soft and flabby, two more of long, thin things that rattled, a small bag of something light and a tin that had inscribed on its label: CONGEALING LIQUID. My load was completed by a long wooden spoon. Then I signed an invoice with a red ball-point pen and was sent on my way by the little man, who patted my horns with a kind of grim relish.

'As fine a pairs of horsns that I'se seen for lonsh time. Happy rizing daysh.'

The moment I arrived back home, Mother made me carry all the stores up to the bathroom, and there I piled them against the far wall, while trying to subdue the torrent of questions that were bubbling up at the back of my mind. For the first time that I could remember Mother kissed me on the cheek.

'Tomorrow,' she sighed happily. 'Tomorrow is the day.'

We worked hard for the rest of that day; cleaning the house, beating carpets, polishing floors, wiping away dust that had accumulated over the years, and finally decorating the dining-room with green paper-chains. Mother brought them out from an old suitcase: long, green, home-made paper-chains constructed from narrow strips of paper pasted together. These we hung across the room and looped around the walls, so that after a while the house seemed almost gay – in a sombre sort of way. Then Mother wiped away her smiles and taking my hand led me into a small room that was situated at the back of the house. It was furnished with a table, a large walnut cabinet, two chairs and a brass oil lamp. Mother, after closing the door, motioned me to a chair, then unlocked the cabinet by means of a key which she wore on a chain round her neck.

'Light the lamp,' she ordered. 'The time has come for me to explain certain facts to you, so tomorrow you won't go all silly when I make up the rising recipe.'

I lit the lamp and Mother unrolled the parchment she had obtained from the cabinet and anchored it down on the table by means of four large bones that had presumably come from the same place. She then sat down beside me and began to speak.

'First of all you must understand you are what the world calls a monster. A minor monster, one might say, a very mixed up monster, but you must certainly have a right to that title. To be precise, you are, as I believe I mentioned before – a mock. A corruption of mongrel-mon. Your father is a shaddy and I am a maddy. Are you following me?'

'No.'

Mother sighed. 'You certainly aren't very bright. Now study this ancestral table that your maternal grandfather drew up and perhaps a little light will penetrate your darkness.'

I turned my attention to the parchment on which was inscribed the following table:

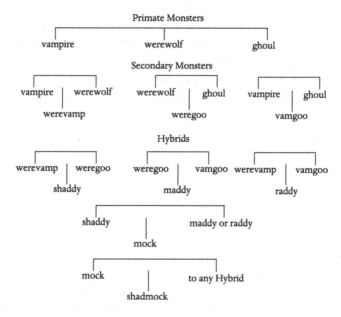

Basic Rules: Vampires – sup; Werewolves – hunt; Ghouls – tear; Shaddies – lick; Mocks – blow; Shadmocks – only whistle.

Having studied this table with mixed feelings, I looked up at Mother and for the first time took particular note of her long, white face and the fringe of black hair that decorated her pointed chin.

'Then I am descended from a vampire, a werewolf and a ghoul?'

'You are highly connected,' Mother agreed. 'Of course this table does not cover every branch of the monster species. For example, no mention is made of the batman, a cadet line of the vampire family. Or the waspwoman, who originally came to this country with the returning crusaders. Then there are the dreaded Fly-by-Night, the shadow people and many others. But at least you are now conversant with your immediate ancestry.'

'But my father – where is he?'

'All around you.' Mother rolled up the parchment. 'Let me explain. Cross-breeding has curious side effects, and particularly so in the case of the male Shaddy. Up to the age of twenty-one your father looked much as you do. He was gifted with long eyeteeth, a throw-back to his paternal grandfather, and these he successfully hid by growing a beard. Perhaps his ears were somewhat large, this being a donation from his maternal grandfather, but worse specimens have sat in the House of Commons. But after his twenty-first birthday the warring elements in his blood began to take their toll. He grew thinner, but did not decrease in size. His bones became fluid, his teeth fell out, his flesh became transparent, and he started to quiver like a water jelly when the table is shaken. Then one day he collapsed in the bath and slid down the plughole and I took advice from the wise ones of our kind.'

Mother wiped away a single tear that trickled down from her left eye, then continued.

'They told me that for eighteen years he would only be reflected on water or any shining surface. But on the eighteenth anniversary of his sliding down the plughole – that would be his rising day. Then I must make a substantial body for him in the very bath that witnessed his dissolution, so that he might rise up and be with us for another twenty-one years.'

'So those tins and sacks . . . ?' I left the question uncompleted.

'Contain the essential ingredients to build your father anew. Only . . .'

'Only . . . ?'

'He'll have no teeth. So I fear he will only be able to lick. But my word, how he will lick.'

I shook my head and pondered on the advantages and handicaps of being only able to lick. Then I shuddered as I remembered something that affected me.

'Mother . . .'

'Yes, son.'

'I am a . . . mock?'

'You are.'

'Well, the document said mocks blow!'

She kissed me on the forehead, yet another unusual gesture of affection.

'That is to come, son. After you have been planted.'

'Planted!'

'Put the kettle on and make your mother a nice cup of tea.'

We were up early next morning, for Mother maintained there was much to do, and in any case she was far too excited to sleep. She put on her best black dress and I was instructed to don my corduroy suit as this was hard wearing and I had quite a bit of carrying to do. Then Mother, after a final look in the mirror, took me firmly by the arm, and together we mounted the stairs on our way to the bathroom. Here I found the tins and sacks exactly where I had stacked them the day before, but I saw that the bath had been meticulously cleaned and the plug jammed firmly into its hole.

'Put this on,' Mother ordered, handing me a butcher's apron. 'You don't want to get yourself messed up.'

I tied the apron firmly round my waist and stood by for further instructions.

'Open each tin and pour the contents into the bath.'

I prized the lid off the first tin and found it was filled with a deep red powder. I looked enquiringly at Mother.

'Instant blood,' she explained. 'What did you imagine it was? Tooth powder?'

By the time I had emptied the six tins the bath was almost half filled with the instant blood powder, and Mother nodded her satisfaction. 'Should make up into a nice mixture, particularly when we have put the solids in. Now, pour six full cans of water on to the blood powder and stir it with the wooden spoon.'

I obeyed. The resulting fluid was rich, frothy and every now and again would erupt into a series of exploding bubbles. It really looked most appetising.

'Let it settle,' Mother whispered. 'Then, keep quite still and you will see the beginning of your father.'

We waited. The bubbles ceased, the foam evaporated and we were left with a dark red surface that gleamed like polished onyx. Suddenly there was a faint ripple and the face I had so often seen before, flashed into being. It looked nothing more than a reflection, as though someone was poised, face down over the bath, but every feature stood out in stark relief. The little eyes gleamed, the bearded lips were parted in a toothless grin, and I fancied I saw a faint resemblance to my own unattractive visage. My mother crooned her delight.

'Hullo, my darling.' She nodded and smiled at the reflected face. 'Soon be up. I said, soon be up. Sonny is going to put the solids in and stir it all up into a lovely paste. Then you'll be up and about. Yes, you will.'

The grin widened and one eye closed in an awful parody of a wink and Mother turned to me in a frenzy of excitement.

'Quick, open the sacks. The big ones first.'

I tore open the first plastic sack and found it contained what appeared to be pink and white mincemeat.

'What . . . what is it?' I enquired.

'Don't ask silly questions,' Mother snapped. 'Tip it into the bath and hurry. My poor darling has waited long enough.'

I emptied the two sacks of mincemeat into the bath, while Mother tore open the ones which contained the long, thin things that rattled. This proved to be a mixture of bones. When I emptied the second sack, a round, smooth skull rolled into the by now, gooey mixture and slowly sank from sight. I shuddered and Mother snarled her impatience.

'Don't be so stupid. Your dear father must have a skull. Really, I have no patience with your lady like stomach. Put the hair in, then begin the first stir.'

'Hair!'

'Yes, this.' And Mother emptied the last sack which I had noticed was very light, and out came a mass of tangled, black hair which lay on top of the red mixture, like some coarse stuffing from a de-gutted sofa.

'Start stirring,' Mother ordered. 'Put your back into it. My poor darling is getting impatient.'

And indeed the face, or rather what could be seen of it through the heap of hair and general array of bits and pieces, did appear to be grimacing in a most alarming fashion. I grabbed the large, wooden spoon and began to stir with all my strength, and in no time at all the mixture was gurgling, spluttering, thickening and taking on weird shapes, while the face elongated, widened, twisted and eventually became a misshapen monstrosity that spread out in every direction.

'Now for the congealing liquid.' Mother was opening the small tin. 'Leave the spoon where it is and stand back. It is now that the expert takes over.'

The mixture was by now so stiff, the wooden spoon remained upright, and I lacked the courage to look down and see what shape it had taken. Mother stood with open tin raised above the bath, and after closing her eyes, began to chant the following words:

> Rise up now, my darling Shaddy,
> For your son wants his daddy.
> Mummy is waiting with open arms;
> Fingers stiff and wide spread palms.
> For she knows the age long rule;
> Maddies yawn and Raddies drool.
> Shaddies lick and Mocks do blow,
> Shadmocks whistle, Humans sow.
> Blood and flesh with bones added,
> Make a body that is nicely padded.
> So rise up now and please your Maddy,
> Be a good and obedient Shaddy.

She poured the contents of the tin into the bath. The imme-diate effect was electrifying. The mixture spat, writhed, seethed and roared, while a foul, black smoke rose up and hid the entire proceedings. 'The second stir,' Mother shouted. 'Don't stand there like a monk at a vampire's picnic. Stir.'

> Twirl it around and pat it down,
> Make a stiff pudding, nice and round.
> Bash it here and poke it there,
> See what happens and don't ask where.

It was awfully hard work. I could not see what was going on because of the smoke, and the mixture was so solid it is a wonder the spoon did not break. Then I detected some kind of movement that had nothing to do with my ineffectual stirring action, and Mother pulled me back while giving vent to a snarl of triumph.

'He's coming up. Praise be to Lucifer and all his angels – he's coming up.'

We waited. There came a soggy, flapping sound as though a large dog were shaking water from its coat, and this was followed by a kind of rasping growl. Then a black shape emerged through the smoke and gradually the bearded face of my Shaddy-Daddy came into view. I cannot truthfully say my heart was filled with filial love. In fact, if I had obeyed my natural impulses I would have turned on my heel and run. To be honest, the Shaddy-Daddy who climbed out of the bath was not pretty, indeed he was possibly uglier than I and much more fearsome. Try to imagine a body that was squat and a strange mottled red and white colour, as though all that mincemeat had become congealed in all the wrong places. It was also covered with coarse, black hair that was matted into strange lumps and seethed in a revolting manner when he moved. He had very long arms that terminated in oddly short fingers, and I was forced to wonder if I had not stirred as well as perhaps I ought.

But it was quite clear that Mother was prepared to accept him, mottled flesh, seething hair, short fingers and all. She took the grotesque figure into her arms and drooled over it, wept on it, made strange noises in its ear, then to my intense disgust, kissed it. In return, Shaddy-Daddy growled, crooned, dribbled and finally licked. Dogs do it when they wish to display affection; cats do it when they sample their food; human children do it when they eat ice-cream. Shaddies do it because it is their nature. They also do it when they are angry – or fight. I felt no inclination to blow. But without doubt, one day I would.

When the first fires of their emotional storm had died down, they parted and slowly turned their attention to me. Shaddy-Daddy bared his toothless gums in what I hoped was an affectionate grin, then advanced towards me. I take credit for the fact that I did not retreat, but stood absolutely still and made a mental resolution that I would not flinch, grimace or shudder when he touched me. After all, there were Mother's feelings to consider.

His hands were cold, but not excessively so. I think the congealing liquid had something to do with that, or maybe there was some kind of internal combustion taking place. I honestly don't know. There are a lot of questions for which I never received satisfactory answers. All I know is, he sighed with quiet satisfaction and said in a deep, husky voice.

'My little Mock. He's a fine, handsome pup and favours his grandmother, who was one of the most beautiful were-goo's who ever graced a churchyard.'

Mother nodded, her eyes shining with pride.

'I always told him that there were some who would consider him handsome.'

'He'll soon be ripe for planting,' Shaddy-Daddy said, feeling my arms and staring intently into my ears.

'Aye, you've only just risen in time,' Mother agreed. 'Let's put the kettle on.'

Shaddy-Daddy settled in very nicely in the circumstances. Mother dug out some clothes from the attic and although they were rather old fashioned and extremely shabby, they fitted him quite well. When we went out walking together, passers-by had a habit of giving us a wide berth, or staring at us in a most disconcerting manner. Shaddy-Daddy poked his tongue out at one or two, and as this was extremely long – a good eighteen inches – it had the effect of making them run.

Naturally, with a father to talk to, I began to ask questions, and he was certainly more forthcoming than Mother.

'Daddy, if Mother is a Maddy, then she is your first cousin.'

Shaddy-Daddy nodded. 'Right, lad. We're both third generation monsters.'

'Then how is it she didn't fall down the plug hole?'

'A matter of genes, lad. Dissolution misses the female line. Mind you, she could have a change of sex when she reaches the change of life, and then it will be another story entirely. But we must hope for the best. Funny thing, cross-breeding, you never know what to expect.'

Then I asked the question which was very close to my heart.

'Daddy, what did Mother mean when she said I would soon be planted?'

Shaddy-Daddy led me to a park bench and a little old lady who had been feeding the birds, beat a hasty retreat.

'Well, lad, it's like this. Basically speaking we all come from the grave, and the urge to get back there is mighty strong. It takes all in different ways, but the Mock – that's you, son – has a very mixed up blood-stream, and powerful instincts that sooner or later insist you go underground. The same that makes us Shaddies dissolve. Presently you'll start to feel very sleepy, and you'll dig holes in the garden, or any bit of naked ground. Then one day you'll flop out and it will be time to plant you.'

'Then . . . then I'll be dead.'

Shaddy-Daddy roared with laughter and shook his shaggy head.

'Not a bit of it, lad. Not a bit of it. When the new moon has grown full and ripe, you'll be a-kicking away down there, and we'll be standing by to dig you up. Then there'll be a change. What! I should say so. You'll be like a butterfly breaking out of its cocoon. Little claws on your feet, little fangs in your mouth, a two inch tail just above your behind, and you'll be able to blow to your heart's content.'

'Blow!' I paused. It was such a terrible question, and really I dreaded to receive an answer. But I had to know. 'Why do mocks blow?'

Shaddy-Daddy patted my arm. 'Look at it like this, son. Why do vampires sup, or ghouls tear, or werewolves hunt? The answer is simple. It's their nature. You'll blow for the same reason.'

'But shaddies lick . . .' I began to protest, then saw Shaddy-Daddy was nodding violently.

'Too true, son. When I lick in earnest, I can bare an arm to
the bone. We monsters may sometimes be objects of ridicule, but
we're not funny. Not really.'

'But blow . . . I don't see . . .'

Shaddy-Daddy rose and yawned, and six bluebottles flew into
his open mouth. He closed his jaws with a snap. 'You will, lad. You
will. Now, let's make for home. Your mother will have the kettle on.'

The sleepiness crept upon me gradually. First there was a reluctance to wake up in the morning, then I began to doze off during
the day, and in the final stages a delicious languor weighed down
my limbs and I longed for a deep, deep repose, while I wrapped
myself in a cocoon of black earth.

The earth. It became to me as a woman whom I must embrace
with all my body; clog my eyes and ears with her damp softness, fill
my mouth with her essence, sleep with and in her, and only wake
every hundred years, so that I might turn over and sleep again.
Sometimes Mother and Shaddy-Daddy would come down during
the small hours and prize me out of an indent in the garden, which
I had clawed out from the rich loam while in a deep sleep. They
murmured soft words of reassurance and escorted me back to
bed, where Mother kissed me on the forehead and Shaddy-Daddy
licked my hand.

The periods of sleep became longer. The visits to the garden
more frequent. The world, as up to that time, I had known it, began
to swiftly slip away.

Voices babbled on the frontiers of consciousness, then went
echoing out to a distant horizon. Once in a long while the bearded
face of Shaddy-Daddy looked down and it radiated a kind of un-
shakable self-confidence, before vanishing and allowing the world
that is without sight or hearing to close in.

Then came dampness, a sense of being shut in, the glorious cloy-
ing aroma of raw earth, and a great and wonderful peace. Some
sense that did not sleep, sent out invisible fingers and felt the earth
that lay beneath, on either side and above, and took joy from its
surroundings. Then that too shut down and for a while there was
nothing.

A hand patted my cheek, a tongue licked my hand, a voice caressed my ears. 'Wake up. It's rising day. Get up little Mock. The sky is clouded, the rain is falling, and the dead keep watch in secluded places.'

The curtains were closed, the light was dim, but my eyes could see every object, every feature of the two faces watching me, as though the room were floodlit. My body felt light and was silent. I could feel no heartbeat, no pounding of blood behind the ears, no perceptible breathing. I was as a creature of air and water, who had borrowed an undamaged dead body.

'Up you get,' instructed Shaddy-Daddy, 'and have a look at yourself.'

I stood in front of the wardrobe mirror and examined my new self. They had washed away the earth stains, but my flesh was now dark brown. I was leaner, perhaps smaller than of yore, but much better looking, once the pointed ears were accepted; the longer horns, the long eyeteeth, the stub of a tail, the taloned feet, and the matting of hair that covered me from neck to ankle. I was no longer repulsively ugly. I was repellently handsome.

'Come downstairs and get some nourishment,' Shaddy-Daddy ordered, 'Get your strength up.'

Mother helped me to dress and sighed when it became apparent that all my clothes were now too large, but by a dint of belt tightening and the assistance of safety pins, I was attired after a fashion. Then we went downstairs and I went straight to the dining-room, to stare woefully at the unlaid table, and become aware that there was not a sight or smell of food anywhere. Shaddy-Daddy roared his merriment and Mother smiled her amusement and said: 'Come into the kitchen.'

I was seated at the kitchen table and with impressive ceremony, Mother placed a silver, covered dish before me. She took a deep breath, then with a flourish removed the lid and I looked upon my post-rising breakfast with wide-open eyes. A long, succulent, speckled snake slowly uncoiled and raised its hissing head, and instinct told me what to do even before Shaddy-Daddy whispered the single word.

'BLOW.'

There was a rasping rattle in my lungs as I built up pressure, then with a roar that made the windows tremble – I blew. The snake quivered, became as rigid as a pointer's tail, before flopping back into the dish. And still I blew. The plastic table cloth turned brown, a paper napkin curled up and began to smoulder, and the snake's skin split like an over-cooked sausage and the pink flesh began to sizzle. My virgin blow lasted for three and a half minutes by the kitchen clock (Mother proudly timed it) and when I at last closed my mouth, the snake was done to a turn.

My parents applauded and Mother said: 'Blow hard, blow soft. Cook, kill or wither.'

It was decided that Shaddy-Daddy and I would share a rising party and invitations were sent to all of our widespread family. This included vampires, both highborn and lowly, werewolves, be they in season or out, ghouls, if their nocturnal activities permitted, and all the numerous hybrids that reside mainly in tall blocks of flats. As an afterthought I sent an invitation to Sheila Benson, knowing curiosity would make her accept. After all, no one had seen the inside of our house before.

To save embarrassment we made it a fancy dress do, so that those who wished could hide fang or claw under mask or robe, and the aristocrats could mingle with the cadet branches without loss of face. Mother was very excited, for since Shaddy-Daddy's evaporation she had not mixed with society, and this for her, would be in the nature of a coming out party. I again went to the house with the red door and returned with a pile of goodies, which included tinned blood for those who partook, various items that were guaranteed to tempt a ghoulish appetite, half a dozen caged incubi, so that the werewolves who were in season could satisfy their hunting instincts, and a bag of mixed reptiles for young Mocks like myself.

The main rooms were again decorated with green paper-chains, the furniture polished, the carpets beaten, the windows cleaned and lots of willow-patterned chinaware brought up from the cellar. Shaddy-Daddy and I washed all our hair and Mother had a shave.* Then the great day arrived and we prepared to meet our guests.

I chose a red devil's costume as this had a hood that was equipped with two sleeves into which my horns slid with ease,

* A forbidden practice.

and it conveniently covered my ears. A matching muffler masked my lower face. Sheila Benson should not be too alarmed by my appearance – not at first.

The band, which was on loan from the monster club, arrived first, and this I installed in the window bay, having ensured that a plentiful supply of vampirical refreshment was close at hand. Then a mini-bus of hired waiters drove in through the front gate and Mother was in a state in case they should think we were not used to servants. Which we weren't. They were mostly vampires of low origin, with one or two werevamps and vamgoos, and I led them into the kitchen and explained the drill as best I could. This should have been Mother's job, but she was so worried lest the first guests arrive while she was in the kitchen, all administration was left to me.

As it happened, she need not have been so concerned, for the first guests turned out to be small fry, who did not care if they were welcomed or not. They were a pair of vamgoos from Hounslow, who practically ignored Mother's: 'So pleased you could come,' and made straight for the refreshment table. A pride of werevamps followed and they at least displayed some traits of good breeding and wished me a happy rising day and many blowing returns.

From then on they piled in, and the band struck up the first waltz. Shaddies danced with maddies, raddies pranced with were-goos, vamgoos led out shadmocks, mocks begged the pleasure from raddies, vampires hugged ghouls, werewolves tripped the heavy fantastic with maddies, and there was an awful lot of excusing and interchanging of partners, so that Mother became rather disturbed that some form of impropriety was taking place.

It was past eight o'clock when a waiter nudged my arm, and after wiping the moisture from his lower lip, whispered: 'Beg pardon, Sir, but a hume's arrived.'

I frowned. 'A what?'

'A female hume, Sir. A woman donator.'

I hurried to the hall and there was Sheila Benson, looking very beautiful in a Regency costume that left her shoulders and arms bare. I had to subdue the urge to blow there and then. She greeted me coolly.

'I can't stay long. Since you took the trouble to invite me, I thought it would be impolite, even unkind, to refuse. But . . .' She looked round our hall, which would have been improved by a spot of decorating. 'But, this is hardly my scene. I don't mean that un-kindly of course. No one can help their background.'

I said: 'So long as you're here. Come and meet my parents.'

Fortunately Shaddy-Daddy had chosen a monk's costume, so he was well covered up, but even so Sheila looked at him with some distaste. Mother, who was decked out as Queen Elizabeth I, looked quite presentable since her shave, but her eyes glittered and she said rather too heartily: 'I *am* pleased to meet you.'

I could do no less than ask the girl to dance, and she accepted with ill-grace. We circled the room while Sheila eyed the other guests with a bold, speculative stare, then asked in a rather too loud voice: 'Do they really look like that, or is it make-up?'

'Sheila,' I said gently, 'people can't help their faces.'

'No, perhaps not. But they could stay at home.'

I don't know how the word got round, because Sheila's good looks were not in themselves a giveaway, for many of the female vampires were quite fetching. But when I looked up all I could see were rows of gleaming fangs and drooling mouths. Then a great hulking vampire from Chorleywood was butting in with a mut-tered: 'Excuse me,' followed by a: 'How thoughtful, but are you sure there's enough to go round.' I glared at him for I could only regard such behaviour as downright greediness, not to mention bad manners.

But of course I had to give way. As the son of the house it would have been gross impoliteness to refuse a guest the courtesy of the dance floor, so I surrendered Sheila to him, but made sure I wasn't more than six feet from them at any time. He was not bad looking, if one overlooked the jutting fangs; tall, with blond curling hair, and he was leering down at Sheila in the manner to which I assumed she had grown accustomed. Then I heard her say: 'I hope you don't mind my mentioning it, but shouldn't you get those teeth attended to,' and waited for the explosion, for your pure-bred vampire is rather touchy about his essentials. But for-tunately a werevamp from Thames Ditton butted in and her late partner was left standing in the middle of the floor, looking as if he had been hit over the head by a brace of crucifixes.

She had six partners in as many minutes and may have assumed she was the belle of the ball. And so she was in a way. Then a tall, fat vampire who had come all the way from the wilds of Kensington, asked: 'Would you care for a turn on the terrace?' and I was in like a stoat defending its young.

I led her unprotesting across the floor, but the expression on her face warned me of the pending storm. When we reached the hall, she opened her mouth, but before words could mature, I jerked her into a small side room and slammed the door. Then the dam erupted and I was submerged under a torrent of words.

'I have never been so humiliated. Those awful creatures with their terrible teeth and clammy hands. I should have known better and never given in to my tender feelings for the afflicted. Common sense should have told me that anyone as ugly as you was bound to have repulsive relations. Don't you dare touch me.' For I put out my hands in protest. 'I feel soiled as it is and frankly I simply loathe you. Loathe.'

'Sheila,' I said, 'please listen.' But as she continued to shout and make her beautiful face ugly with hate, I raised my voice and bellowed: 'I said – LISTEN,' and she became silent and still, looking up at my masked face with growing astonishment. I continued in a quieter voice. 'Ugliness can be transformed into a new kind of beauty if someone takes the trouble to look at it in the right light. But that person must have love and compassion in her heart and the ability to forget self. I loved you, but you spurned me with cruel words. Now I come to you again. Surely there must be a spark of beauty hidden deep within me that deserves to be fanned into an enduring flame.'

She laughed. A cold, silver sound that resembled the pealing of bells, heard across the width of a frozen lake. 'Ugliness makes you repulsive, sentiment makes you insolent.' And raising her hand she deliberately struck me across the face.

It was then that I rightfully came into my inheritance. A cold rage rose up from my stomach and forever swept away the last lingering traces of mercy and tenderness that still chained me to the human race. I saw before me a pretty china doll that had dared raise hand to a mock. Had had the audacity to strike the heir of the dark princes who had ruled the earth in the days before Christianity had soiled the minds of men. I felt my lungs fill, heard the ominous rattle in my throat, and with a savage gesture I jerked the concealing muffler from my face, and the hood from my head. Sheila Benson had the privilege of looking upon a newly arisen mock in all his ferocious glory.

Monster advanced towards fear-stricken beauty. Clawlike hands went out and clasped white flesh and the moaning whimpers were soft music, the terrified eyes, superb mirrors that reflected the dread of long-dead centuries. I drew her towards me and blew gently on her face, and beauty shrivelled like a flower in a frost-laden wind. I breathed into her small ears, fanned her golden hair, ripped her clothes and destroyed the sheen of her white skin, the perfection of her breasts.

I worked slowly and well and when I had finished I left her on the floor to mature. She would not die for a hundred years.

Back in the large withdrawing-room there was a quarrel. It always happens when thoroughbred meets cross-breed. Shaddy-Daddy was standing up to the large fat vampire. I was in time to hear the end of his grievance.

'. . . share and share alike, that has always been the rule of monsterdom. Yet, what happens? Your son introduced a grade A donator, flaunted it before our very noses, then whisks it away for his own nourishment. Although what a "breed" wants with a donator is beyond my comprehension. I demand it be returned at once so that your betters can sup.'

Shaddy-Daddy growled and shook his head. 'No one demands in my house. My son brought the donator in as a guest. A guest is not nourishment. It is the host's own property.'

The vampire went quite grey in the face and bared his fangs.

'Will you, or will you not hand the donator over?'

Shaddy-Daddy grinned. 'You'd best ask my son.'

All eyes were turned on me and I shook my head.

'What blood is left, is parboiled.'

The fat vampire turned back to Shaddy-Daddy and he was fairly shaking with rage.

'I demand satisfaction.'

Nothing more was said, but everyone drew back so that the antagonists had a rough circle in which to fight. But there was a murmur of satisfaction, because I should imagine the party had been becoming rather boring and a fight always livens things up. The vampire removed his coat, but Shaddy-Daddy did not bother, after all he did not fight with his fists. As for that matter, neither did the vampire, but I suppose he wanted to show he meant business.

They circled each other, the vampire with bared fangs, Shaddy-Daddy with his mouth open. Then the vampire roared and rushed in and just as quickly withdrew, for there was a six-inch strip of his left cheek bared to the bone. Shaddy-Daddy gulped, then opened his mouth in readiness for the next attack. I was amazed at the speed with which his tongue had struck. For all I had seen was a long, dark streak dart from his mouth, then the howling vampire was retreating, nursing a depleted cheek. Next time the blood feeder came in with lowered head, hoping no doubt to fasten his fangs into a leg and throw his opponent before that deadly tongue could be brought into action. The Shaddy waited until the sleek head was within six inches of his stomach, then he became blurred movement, and instantly the vampire turned into a writhing figure on the floor with a deep furrow running from the top of his skull to the base of his neck. Shaddy-Daddy chewed appreciatively.

The fight was over. The truth is, of course, that the aristocratic and bourgeois vampires have grown soft. They no longer hunt, but are content to sup from tin or bottle. Now they raid the blood bank – not the neck – and have to pay the price. The vampire's friends carried him away and shortly afterwards the party broke up. I could see there was a considerable amount of ill-feeling and wondered if this incident might not lead to war in monsterdom. When the last guest had departed, Shaddy-Daddy approached me and grinned shyly.

'You young dog. What did you do with her?'

I shrugged. 'Blew on her. She insulted me.'

Shaddy-Daddy nodded. 'It was to be expected. You had to have your first angry blow. But don't keep her all to yourself. Remember you've got parents.'

Mother kissed me and said: 'I hope you had a nice time, darling. Leave everything as it is, we'll clear up tomorrow morning.'

After they had ascended the stairs and closed their bedroom door, I went into the little room and stared at that which stood against the wall. I had not blown on her brain, she was fully conscious and felt no pain. I had blown well. I walked towards her.

'I fear I cannot marry you. Do you want to know why?'

She tried to make a noise, but had not yet learned how.

'Very well, if you insist. You are so ugly. I am sure you are far too intelligent to resent being told the truth. But please stop me if I hurt your feelings.'

She made a little noise. Not much, but she tried.

'Being ugly would not matter all that much. Some ugly women are quite attractive. But you are repulsively ugly.'

She croaked. A funny little croaking sound. Rather like a crow that has a sore throat.

'I don't know what it is that makes you so repulsive, perhaps it is your ears. They remind me of dead – long dead – brussels sprouts. Then there is that awful, yellow, wrinkled face. I don't want to be rude, but if I were to kiss you now – I'd be sick. Honestly. Then there's your hair – what's left of it – green, nasty green, and all frizzy . . . I say, I haven't gone too far, have I?'

Sheila was improving. She made a muted shrieking sound.

'Oh, good. Because I'm telling you this for your own good. I could mention your limbs are like decomposed sticks of celery, but I won't. I could refer to your breasts as deflated apple skins, but that would be unkind. I'm sorry . . . Is there anything wrong? Can it be anything I said?'

She was twisting her head round, contorting her throat, trying so hard to communicate. Then – she was rewarded. A tiny shriek slid up from her throat and gradually grew into a long, long, drawn out whistle.

I overcame my feeling of revulsion for her extreme ugliness. Pardoned her crime, and drew her into my arms where she basked in the warmth of my undying hate. I laughed softly.

'I must mate you with a shadmock. For shaddies may lick and mocks may blow, but you – fortunately – can only whistle.'

Monster Club Interlude: 2

There was quite a crowd round the table when the mock at last finished his story, and Donald was becoming a little worried because some of the newcomers were observing him with more appetite than politeness. Eramus, bored by a story he had heard so many times before, was fast asleep, and the werevamp was displaying signs of profound distaste, although whether these were assumed or genuine, Donald could not determine.

'Every time I hear that story,' the werevamp announced, 'I find it more disgusting. Right – I'm a monster – we all are, but hell below, there are limits. As I see it, you messed up a nice piece of homework because she told the truth. She called you ugly, and so you are. Bloody ugly.'

The mock scowled and there was an ominous rattling sound that originated in his throat. 'You half-breeds think you're devil-almighty because you happen to be half of one and fifty per cent of the other. I'm a mock – and proud of it, I might add. Because I am a mock, I blow, and that wench was definitely blowable. And if you want to make something out of it – come outside.'

A dignified ghoul who had listened intently to the werevamp's story, hastily intervened.

'Gentlemen, please. There is really no need for us – if I might coin a phrase – to heat our blood – hell alone knows, there's little to spare.'

He paused to allow the titter to die away, then continued.

'We all follow the path that the Black One has laid down for us, and it ill becomes any member of this club to criticise the nocturnal habits of another. In particular must I take exception to remarks concerning anyone's pedigree. I would request everyone to remember the club's irrevocable rule: – "All monsters are equal".'

There was a rumble of hear, hear, and the two antagonists displayed signs of embarrassment. The mock was the first to tender his apologies.

'Sorry, old man. Lost me temper. Take it all back.'

The werevamp was not to be outdone by this magnanimity and extended his taloned hand in a gesture of renewed goodwill.

'Forget it, my dear fellow. Entirely my fault. Damn it all, if you must blow – then, blast it, you blow. And may I add, if some mortal women were blown on at regular intervals, the world would be a better place than it is.'

Everyone in the immediate vicinity applauded as werevamp and mock gravely shook hands and the ghoul permitted himself a tiny smile of approval.

'I am gratified, gentlemen, that I did not overestimate the generous – the noble – feeling of good fellowship, which is a by-word of our august organisation. And I cannot but help feel that this auspicious occasion calls for a rousing rendition of the first verse of the "Monster's Anthem".'

An undersized weregoo, who had been consuming whatever was left in the glasses while everyone was enthralled by the ghoul's discourse, shouted: 'Baddie, baddie, a sing-song!' and thus earned himself a united admonishing scowl.

'Let us sing heartily, but with reverence,' the ghoul warned, watching the offending weregoo with cold disapproval. 'Now, gentlemen,' he picked up a fork and banged it three times on the table, 'all together.'

Mouths, snouts, jaws and muzzles were opened and everyone bellowed, roared, screamed or simply sang the following words.

> Monsters all, we stand together,
> In windy, fine or rainy weather.
> Jaws, claws or dripping fang,
> It matters not when vault doors clang.
> Then we march forth, snout to jowl,
> A glorious army straight from hell,
> Sup, hunt, tear or lick,
> We'll make humans deadly sick.
> Blow, yawn or simply whistle,
> Mortal hair will rise and bristle.
> So let us give one mighty shout,
> Jaws wide open, gaping snout.

Monsters all, we stand together,
In windy, fine or rainy weather.

The last two lines were roared out in a bedlam of sound, and
when the last voice had died – which, of course, was that of the
little weregoo – there was a spontaneous outburst of emotion.
Werewolves hugged vampires, ghouls embraced either, mocks
blew very gently on werevamps, vamgoos pounded the backs of
raddies, shadmocks whistled at maddies, and some of Baron Frankenstein's mistakes did unspeakable things to anyone who happened to be in their immediate vicinity. When at last the tumult
had died down, the ghoul wiped his eyes and reseated himself in
the nearest chair.

'Not since . . .' he gradually mastered his emotion, '. . . not
since the Ghoul cemetery feast of '54 have I been so moved. Now, I
know I was justified, when in my after dinner speech on that occasion, I said: "Let them come with rolled umbrellas or sharpened
stakes; let them come with garlic flowers or burning crosses, and
we will defeat them".'

Eramus, who had been awakened by the singing of the 'Monster's Anthem', yawned and several of the other monsters began to
look bored. There was a consensus of opinion that the ghoul was
rather overdoing things.

'As I was listening to our friend's interesting and colourful narration,' that personage went on, 'I could not but help recall a story
that was recounted to me by a distant relative. And it has occurred
to me that you may all derive pleasure and profit if I were to exercise, what my good spouse is pleased to call or describe, as my
exceptional histrionic powers. In short, read the story which I had
the foresight to commit to paper.'

And without further words the ghoul fumbled within his shroud
and brought forth a rather dirty looking manuscript and laid it
carefully on the table.

'Satan Almighty!' Eramus exploded. 'Not another damn story!
Is there never going to be an end of this baring of souls and uncov-
ering of skeletons? Frankly, I'd rather . . .'

'As president of both the wine and blood committee,' the ghoul
stated, coolly ignoring the interruption, 'I think it behoves me to

ensure that all lips are moistened and all tongues bathed. In short
– to order drinks all round.'

Faces came alive, bodies sat up, tongues came out and Eramus
ceased to object. When everyone had been supplied with his choice
of needful refreshment, the ghoul opened the manuscript, and
after adjusting a pair of rimless spectacles on to his extremely large
nose, began to read in a slow, well-modulated voice, the story of:

The Humgoo

Gerald Mansfield was lost, a not unusual occurrence, being the kind of person who has no sense of location. He knew he was somewhere in Hampshire, that Portsmouth lay possibly thirty miles or so to the south, that he was driving through narrow lanes, having turned off the main road while suffering under the illusion that he would thus cut short his journey.

Suddenly he saw the sign. A long, white plaque with embossed black letters, which stated quite clearly – LOUGHVILLE. Gerald thought of a petrol station – the tank was nearly empty – a restaurant – his stomach being in like condition – and some intelligent person who could put him back on the shortest route to Portsmouth.

At first glance Loughville looked promising. A narrow main street, lined on either side by terraced houses, and what appeared to be a pub, backed by an old church at the far end. But when Gerald examined his surroundings more carefully, he found a general atmosphere of age and neglect. The cottages were not only old, but decrepit, with crumbling mortar and flaking paint, while the tiny front gardens displayed tall grass and wild flowers, which was in keeping with the tumble-down gates and reeling fences. He might have supposed the place to be deserted, were it not for the occasional plume of smoke that drifted up from almost every chimney and the thick and dirty net curtains that masked every window. As his car crept down the street, he had a suspicion that some curtains stirred as though a ripple of interest had roused the houses from an afternoon nap. And there was no doubt at all that one door opened very slightly, thus allowing a single, cold eye to peer round the edge.

Gerald drove into a narrow courtyard which lay before the inn and looked up at the building that could have been mistaken for another cottage, were it not for the dilapidated sign which hung over the solitary, green painted door. This depicted a man in what appeared to be a white smock, and immediately below was the inscription: THE LOUGH INN. Gerald got out of his car, crossed the drive, and after some hesitation, opened the green door.

He entered a long, evil smelling room and looked round with some surprise. A plain, unvarnished counter ran three-quarters of the length of the room, and terminated where a flight of stairs led to the upper regions. A large beer barrel stood at the right end of the bar, and the counter top was littered with a number of earthenware mugs. Two oak settles flanked an old-fashioned fireplace, and a long, backless bench stood against the wall on either side of the door. The floor was coated with filthy sawdust. There were no decorations of any kind, no advertisements which even the meanest of inns usually displays – nothing but bare essentials.

Gerald approached the bar, and as there was no one in attendance, rapped smartly on the stained counter. He waited for a full minute, then rapped again and looked expectantly at a ragged curtain which masked an open doorway set in the facing wall. Presently this stirred, a long-fingered and extremely dirty hand pulled it slowly to one side, and a tall, lean man emerged into view. He shuffled to the counter and stared at the visitor with mouth-gaping astonishment. Gerald decided that here was an individual he would not care to meet on a dark night.

The face was unnaturally long and narrow; the eyelids were hooded and hung down over the watery eyes as clusters of wrinkled skin; excessively large ears stood up on either side of the completely bald head; a hooked nose jutted out over a mouth, which being open, revealed yellow, pointed teeth. He was dressed – if that was the right word – in what Gerald could only suppose to be a suit of filthy, striped pyjamas. The young man tried to veil his repulsion by a nervous smile and a polite voice.

'I wonder if you can help me? I seem to be lost. I was driving to Portsmouth and . . .'

'You cum by motor . . . car?'

The question was asked in a thick, slurred voice, which suggested its owner had either a vocal-cord ailment or mucus-filled bronchial tubes. At the same time the watery eyes, in so far as they were capable of expression, gleamed with pleasurable surprise.

'You cum by motor . . . car from . . . outside?'

Gerald frowned and considered the possibility of backing

towards the door. 'Yes, I've driven down from London and intended
to be in Portsmouth before nightfall. But, as I said, I seem to have
lost my way. I was hoping you could direct me back to the main
road.'

The man nodded. A very slow jerking of his head, then, as
though struck by a sudden thought, turned and shuffled back to the
doorway. Gerald heard him mutter something in a low, growling
voice, and almost at once a child dashed from behind the curtain,
and after ducking under the bar, stood upright for a few moments,
gazing up at the visitor with the same open-mouthed astonishment
that decorated the face of the innkeeper.

Gerald could not determine the child's sex, for the skinny body
was attired in the remains of a little girl's nightgown, but there
was certainly nothing feminine about the long, narrow head that
was surmounted by a mass of tangled black hair. The innkeeper
growled again and the child sped for the door, which Gerald had
thoughtlessly left open.

'Sent for someone,' the man intoned. 'Someone who direct.'

'Very kind,' Gerald murmured, then added, 'but I've no wish to
cause trouble. I daresay if I keep going, I'll find a main road somewhere.'

'Someone direct,' the man repeated. 'Have beer.'

'Yes – well, that's an idea. I'll have half a pint.'

The innkeeper, with the same slow movement which seemed
to dominate all his actions, took up an earthenware mug, and
after shuffling along the entire length of the bar, held it under the
beer barrel and turned a spigot. When Gerald tasted the liquid, he
found it to be both bitter and strong.

'Home brewed?' he enquired.

'Make it ourselves,' the man growled.

'Then you are a free house?'

The question seemed to confuse the innkeeper, for he again
assumed an expression of open-mouthed astonishment and did
not answer. Gerald emptied the mug, then looked with pretended
impatience at his watch.

'Look here, I don't think I'll bother to wait for your friend. I'll
push along and hope for the best.'

'They cum now,' the man said.

And indeed, barely had Gerald time to note that singular had been transformed into multiple, when a large number of persons filed in through the doorway and formed a half-circle in front of the bar. The child, being the last to enter, slammed the door, then hastened to join its elders who were staring at the stranger with disconcerting interest.

They all bore an uncanny resemblance to the innkeeper. Same long, narrow heads, identical large ears and hooded eyes, but a few were endowed with a mop of tangled, greasy hair. Gerald could not avoid the impression that he had caused them all to rise from a loathsome and unsavoury bed. Filthy and torn pyjamas of every colour and design predominated; flannel nightgowns took second place, and one tall, lanky creature was wrapped in what appeared to be a badly stained bedsheet.

'Gentle . . . man lost,' announced the innkeeper.

'Ah!' the tall, lanky one ejaculated, and his Adam's apple went up and down as though it had been motivated by some intense excitement.

'Cum by motor . . . car,' the innkeeper added and instantly two members of the assembly shuffled towards the door.

'Where's he 'e bound for?' enquired a short thing, in a spotted nightgown.

'Ports . . . mouth,' the innkeeper answered.

Gerald, like a man lost in a particularly unpleasant nightmare, watched an awful nodding of heads. It was a slow nodding, which might have suggested that a very simple problem had been solved.

'I reckon that be a goodish way off,' announced something in greenish pyjamas.

'Reckon 'e won't get there tonight,' stated the man in the once white sheet.

'Or tomorrow,' added the innkeeper.

They all tittered. A kind of low, gurgling giggle, such as a crowd of evil, backward children might make, while anticipating the result of an unpleasant practical joke. It was at this point that the door opened and the two persons who had gone out returned. Gerald gathered up his shattered courage and made a statement.

'Thank you all for your kind interest, but I must leave now. Don't worry, I'll find my way somehow.'

''E be leaving,' said the tall lanky one with an expression of profound astonishment.

'Leav . . . ing?' enquired the innkeeper.

'Ah.'

'Well,' Gerald managed to grin. 'I'll be on my way. Thanks again.'

He strode purposefully towards the door and the half-circle obligingly parted in the centre and allowed him to pass. He reached the door, opened it and, feeling like a man who has against all expectations been released from prison, stepped out into the dying afternoon. He all but ran to his car, as though it were a refuge that would protect him from all danger, or a bastion from which he could fight off a horde of grotesque attackers. But when he was safely inside, the door closed and the ignition switched on, he saw them clustered round the inn door, watching him with amused interest. Before he pressed the self-starter, he actually waved to them, hoping that this would be accepted as a gesture of cheerful unconcern. No one bothered to wave back – neither did the self-starter respond to the urgent pressure of his foot. The continued silence, which should have been broken by the comforting roar of the engine, made his heart thump and he pressed his foot down until it seemed it must go through the floorboards – but to no avail. A sideways glance told him the line of night-attired figures was very slowly advancing, only now the hooded eyes were alight with malicious pleasure, and the child was dancing as though in anticipation of some unexpected treat.

Gerald had no alternative but to climb out and walk with assumed unconcern round to the front of the car. He raised the bonnet and the reason for the self-starter's non-cooperation became instantly apparent. The distributor had been smashed and every length of wiring pulled out. Uneasiness – active fear had not yet crossed the border – was temporarily swept away by a hot surge of rage.

'Who did this?' he bellowed at the now stationary, but interested audience.

'Be it broke?' asked the innkeeper.

'Of course it's bloody well broke. Who did it?'

One white face looked at another in a parody of helpless enquiry, then the tall, lanky one expressed an opinion.

'Be them vermin. I lay it be them vermin.'

The something in greenish pyjamas nodded with awful solemnity. 'Real monsters, they be. Nothing be safe.'

Gerald's range evaporated and fear was willing and ready to fill its place. He looked hopefully up and down the road, then proceeded to ask what proved to be a silly question.

'Can anyone direct me to the nearest telephone?'

'No tele . . . phone . . . no tele . . . phone . . . no tele . . . phone . . .'

The tortured words rumbled mournfully along the line, then dropped down to the child, who, lacking his elders' histrionic powers, repeated them as a cry of triumph.

'NO TELE . . . PHONE.'

'How far is it to the nearest garage?'

The same enquiring looks were exchanged, but now heads were shaken and the innkeeper, who seemed to exercise some kind of authority, murmured: 'Gar . . . age! No gar . . . age.'

'For heaven's sake!' Gerald looked anxiously from side to side. 'Surely you can suggest something. What can I do?'

They all spoke in unison. 'STAY HERE.'

'STAY HERE,' yelled the child.

'Soon be dark,' said one.

'T'aint safe in dark,' said another.

'Be snug in pub,' comforted yet another.

Dirty white fingers plucked at his coat sleeves, an elbow prodded his back and Gerald was half led, half forced back into the Lough Inn.

Gerald was given a room with an excellent view of the churchyard.

After a swift glance which evoked an involuntary shudder, he released the dust-grimed curtain and examined the room in which he was expected to spend the night. Like the bar no effort had been wasted on non-essentials. A narrow wooden bedstead, on which lay a rumpled pile of bedclothes: a battered tallboy with tantalisingly familiar brass handles and a wooden chair. The floor was bare, faded wallpaper hung in drapes from crumbling plaster, while festoons of cobwebs decorated the cracked ceiling. Gerald decided that there would be no communication between himself and the bed and if he must spend the night in this room, the chair would be his only resting place. Even as he reached this decision, the door opened and a girl entered.

She was as a diamond among pebbles. Or perhaps a better simile would be – a lamb among wolves. Her face was long, but not unnaturally so, her eyes, large and a deep cornflower blue, which contrasted with her shoulder length black hair. She was dressed in a comparatively white nightgown and gave the impression that – unlike her associates – she was at least on nodding terms with soap and water. Gerald gaped at this beauty that had so unexpectedly emerged from the grotesque and watched her place a tray on the edge of the bed. She spoke with the same husky voice that seemed characteristic of the entire village, but it lacked that horrible gurgling quality.

'Dadda said you eat this.'

He looked at the basin of brown stew from which lumps of meat jutted out like rocks in a calm sea, and wondered if his stomach would accept anything that had been cooked in this dirt ridden place.

'What is it?' he enquired.

She smiled and her teeth were even and white.

'Stew rabbit. I cook.'

He looked, sniffed, and after taking up a battered dessert spoon, finally tasted. 'It's not bad.' The stomach held a conference with appetite and decided to accept the rabbit stew. The girl watched him eat, then when the basin was empty, she timidly put out a hand and felt the soft texture of his camelhair suit.

'Good. Do all people on outside wear this?'

'Outside!' For a moment he thought that she had made some kind of obscure joke, or this was a clumsy attempt to start a flirtatious conversation, then he saw the wonderment in the blue eyes, and fear, which was never far away, came rushing back.

'Look, you are only a few miles from the main road. An hour's ride in my car would take you to a large town. This isn't the north pole.'

She shook her head. 'I do not understand. Long ago the elders set a gulf between them and us. Only once in many eatings has stranger from outside come through. No one but elders go out.'

A theory formed from the mass of jumbled words that bedevilled his mind, giving a rational explanation for all he had seen and heard. A small community that had interbred for generations, and now was but a collection of semi-idiots who had lost track with reality. That must be the answer. And this girl was a throwback, a misfit who accepted the superstitions and legends that had been passed down and elaborated on by crippled minds. He felt a twinge of pity.

'All people . . .' He paused, then tried again. 'All people on the outside wear clothes like mine. But girls wear prettier ones – and you should too. Tell me, why are you all dressed in nightclothes? Surely you must be cold during the winter time.'

'These only clothes in boxes,' she stated simply. 'No clothes like yours. Only this,' she pointed to her nightgown, 'and others like Dadda's.'

'Boxes!' He frowned and tried to understand. 'You mean you found some boxes filled with nightgowns and pyjamas?'

She shook her head. 'No. Only one clothes in each box. All comes from boxes.' She nodded towards the chest of drawers with the brass handles. 'Dickon, who work with hands, made that from boxes. Bed made from boxes. Chair made from boxes.'

Gerald looked at the tallboy with renewed interest. It had been constructed from polished elm and was fitted with brass handles that were still tantalisingly familiar. The workmanship was crude, for he could see hammer marks where the craftsman had missed his aim and no attempt had been made to remove the numerous stains and scratches.

'Where did your people find these boxes?'

She nodded towards the window. 'In ground. On gathering night. All come from boxes. Clothes, wood – food – for big eating.'

Almost against his will, Gerald moved over to the window and looked down on to the churchyard. There was the church, grey, forlorn, with broken windows and gaping doorway, and there was a rugged crop of reeling tombstones that looked as if they had lost a long battle with a raging typhoon. But instead of graves were row after row of earth piles and yawning holes. The girl's voice came from behind his left shoulder.

'No more boxes left. All gone.'

Gerald turned and for a thought-frozen moment, stood looking down at the white, beautiful face, then when understanding wriggled into his mind like a bad-intentioned snake, he sprang into violent and purposeful action. He reached the door in three running strides.

The innkeeper watched him pass with his habitual look of profound astonishment; three night-clad creatures who were propping up the inn wall raised their heads as he stood in the narrow courtyard and looked anxiously from side to side. The car had disappeared. There had been some wild notion of doing some running repairs, or at the very worst locking himself in – but now even these frail dreams evaporated and merged into the stream of cold despair. There was only one recourse; to keep running.

He ran down the road that skirted the church and disappeared under an archway of trees. He ran until it seemed his heart must burst and the most glorious pleasure would be to lie down in the tall grass and let his soul float away on a cool breeze. Eventually he stopped and looked back. No one had either been able or could be bothered to follow him. He remembered those slow-moving figures and gave a loud sigh of relief. He had now only to follow his nose and sooner or later he would reach a main road, or, at the very least, a telephone.

He walked for an hour. The road twisted, did a complete turn, ran between untilled fields, turned again, slid under an avenue of interlocking trees – and Gerald found himself back in the village street. He mastered a wave of near panic and decided that if the road was not to be trusted, he would take to the open fields. He climbed a low bank, wended his way from tree to tree and presently came out into a large open space that rose gradually to a far-off crest. As he walked Gerald had the silly notion that he was getting nowhere, almost as if – and this was even more silly – the ground was moving and he was marking time. The notion appeared to have some substance when he crested the slope, for way down below lay the desecrated churchyard and the twin lines of huddled cottages, that at this distance looked like two long brown caterpillars on either side of a grey ribbon.

Gerald Mansfield wandered for the rest of the day. He walked away from the sun, he walked towards it. He crashed through overgrown hedges, jumped waterlogged ditches, waded through waist-high grass, crossed the road several times – and always came back to the village. The sun was setting when he reeled into the main – the only street – for the last time, and they were waiting for him.

'Had nice walk?' the tall, lanky one enquired.

'Been goodish distance?' asked the thing in greenish pyjamas.

'Eating time,' announced the creature wrapped in a bedsheet.

''Ot rabbit stew,' promised the innkeeper.

He was escorted back to that awful bedroom, the door was shut and bolted on the outside and there followed the simple peace that follows a complete defeat. Gerald was so tired he actually flung himself down on the bed, but did not of course attempt to climb between the sheets. Apart from other considerations, there was an exciting suspicion that they had been made from a well-used shroud.

It was dark when the door opened and the girl, holding a candle in one hand and a tray in the other, entered the room. Gerald sat up and blinked at her. He had no idea how long he had been asleep, but his body was refreshed, if somewhat stiff, and his brain fully receptive. Horror rode in on the back of memory, but Gerald tried to ignore it. Fear would freeze his mind, paralyse his reasoning powers and therefore destroy any faint hope that this pretty young thing could be made to render assistance. He smiled with assumed cheerfulness as she laid the tray on the bed and pointed to the steaming basin.

'Rabbit stew again? ' he enquired.

She shrugged. 'Boxes empty. We have to make do.'

He shuddered, although he could not really believe that the nightmare of medieval mythology could become stark reality. There must be another answer. The girl seated herself on the only chair and watched him eat and because curiosity would not be denied, he had to ask questions.

'You are different from the others. Do you know why?'

'My mother outsider. When I born . . . she got into box. Then dug up for great eating. All happy.'

Gerald put the half empty basin down and did not wonder why his appetite had fled. He began to speak quickly, the words tumbling over one another in a vain effort to dislodge terror and re-establish reason.

'This is some kind of game, isn't it? People – cars – they must come through. It is impossible to think otherwise. If what you expect me to believe is true, then beauty, the commonplace – all – is only a brightly coloured veil which hides the horrific. Why – God in heaven – the entire world is but a pretty ball, pleasing on the outside, a mass of seething maggots on the inner.'

'Not understand.' She shook her head. 'Sometimes elders come in on day of great eating and there is much dancing round fire. They bring in boxes.'

A tiny spark of hope flickered across the darkness of his despair. 'Then someone does come in! Tell me – please think carefully – when is day of – great eating?'

She was looking aimlessly out of the window and Gerald wondered if he were beginning to frighten her with all these questions. She answered him in a low voice. 'When nightlight is big ball over big house.'

'Big ball . . . nightlight?' His brain played with this imagery, tossed words to and fro and came up with the simple answer. 'When the full moon is over the church! Tell me . . . what is your name?'

'Name?' She frowned and stirred uneasily and he knew that he would not retain her much longer. 'You mean how am I called? Luna.'

'Then, Luna, can you remember how these . . . what do you call them? . . . how these elders come. Do they walk?'

She giggled. It was the first natural girlish sound she had made and it seemed she was a little nearer to him because of it. 'No. Elders come in motor-car. Big motor-car.'

He leaned towards her and she did not shrink away. 'One more question, Luna. I promise, just one more. You said your mother was an outsider. How did she get in? Did she come in . . . did she come with the elders?'

Again that childish shaking of head. 'No. Dadda say she caught in trap. Like rabbit. Like you and motor-car. Trap not catch many. Last – ten great eatings ago.'

'Luna, what will they do with me?'

'You say . . . only one more question.'

She got up and moved towards the door and it was then that the cords of reason snapped and he was clutching her arm, pouring out his terror born words.

'Luna . . . tell me . . . in the name of mercy, tell me. What will they do with me?'

She was writhing in his grasp, struggling to break free, and her beautiful eyes were wild with alarm.

'Me not tell . . . Dadda beat me if I tell.'

'He will never know. I promise. But I must know. Please tell me and I will let you go.'

Luna became quieter, then she turned her head and whispered as though afraid the paper-draped walls might overhear the dread secret.

'You wear clothes like this,' she pointed with her free hand at the nightgown, 'then you go into box and bury in ground near big house . . . and when nightlight round they dig you up . . . and there will be great tearing and eating . . .'

Gerald's hand dropped away and Luna finding she was free, slipped out through the half-open door and slowly bolted it behind her. Gerald paced the room, clasped his head between shaking hands and tried to come to terms with truth – as he saw it. One fact was certain, he was in the hands of imbeciles with a mania that included murder and – he might as well face the fact – eating their victims afterwards. Luna's last words raced across his brain: 'And there will be great tearing and eating.'

He went to the window and looked down. A drop of at least twenty feet and it would not be pleasant if he were to break a leg and be helpless to move when they came for him. But the bed-clothes! He could make some sort of rope from them, and surely if he tried really hard, he must find a way back to the main road. It would be a great help if he knew where he was. Then he remembered the road map in his jacket pocket.

He spread it out on the bed and by the light cast by the guttering candle, anxiously studied the meandering lines that denoted roads and tried to pinpoint the position where he had turned off. 'I passed that roundabout,' he spoke aloud. 'Yes, and that farm, so . . .' he jabbed his finger down, '. . . here is where I turned. It must be. The only side road for miles. That being the case, where the devil is Loughville?'

His finger followed the line of the road and came to a space of open countryside and woodland. He widened his search area and muttered the names as they came within his line of vision. 'Corhampton . . . Wickham . . . Tapnage . . . Farnham . . . but no Loughville.' Then, desperate for a straw of hope, hungry for a crumb of reality, he grabbed at the improbable. Perhaps the map-makers had spelt the name wrongly. Or there was a misprint. Suppose there was a G where an L should be, or an O in place of a U. 'Treat the name as an anagram and see what you come up with.' Gerald thought hard. 'HOUGL – ville? No. OUGHL – ville. Extremely unlikely.' Then he exchanged one letter for another and stared with bulging eyes and gaping mouth at the result. GHOUL – ville. Ghoulville. The place of the ghouls.

Had he been in any other situation Gerald would have laughed most heartily at this macabre joke. He would most likely have experimented with a few more place names and possibly have come up with one or more bizarre results. Good heavens – the anagram of Slough was ghouls. Was it possible . . . ? The arm of coincidence could not be that long. He was in the hands of ghouls.

The sheets – or shrouds – were made from tough, unbleached linen, and had it not been for his penknife, he would never have been able to tear them into long strips. The rest was easy. Five minutes later found him with a reasonably strong, knotted rope, which would more than reach to the ground. He pulled the bedstead up to the window, tied one end of his rope over the footboard and tossed the other out of the window. Then he prepared to climb down and found the task more difficult than he had supposed.

A bedstead made from coffin boards was not very heavy and the instant Gerald slid over the window-sill, the footboard left the floor and came crashing through the window-frame. This meant he was jerked out from the wall and was left hanging like a hooked fish over a patch of unkept, back garden. By a dint of sliding and going down hand over hand, he finally reached the ground and prepared to set up an all time record for the hundred yard sprint. It was then that he found that his labour and ingenuity had been completely wasted.

They moved in from both sides. Pyjamas, nightgowns, shrouds, faces faintly phosphorescent in the semi-darkness, two dozen or more nightmare figures shuffled in, bringing their gurgling voices with them.

'That were a goodish drop,' Long and Lanky stated.

''E made a fine old muck-up of your winder,' observed Green-ish Pyjamas.

'I reckon 'e be going for a walk again,' Bedsheet suggested.

'What do you reckon we ought to do with 'im?' enquired the innkeeper.

'COFFIN 'IM,' shouted a shrill voice that was very near the ground.

The suggestion found favour with an overall majority – less one. Whatever courage Gerald still retained, melted when cold, seem-ingly boneless hands grabbed his arms, caressed his neck, embraced his thighs and ankles and he was frog-marched round the inn and through the front door. His screams caused a certain amount of low, throaty laughter, and the child, whom he had come to dread more than the full grown, slobbering adults, took full advantage of his helpless condition, to poke him in the ribs, scream in his ear and bite his writhing fingers.

They passed him over the bar – and here there was a little ill-intentioned horseplay, pulling of arms, twisting of legs – through the curtained doorway and into a small room beyond. All had been prepared. The coffin was not one to be proud of. It was old, earth-caked, the wood cracked here and there, but for the lack of some-thing better, still serviceable. Gerald was undressed with the greatest of care, for even he could appreciate that his wardrobe was of ines-timable value, and when shared would replace worn out pyjamas, nightgown or shroud. When he was naked they all gathered round and drooled. He was the uncooked joint, the peeled potatoes and washed greens, the plum pudding or apple tart – and there was clearly a great hunger for food. Fingers clawed his bare leg, pointed teeth were bared, but Luna screamed out the merciful words: 'DON'T TEAR . . . HE NOT DEAD YET.'

Like the coffin the nightgown had seen better days; stained with unthinkable splodges, torn, smelly, but it fitted where it touched. They bound him with coffin-lowering ropes then, with surprising gentleness, laid him in the coffin. Dinner was now ready for the cold oven.

As the coffin lid was lowered he saw the circle of open-mouthed, hooded eyed faces, and all were dribbling, gloating, lip licking – save one. If hope still lived, it lay hidden in a pair of cornflower blue eyes that wept. Two large tears were creeping down the white cheeks, when the light was blotted out and he was shut in.

Age is sometimes ugly. It can also be spiteful, malicious or down-right cruel. It can also, on occasion be kind. Age had robbed the coffin of its former polished sheen, warped its wooden planks, tarnished its brass handles, but it had also given it some long, gaping cracks and these enabled Gerald to breathe. He could also hear, which was not quite so fortunate.

'Bury 'im now?'

'Aye. Then 'e be nice and ripe for great eating.'

'I fancy's leg, meself. Rare and tender that be.'

'Ah, but arm be tasty.'

The voice of the innkeeper had an authoritative ring.

'Get 'im planted furst. Then when nightlight be big we tear and eat.'

Gerald found himself being lifted up and there was a general swaying, which was occasionally disturbed by a violent bump, when the coffin made contact with doorpost or bar. Then the night breeze seeped in through the cracks and he knew he was on his way to the churchyard. There was no burial service and really he did not expect one; for what housewife says a prayer when she drops the steak into a pie-dish? Just an ungentle lowering into a second-hand grave, then – and it was now that Gerald learned to pray – the hurried shovelling of loose earth, that crashed down on the coffin lid like rocks on a drum.

He tried to resign himself to death, but the body was young and healthy and it wanted to live, and the brain gave a great cry of terror when it saw the black, rolling plains that lay ahead. Gerald arched his bound legs, and his knees smashed up against the coffin's lid. Again age came to his assistance, for the wood was rotten and broke easily, rearing up through the loose earth in jagged splinters, so that his supply of air was reinforced by means of a narrow tunnel. Gerald held his breath, terrified lest the noise had attracted the attention of his grave-fillers, but it must have been masked by the sound of falling earth, for the shovelling continued without interruption and he increased his upward pressure when a trickle of earth seeped down into the coffin. Presently the, by now, faint thudding ceased, and after waiting for as long as he dared, Gerald pressed his head against the coffin lid and was rewarded by a soft popping sound as corroded screws flew from enlarged holes, plus the knowledge that the loose earth was giving way above him. Fortunately his burial had been more symbolic than actual, for those who put him down had every intention of shortly bringing him up again, and ghouls were not apparently addicted to hard work. Spluttering, sweating, with scratched face and soil-caked hair, Gerald Mansfield came up from his grave and looked anxiously round the deserted churchyard. The moon, which was but a nibble away from being full, lit up the gothic scene, highlighted the grey stone church, the desecrated graves and reeling tombstones. The night breeze came rustling across the tall grass and made the young man shiver. By a miracle he was free from his coffin, but his position still bordered on the hopeless. Clad in a nightgown and trussed up like a roasting fowl, it would take all his strength and ingenuity to climb out of the grave, let alone put distance between himself and the sinister village.

His head was just above ground level, but by leaning against the grave wall, he was able to draw his feet up and stand on one side of the coffin. Then followed ten minutes of wriggling, heaving and kicking the loose earth downwards, until he was able to at last roll over on to solid ground. He lay still for some time and gradually regained his breath and strength, then he looked up and all but slid back into the grave. A white figure was wending its way between the tombstones towards him.

Fear chased thoughts round into a mad circle and despair looked down from the night sky. One of them was coming back to finish the grave-filling operation, or perhaps the noise he had made when breaking out of the coffin had been heard and its implication only just realised. Gerald buried his face in the coarse grass, and, overcome by weakness, shock and cold terror, cried. He heard the slow footsteps draw nearer and waited for the clutch of flabby fingers and the harsh cry of a gurgling voice. The footsteps ceased when they had reached a spot but a few inches from his shaking head and a low voice said: 'You get out! I afraid you not get out.'

It was some time before Gerald dared to look up and when he did it was hard to believe that fortune still smiled upon him. Luna stood looking down at him, a gleaming carving knife in one hand, a spade in the other. When she bent over him with outstretched knife he shrank back with a little cry. She looked anxiously over one shoulder.

'No make noise. I cut loose.'

She hacked at the confining ropes, and when they had fallen away, he still did not move, but lay staring up at her with wide eyes. Luna sat down beside him and looked sadly at the open graves.

'I could not let them do this to you. Others, old and fat and squeal like trapped rabbit. But you different. I feel sadness for you.'

Gerald sat up and he felt pity, even tenderness for this lovely creature who belonged neither to monster world or human, but fear, the urgent demand for self-preservation left no room for gentle emotion. He could only ask the all important question.

'Where can I hide?'

Luna pointed to the moonlit church. 'In big house. They not go there. It is – not good. They fall down if go in there.'

The old grey building with its broken windows and sagging doors, was at once a place of sanctuary, a mecca for the hunted, a resting place where hope could be reborn. He laid his hand on the girl's arm and she started as though his touch were a branding iron.

'Can you go in there?'

She nodded. 'Yes. I am not as them. Dadda say I am humgoo. I have mother's blood. I too would go into ground, but Dadda chief and elders say I be left alone.'

'How long must I stay there?' he asked.

'I not know. I bring you food when others not watch. But must be careful.' She shuddered and again looked fearfully back at the inn. 'They must not know or I suffer bad things.'

'I'll go into the church now,' he said. 'And thank you. Thank you.'

He rose and there was a fleeting thought that he should reward her bravery with a light kiss, but the shuddering suspicion of what food had passed those full, red lips, and what tasks had been performed by the long, white fingers, made him draw back. Without so much as a backward glance he ran towards the church and left her standing like a pathetic, white ghost among the dejected tombstones.

Time had breathed upon pews, floor and altar, and left behind a thick coating of dust, which sometimes stirred when a breeze slid in through the gaping windows, and rose up as nebulous spirals that drifted across deserted aisle and desolate chancel. Giant cobwebs hung from the roof and window-frames and Gerald occasionally heard the twitter of a sleeping bird that had nested high up among the shadowy beams. He walked slowly, not knowing, even here, what might be waiting for him, and his naked feet left their imprint in the thick carpet of dust – a giant among the pygmy trails that marked the passage of minute life. He went into the vestry and it was here that horror put on a new face and shot out a cold fist that hit him in the stomach.

The vestry was lit by a single, plain, glass window – miraculously unbroken – and through this the moon sent a bright beam of light that illuminated a small oak table and a highback armchair. Seated at the table, dressed in a black, dust-coated cassock, was a grinning skeleton. In places the skin hung in wrinkled folds, and on the skull was a meagre mop of white hair, but otherwise it was a collection of white bones that glimmered softly through rents in the tattered cassock. It leant sideways and was only held in position by the chair arm; one bony hand still lay on the table, but a few inches from a dust covered book and an old fashioned quill pen.

When the effects of shock had died away, Gerald forced his legs to move across the vestry, and because – for no reason he could bring to mind – it seemed an important thing to do, he leaned over the table and pulled the book towards him. The skeleton appeared to nod, as though in approval, then, possibly disturbed even by this slight movement, slid sideways and fell with an awful clattering sound to the floor.

It was some while before Gerald was able to look for candles, but he finally found some in an unlocked cupboard, together with a number of moth-holed cassocks and a box of long, sulphur matches. When he had lit the candles and the most wearable cassock had given at least the illusion of warmth to his chilled body, he pulled a stool up to the now vacated table and opened the book. Half the pages appeared to be filled with clerical engagements. Baptisms, weddings, funerals, they were all there, but Gerald turned the pages over impatiently and it was on the last, under the date 21 June 1872, that he found what he had been unconsciously looking for. The candles flickered as he read, casting shuddering shadows over the yellowed paper and the thick, faded writing. 'Even as I write I can hear their howls. Almighty God, if you still live, listen to the prayer of your miserable servant and give him the power to set down the unthinkable evil I have witnessed. Although whether any eyes than mine will ever read these words is unlikely, for there seems no way to leave or enter this village. And I have tried . . . tried . . . tried. I must believe that we have been forsaken by God and man and handed over body and soul to the evil one.

Lord have mercy . . . mercy . . . for our sins are black and we have wandered from thy ways. Amen.

My flock was small, but fifty-five souls, and now they have gone and I, an old man, by virtue of this hallowed place, still live. We should have destroyed the first one. Crushed it under foot, burnt its foul carcase and tossed the ashes to the winds. But, I – may I be forgiven – did implore mercy for the creature that bore a semblance to man when it squatted on a tombstone and did gibber upon us. I took it into my house and washed away the filth and clad it in clean raiment and laid it on a soft bed. All, as instructed by holy scripture. Where did I sin, merciful God? For should we not succour the afflicted, give good for evil?

Then one night when the moon was full, I saw it – cursed be the eyes that see, the ears that hear – *feeding* in the churchyard. Mud on the hands, sitting on a pile of earth and gnawing . . . gnawing . . .

We chased it away and sent for the constable, but he was a man of little sense and did not believe. For the one we drove away, twelve did return and they danced round the village bounds and since that day no *mortal* soul has come in or gone out.

I am weak, for I have not eaten these many days, so what I have to tell, must be written quickly. Others of their kind come in once a year when the moon is full and its light streams in through the north window. This I have noted. Should – by God's infinite mercy – one who has escaped them read these words – pay heed. Take the crucifix from the altar – for they fear it – and when the full moon paints a silver streak on the aisle beside the third pew from the chancel, then go you forth. Hold the crucifix on high and run . . . if you hold your soul dear . . . run . . . run . . . and if God be with you . . . the barrier may be crossed.

Their howls are louder and I hear screams . . . Lighten thou my darkness, I beseech you, oh Lord . . . for I am lost in a valley of darkness . . .'

There was a blot after the last word, followed by a thick, straggling line, which suggested the pen had dropped from fingers too weak to hold it. Gerald got up and leaving the book open upon the table, ran into the church and sat down in the third pew. He remained there for several hours, anxiously watching the yellow streak of moonlight as it crept slowly down the chancel and along the aisle. It came as far as the second pew, then began to fade as the moon moved gradually to the east. Tomorrow night – if the old man had not been mad, and if he had got his facts right – there were so many ifs – tomorrow night he would make his last – his very last bid for freedom.

The moonlight died, darkness closed in and despite the constant presence of terror, Gerald fell into a dreamless sleep.

He was awakened by sunlight and birdsong.

The church, flooded with golden light, looked even more desolate and sinister than it had the night before. The ever moving spirals of dust whirled and leaped across the floor, like minute, restless ghosts. The altar drapes twisted and flapped, the vestry door opened and closed, while its oil starved hinges groaned a mournful protest. In striking contrast to all this gloom was the army of birds that swooped and dived among the roof beams and sent out a chorus of twittering, whistling and early morning song, that under the circumstances was rather distracting. Gerald could not dismiss a ridiculous notion that they resented his intrusion and were loudly proclaiming his presence. A black starling alighted on a pew back and examined him with bright, inquisitive eyes, then as though not at all reassured by what it saw, gave a startled cry and flew swiftly towards the altar. Gerald rose and stretched his aching limbs. He was stiff, cold, and now he came to consider the matter, very hungry and wondered if and when Luna would bring him some food. He climbed up on to a pew seat and peered cautiously out of an empty window-frame. His range of view included most of the churchyard and one side of the Lough Inn, and his morale was not improved when he saw his own freshly turned grave. The ghouls – and he shuddered when this designation slipped uninvited across his brain – had not struck him as being particularly intelligent, but even the dimmest must surely soon realise, that that which had been put in, had unaccountably come out.

As though to substantiate this belief, the child suddenly ran out from beside the inn and went leaping across the churchyard, looking like a particularly unpleasant species of monkey on its way to a bone picking session. It reached Gerald's one-time grave and after dancing round it with joyous anticipation, suddenly stopped and dropped down on all fours. The monkey image was now replaced by that of a vicious dog which has conceived the well-founded suspicion that it has been robbed of a succulent bone. This conception was dramatically enhanced when the child began to claw at the disturbed grave with both hands and toss up the earth in a frenzy of excitement. An agitated beaver could not have done a better job. Gerald watched the displaced earth grow higher and the head and shoulders of the burrowing child go lower, until all he could see was a skinny rump and a pair of jerking legs. Suddenly it sprang upright and after giving vent to a harsh and prolonged howl, went bounding across the churchyard towards the inn.

Gerald did not have to wait long. In no time at all a crowd of gesturing, prancing and clearly unhappy figures were congregating round his grave and appeared to be accusing the innkeeper of some misdemeanour. That personage apparently did not believe what he could not feel, for he flung himself down on the ground and plunged his arm into the loose soil. Gerald thought he looked like a plumber trying to remove an obstruction from a choked manhole. His probing efforts clearly confirmed everyone's worst suspicions, and when the innkeeper had regained his feet, the incriminating argument broke out all over again, and was only terminated by the child screaming some unintelligible words and pointing towards the church.

Gerald fled to the vestry, where he barricaded the door and prayed for nothing to happen. The ensuing silence was more nerve

racking than a chorus of voices demanding – allegorically speaking – his blood and presently, finding his prayer appeared to have
been answered, he unbarricaded the door and crept back into the
church. Finding it empty he walked boldly down the aisle and
peered out into the sunlit road.

There was absolutely no doubt that the ghouls entertained a
respectable fear for the church and its immediate vicinity. Gerald
counted seven of them leaning against the inn wall, and although
his appearance caused an unwelcome stir of interest, not one attempted to approach the church. Dinner stood looking at prospective diners and for the time being there appeared to be no prospect
of either making contact with the other. In consequence, Gerald
felt a heartening revival of confidence and decided to try an interesting experiment. He walked swiftly to the altar and was delighted
to find a tall, processional cross leaning up against the left hand
wall. He wiped away the worst of the dust with his cassock sleeve,
then held it on high and marched with due solemnity back to the
front door. His reappearance was greeted with a prolonged howl
and the ghouls hastily averted their faces and jog-trotted back into
the inn. Gerald, whose, to date, only close-up view of a cross, had
been on a hot-cross bun, decided this one would never leave his
side, and it had more protective value than a loaded bren-gun.

It was possibly an hour later when he heard a series of gasp-
ing screams and looking out he saw Luna suddenly emerge from
the inn doorway, carrying a heavy iron saucepan in one hand and
a tablespoon in the other. She ran towards the church, hotly pursued by the innkeeper who was brandishing a stout stick, while
the remainder of the ghoulish crew remained clustered round the
doorway, where they encouraged their leader with advisory howls.
Gerald seized the processional cross and waved it wildly back and
forth in an effort to assist the pursued and check the pursuer. He
succeeded on both counts. The innkeeper stumbled and appeared
to be in some distress, then shrieked when he saw the cross which
Gerald was waving with more fervour than reverence. Luna passed
through the doorway, while her terrified sire trotted back to the
gesturing group of ghouls.

She placed the saucepan down on the front pew, then seated
herself and raised tearful eyes to the young man who was more

concerned with the steaming stew, than her distress.

'Dadda beat me because they say I cut you loose. So I take pot and come here. I not go back.'

'Oh, dear,' Gerald took a seat beside the saucepan and looked meaningfully at the battered spoon. 'Sorry, if I got you into trouble. Is it – rabbit stew again?'

'No.' She dabbed her eyes and sniffed. 'Small animal and birds.'

'Oh!'

'There will be much anger because I have taken it.'

'Yes, I expect there will be.' Gerald paused before allowing hunger to overcome restraint. 'We mustn't let it grow cold. Are you hungry?'

Luna shook her head. 'I eat this morning. For you.'

Gerald seized the spoon and such is the nature of man, far from feeling any sense of gratitude for this act of devotion, he experienced a twinge of irritation because she had not brought something to drink. The girl sat and stared wistfully at the north window, in which a few fragments of stained glass still remained, and occasionally sighed deeply and loudly as though to draw attention to her distress. When his hunger had been appeased, Gerald laid down the spoon and looked at her with some concern.

'Look here, you mustn't give way, you know. Did . . . did he hurt you?'

Now tears seeped from the beautiful eyes and Gerald felt some surprise that a – what was she? – a humgoo, could cry like a normal human being. Despite her undoubted beauty, he could not forget her relationship to the things whose culinary designs on his person was still a matter of fearful concern. She poured a torrent of words, using the full extent of her limited vocabulary in an effort to make him understand.

'You no care if I be hurt or not. I only animal who cut ropes, bring food. If you go, Luna will be left behind and you not care if bad things be done to her.'

This was so near the truth, conscience stirred and put a gentle tone in his voice. 'Nonsense. I am very, very grateful for what you have done. And if – when I escape, you must come with me. You must leave this place and live like a pretty girl should.'

She stifled a sob and turned a face to him which was lit by a dawning smile of delight. 'You take me outside? And I wear clothes like yours?'

'Better. You'll be able to have some nice dresses from Marks & Spencers and wear shoes and stockings and watch television. You can't imagine what it will be like.'

She jumped up and down on the hard seat in childish delight and Gerald wondered wryly how the monsters here would compare with those she would meet on the outside.

'You really take me outside? I do all the things you say and ride on tube?'

'Good heavens, what do you know about tube trains?'

Her smile was that of a beautiful, innocent child.

'Elders say, there much good eating on tube.'

Whatever retort Gerald might have made to this statement, was cancelled by a whirling sound as a stone flew in through the open door and crashed against the chancel step. He jumped to his feet as Luna grasped his arm.

'Do not go near door. They use throwing sling and stone kill if it hit head. They kill many animals that way.'

Another stone the size of a fist came in through a side window and chipped a fragment of wood from a pew back. Gerald grabbed the girl round the waist and half-dragged and half-carried her into the vestry, where he shut the door and retreated to a far corner. Then he turned to Luna.

'How long will this go on?'

She shrugged. 'Not long. They not like long effort and will soon be tired. They wait for elders to come for great eating. Elders not like us. Have much wisdom.'

'The . . .' Gerald swallowed and forced himself to ask the question. 'The great eating . . . is that tonight?'

She nodded. 'Elders bring in special . . . things and there be much dancing round fire in harvest place. We go before elders come. No escape when elders here. They have great magic and kill with bang.'

'Fine.' Gerald nodded grimly. 'That's all I needed. A pack of gun-toting ghouls. Well, it seems the stone throwing session is over for the time being, so I guess we had better try to get some sleep and get our strength up for a lot of running.'

She giggled and looked at him shyly from under long lashes.

'You talk funny. Lots of words which I not understand. But I do all things you say. You say sleep – Luna sleep. You say, Luna wake and run. I wake and run.'

'Good girl. You do what I tell you and we'll get out of here somehow.'

There was something terribly pathetic in the way she accepted his assurance with simple, unquestioning faith and obeyed his instructions with almost cheerful obedience. She sat down on the dust covered floor in one corner of the room and was instantly asleep. Gerald sat watching her for some time and wondered how she would fare if they won free and reached his workaday world, where the only ghouls he knew were confined to property speculators' offices and 'great eatings' to businessmen's lunches. Then he heard another stone rattle across the church floor and fear flared up to drive all but the immediate future from his mind.

The day passed slowly and a fresh spectre came to haunt the little room. Suppose there was no moon tonight and he was unable to judge the exact time when it would be safe for them to run from the church? He looked anxiously out of the small window. So far as he could see there was no sign of cloud, but there were still eight or nine hours before the moon would be in a position to advance a beam of light to a point in line with the third pew. One worry begat another. The ghouls – at least the adult ones – did not strike him as being fond of exercise, but how fast could they run when proposed nourishment was going all out for wide open spaces? Also – and Gerald experienced a new kind of shudder – a hail of well-aimed stones could bring him down before he had run two steps. He would have to run fast, weave from side to side and take advantage of every inch of cover, and all the time be hampered by the presence of a girl. Such was his fear, he even considered the possibility of leaving her behind, then he remembered that he would not be free now, but for her courageous act of cutting him loose, and knew, whatever the cost, they would leave together.

He too was asleep when the sun set, and awoke in total darkness, save for the reflection of dancing flames which flickered over the far wall. Gerald jumped to his feet and after climbing up on the bench, peered out of the vestry window. An immense fire was blazing away on the edge of the churchyard.

They – and this seemed to be a natural appellation – were feeding the fire with dead wood, which was being dragged from the near-by woods. Gerald watched the grotesque figures as they struggled with rotting branches, wrestled with young trees, saw the shower of sparks that rose up to the night sky as each offering was flung on to the flames. A motley collection of chairs and tables had been arranged in a rough circle round the fire, thus – and Gerald found he had the courage to face the fact squarely – creating an open air dining hall, which must be a very necessary part of the forthcoming proceedings.

He looked anxiously up at the sky. Heavy cloudbanks drifted like prowling ghost-hounds across the face of the moon, so at times its silver light was shut off and the dancing flames of the bonfire took on a deeper, more sinister glow, while the moving figures threw long shadows that writhed and caracoled among the tombstones. Gerald climbed down from the bench and after locating the shadowy figure of Luna, gently laid a hand on her shoulder. He whispered: 'Luna, wake up. It's almost time to go.'

Like a young animal, she was instantly awake and sat looking up at him, her face a white blur in the semi-gloom. 'We run now?'

The question was asked in her usual husky voice and he could detect no undertone of doubt or fear. He felt the now familiar twinge of irritation when he realised the full extent of her complete faith in his ability to get them both through this time of intense and unthinkable danger. This was followed by a surge of unexpected pity as he took her outstretched hands and pulled her gently upright.

'I think so. Look, they have a fire burning out there and I saw lots of chairs and tables. Have you any idea how much longer it will be before anything happens?'

Luna climbed up on to the bench and stood looking out over the churchyard. Then she got down and put her head over to one side and he thought how young she looked.

'Not yet. They have to wash in river and put on other clothes for great eating. The elders like us all to be clean. No stink.'

Gerald nodded his approval and decided the unknown elders

might be monsters, but at least they were fastidious monsters.

'We must go into church – big house,' he said. 'Then when time is ripe, we will go out.'

She nodded and waited for him to open the door before walking out into the main body of the church, which was, to Gerald's horror, in complete darkness.

'When the moon – the big nightlight shines through the window,' he whispered, 'and reaches here,' he groped for the third pew, 'then we must run. But the clouds are stopping the light from coming in.'

'Then we go now.'

'No,' he shook his head violently. 'If the road is not open, then they will catch up with us. But if the moon does not come out soon, then I will have to guess when the time is right and hope for the best.'

They waited and listened to the chorus of howls that seemed to be part of the general air of festivity. Once a stone came hurling through the doorway, but Gerald thought it had only been thrown as an act of bravado, or as a reminder that he had not been forgotten, rather than in aggression.

'I not worry,' Luna's voice tried to comfort him. 'We run fast and get through.'

He choked back an outburst of fearful doubts and instead patted her shoulder approvingly. 'That's the spirit. You must think of all the wonderful times you'll have when we get out of this place.'

He heard her sigh of contentment and would have elaborated on the joys to come had not the moon chosen that moment to emerge from behind a drifting cloud. The beam of light glided down the chancel, flowed over the single step and did not stop until it reached the third pew. Gerald gasped, then shook his head in disbelief.

'Talk about a bloody miracle! Where's that damn cross?'

He stumbled around in the half-light looking for the mislaid cross and finally stumbled over it, measuring his length on the floor as though in retaliation for either irreverence or carelessness. He took a firm grip of the polished wood and whispered his final instructions.

'Keep close beside me and don't fall behind. Can you run fast?'

'As rabbit when chased by Dadda,' she announced and Gerald groaned.

'I hope the hell I can. Ready?'

'You say run – I run.'

He led her out into the church porch and caught his breath in dismay. Although the majority of the ghouls were occupied with preparing for the forthcoming feast, they had not neglected to post sentries on the church. Four of the sinister figures – now clad in clean white nightgowns – were lined up by the inn wall and came to instant, lively attention when Gerald and his companion appeared. Gerald took a deep breath and shouted: 'Run.'

With cross held high, yelling at the top of his voice, and running as he had never run before, Gerald and the girl humgoo streaked out into the moonlight. The four sentries scattered before him like leaves buffeted by a mischievous wind, while screaming their alarm to the main pack around the bonfire. The inn was passed, the line of cottages became a menacing row of burrows from which disaster might emerge at any moment, then they too slipped into what-has-been and were replaced by low hedgerows and wide-open meadows that stretched out gently to rolling hills. Presently Gerald dared to look back and received an instant incentive to quicken his pace. The entire pack were less than a hundred yards behind. Running shoulder to shoulder, wedged so tightly together in the narrow lane, they resembled an avalanche of snow that must crush anything or anyone that stood in its path. Suddenly a stone went hissing by Gerald's head and he had time to marvel at the speed and velocity with which it travelled. His terror reached a new dimension when the missile crashed into a tree and became embedded in the smooth, grey trunk, so that his unprotected back became an expanse of quivering flesh, that anticipated a resounding thud and the ensuing agony, long before it arrived. When a stone glanced off his right shoulder, it came almost as a relief. Now he need no longer imagine; the pain was excruciating, but not unbearable and was followed by a merciful numbness that left his right arm limp and caused him to drop the processional cross. A loud howling from the his rear announced the pack's displeasure at this sudden obstruction to progress, which resulted in a temporary respite from the hissing stones. But the girl who ran

beside him with smooth, effortless strides gasped when he involuntarily cried out and said: 'You hurt! Must not stop. Not very far
now.'

The lane gradually curved so that for a brief while they were
hidden from the reassembled pack, but Gerald was not far from
complete exhaustion and there was a feeling that surrender would
be preferable to the agony of labouring lungs and tortured throat,
not to mention sore, naked feet. His pace automatically slackened,
but Luna grabbed his arm.

'No stop. We are there. Look.'

Even before she had finished speaking, he saw the other road.
The lane still continued to curve and if followed would have
doubtlessly led back to the village, but running at right angles to
it was a broader road that shimmered faintly through a thin mist.
Understanding came to Gerald and the words, 'Mind condition-
ing', 'Hypnotic blindness', flashed across his mind as with renewed
energy he ran towards the bridge that spanned the gulf which sep-
arates fantastic from commonplace. When the full moon was in a
certain position you were temporarily permitted to see.

The road to freedom was only a few steps away, when the grisly
hunters came round the curve and their anger was expressed by a
storm of hideous howls which could be likened to that of a pack
of starving wolves who see their quarry escaping. The stones flew
again, but now the aim was far from accurate, which suggested
the hunters were as near exhaustion as the hunted. But one missile
found its mark. Gerald heard a sickening thud and felt Luna's hand
wrenched from his as the girl went hurtling to the ground. Every
instinct told him to leave her, to go on running until he was safely
beyond the barrier of misty moonlight, but another emotion, that
so far had not entered his pampered, sated life, made him stop and
grip the back of the girl's gown. Regardless of menacing stones,
howling monsters and protesting body, he dragged her on to the
side road, through the mist, to finally collapse when he reached
a spot some twenty yards beyond. There he lay and looked back
down the road. Apart from a patch of silver mist there was nothing to distinguish it from a million other roads that interlaced rural
England – nothing that is to say, if the group of white clad figures
could be ignored. Gerald had time to wonder what superstition or

taboo made it impossible for them to advance through the mist barrier, before a groan from Luna made him forget all but the need to comfort.

With his one good arm he eased her on to the grass verge and smoothed the tangled hair from her pale forehead. She smiled up at him and pressed his hand against her cheek. Her voice was faint, but every word was distinct and became an arrow of remorse.

'I hurt bad. Feel nothing from waist down. Back broke like when Dadda hit rabbit.'

He shook his head. 'Nonsense. You will be all right. I'll go and fetch help.'

She gripped his hand so tight he flinched.

'No. Do not leave me. Rabbit die soon when back broke. I soon die. Will never see outside and wear clothes like yours. Never wear clothes from . . . from . . .'

'Marks & Spencers,' he prompted gently and cursed himself for such stupid, unfeeling flippancy.

'It is better so. I would never be anything to you but an animal . . .'

'No!' He shouted the denial, but even as he did so, knew there was some truth in the accusation. 'I never thought of you like that. I . . . I . . .'

She pulled his hand to her lips and caressed it softly. 'Do you like . . . your little humgoo a little? Just . . . a little . . . little . . .'

'A lot. I like . . . love you, a lot.'

For the last time her face was lit up by a joyful smile and she kissed his fingers, while the young man tried to suppress an involuntary shudder.

'Humgoo . . . half and half . . . but one half belong . . . to . . . you . . .'

The last word ended in a sigh that drifted away on the night breeze and Gerald disengaged his hand from the now limp grip, and closed the staring eyes. He sat and looked at the dead face for a little while and remembered that unfamiliar word. Humgoo. It sounded like a breed of horse, or maybe a pedigree dog. But a horse could neigh with pleasure when sighting its owner, and a dog could lick the hand of its master, and love – of a kind – could be transmitted through the barrier which divides king from subject. Such was the love he felt for the pathetic but still lovely corpse that lay before him. Then he remembered that danger still gibbered, gestured and howled but thirty yards away, and rising to his feet, walked quickly away.

Luna rested by the roadside, a sad reminder that oil should not flirt with flame.

Gerald walked for an hour, or at least so it seemed, for road crossed road, turnings met crossroads, and he might have been the last man on earth, wandering in a moonlit maze.

Then he heard the roar of traffic and his strength returned in a last strong flow, so that he was able to break into a stumbling, painful, but joyous run. He came out of a narrow lane into a wide motorway and the joy, the blessed relief, was such that he stood for a moment drinking in this glorious sight, while tears ran down his haggard face. He was free. He shouted the word several times. 'Free. Free. Free.' And several youths on motorcycles whistled at him, being apparently under the impression that he was drunk. And so he was. Drunk on the wine of life, intoxicated on the heady spirit called – he jumbled a mass of words together and came up with the right ones – naked sight. He was seeing the world as it really was for the first time. A place of beautiful motor roads, bright lights, wonderful petrol fumes, exquisite roaring cars – all of which were gloriously breaking the speed limit – and nowhere was there a sight or smell of a ghoul.

He ran, skipped, danced and sometimes walked along the road and presently his joy was crowned by the sight of two stationary vehicles. One was a very large, very shiny, and no doubt, very expensive Rolls Royce – thrice blessed be that name – and the other was an equally large, plain black van. When he drew nearer to this wonderful sight, he was able to count seven people clustered round the Rolls Royce, all of whom appeared to be in a state of great agitation.

'Godfrey, how much longer are you going to be?' enquired a beautiful young woman in a fur coat. 'We're late as it is.'

A tall man in a black overcoat and a white muffler, closed the bonnet and wiped his hands on a silk handkerchief.

'No longer at all. Finished. The old sparking plugs were playing up. If you'll pile in, we'll be on our way.'

'You'll have to step on it,' a short youth in a hideous green over-coat observed. 'You know what happens . . .'

The man who had been addressed as Godfrey, smiled derisively. 'My dear Tony, if you will get back to the goodies van and stop bleating like a demented sheep, no more time will be lost.'

Gerald coughed and made his presence known.

'Excuse me. I wondered if you would be so kind as to give me a lift.'

Godfrey swung round and took in the bedraggled cassock and bare feet of this petitioner for free transportation, with an expression of comical surprise.

'Would you believe it? A tattered priest! Have you met with an accident or are you performing a penance?'

Gerald hastened to make the situation clear, particularly as certain members of the party were looking at him with some distaste.

'I'm not a priest. I've met with a . . . sort of accident, and I want to report it to the authorities as soon as possible.'

Godfrey frowned. 'Well, this is by way of being a club outing, and we are rather late for a bit of a do. But I daresay we can drop you at the end of the motorway.'

'But we're over an hour late,' Tony protested.

'Then ten minutes more won't make all that difference,' Godfrey stated. 'Right, in everyone. And you, sir, if you don't mind squeezing in between Daphne and myself on the front seat, we'll be away.'

Three elegant gentlemen seated themselves in the rear of the car, Tony and another man went back to the black van, and Gerald was sandwiched between Godfrey and Daphne on the front seat. Car and van glided away down the motorway. It is unfortunate that Gerald felt a great urge to communicate his recent experiences to a receptive ear.

'Look,' his voice boomed out in the enclosed space and was perfectly audible to even the passengers on the back seat, 'you won't believe this, but I haven't really been in an accident. I lost myself and landed up in a weird village.'

For a while Gerald wondered if anyone had heard or understood his announcement, for the silence was absolute, save for the gentle purr of the car engine. He decided to elaborate further.

'An awful place, inhabited by – I know you'll think I'm stark, raving mad – inhabited by ghouls.'

Godfrey made utterance. 'You don't say!'

'Yes. I don't blame you for doubting me. If a chap had told me yesterday that there was anywhere on earth where you could be buried alive, then dug up for what they call – this you won't believe – the great eating, I'd have called the nearest copper.'

Godfrey nodded slowly, then as though coming to a sudden decision, swung the car into a side road. Gerald recognised it as the one from which he had recently emerged. He voiced his objection.

'I say, you've left the motorway.'

Godfrey looked out of the side window, then consulted the driving mirror. 'You know, I do believe you're right.'

A dreadful suspicion rummaged around among a host of newly aroused fears and suddenly grew and became a certainty. His question was rather superfluous.

'You're not . . . ?'

Godfrey nodded. 'Yes, we are. The jolly old elders taking in some goodies for the yokels. I say, this isn't your lucky night, is it?'

Gerald began to struggle and Godfrey smiled.

'Daphne, my love.'

'Yes, Godfrey?'

'Have you still got that shooting iron in your bag?'

'Yes, Godfrey.'

'Then get it out, there's a good girl, and poke it into this blighter's ribs. He might break something.'

Daphne obliged and Gerald surrendered his body and soul to the inevitable. He began to sob like a frightened child.

'Cheer up,' Godfrey instructed, 'after all, you are coming back in style. I can't wait to see their simple, honest faces, when you step out into the moonlight. I always find it pays to pamper the lower orders, just so long as you don't overdo it.'

Daphne fingered Gerald's arm. 'When he's had time to mature, he'll tear a treat.'

The hedgerows flashed by and the full moon smiled benignly down on sleeping fields and murmuring trees. It also gently caressed the face of Luna as she lay, silent and still by the roadside, and painted a silver sheen on her wind-ruffled hair.

Monster Club Interlude: 3

The ghoul put the manuscript down, removed his spectacles, then looked round the table. His venture into authorship had not been well received. Both Eramus and the werevamp had fallen asleep, the little vamgoo had been mixing his drinks and was now singing – if the strange noise he periodically ejaculated, could be so designated – a refrain which never progressed beyond the following words:

> Give me blood, give me meat:
> Let me gnaw a dead man's feet:
> And I'll pass the night with you.

Donald, who had been both fascinated and horrified by the ghoul's narration, looked with extravagant concern at his wristwatch, then announced in a loud and much too hearty voice: 'Well, this *has* been a jolly evening, but I really must call it a day. Have to be up early tomorrow.' Instantly everyone was wide awake, just as though a dozen alarm clocks had clanged their strident demand. He was flattered, if somewhat uneasy by the united chorus of protests that greeted his announcement.

'You can't possibly go now,' said Eramus, wiping his lips on an unbleached linen napkin.

'Won't hear of it,' stated Manfred the werevamp.

'We would be forced to think that you did not appreciate our hospitality,' announced the ghoul gravely.

'Please, you must not think that,' Donald protested. 'I have enjoyed myself so much.'

'The evening is still young,' the mock said, then growled in a most disconcerting fashion. 'The film show will begin shortly.'

The little vamgoo banged his glass on the table and broke into another song.

I'm going to the cinema, I'm going to the flicks.
I'll chew salted toes and drop them down Vamie's knicks . . .

'Will you be quiet?' the ghoul roared. 'Really, I must apologise,
gentlemen, for this – this creature's outrageous behaviour. And as
for you, sir, if you do not mend your ways, I'll speak to the committee about withdrawing your membership.'

The vamgoo lapsed into a sulky silence and the ghoul regained
his dignified self-control. 'What is showing tonight, Maurice?'

'The Shadmock,' the mock replied. 'Directed by the up and
coming Vinke Rocnnor.'

'Ah!' The ghoul nodded his approval. 'Did anyone see his From
Behind The Tombstone?'

'I did,' a superior looking vampire said. 'It showed promise. I'm
not at all sure I approve of films which deal with the lower hybrids.
I mean to say, there is an awful lot of bilge talked about the so-
called underprivileged. Who cares if a shadmock can only whistle?
If one came sniffing round a daughter of mine, I'd give him something to whistle about.'

'I care,' said the mock. 'If one day – Satan willing – I sire an offspring, he will be a shadmock, and I'm certain that to his mother
and myself, the most glorious sound in the world will be his shrill
but sweet little whistle.'

'Gentlemen,' announced the ghoul, 'I do think it is time for us
to move into the projection room. Manfred and Eramus, I'll leave
it to you to see that our guest is comfortably seated.'

With a vampire on one side, a werevamp on the other, with a
ghoul in front and the little vamgoo behind, Donald was gently
but firmly led across the restaurant, through an open doorway
and into a small, but comfortable cinema. An usherette – a rather
pretty little vampire – armed with a torch which looked very like
a severed hand fitted with minute electric bulbs in the fingers,
directed them into the back row, where Donald found himself
seated between Eramus and Manfred. They had arrived just in time
for the screen advertisements.

'Have you visited Carlo's delicatessen?' inquired a recorded
voice, as a coloured plate was flashed on to the screen, depicting

a slab covered with some very dubious looking cooked meats. 'We supply the very best – the very freshest – to the very mostest. Something to tempt all appetites.'

'Get your talons trimmed by experts,' instructed a red lettered caption, while a film clip portrayed a dapper werewolf sitting in a barber's shop, having his talons clipped by a glamorous maddy.

Donald closed his eyes when a voice boomed: 'Ghouls, come to Streamcorp Restaurant, where the ripe is waiting to be torn!': and opened them again as Eramus whispered: 'Good, forthcoming attractions.'

Donald gathered that next week's film – *Bleeding Hearts* – was all about a highborn vampire lady who fell in love with a lowly ghoul, who worked in an East End churchyard. Their romance was frowned upon by the girl's father who was someone high up on the stock exchange. Presumably it would all come right in the end, for there was a scene when the ghoul – now dressed in a starched shroud and a pink ribbon – was addressing a clearly moved father, with the words: 'You sup, sir. I tear, sir. But we both get down to the bone.'

Then the lights went up and so did a lot of seats and Donald saw a queue form in front of another pretty vampire, who did a roaring trade in enriched ice-cream.

'It is to be hoped,' said the ghoul, leaning forward and addressing the werevamp, 'we're not going to see a lot of white-smut. I've no time for this modern craze for naked bones and exposed innards. Give me a good old fashioned story of monsters and humans, where bad always triumphs and there's a miserable ending.'

'You're alive right,' agreed the werevamp, 'the immoral is the thing. You're not going to tell me that some of these films aren't responsible for the soaring rate of goodness that is ruining the younger generation. Take my young nephew for example. Every other word he uses starts with H and ends with Y.'

Further conversation was curtailed by the lights being lowered and the screen erupting into life, as the credits slowly seeped into being from a pool of blood. Donald watched the imposing list of names and tried to ignore the strange-looking madgoo with green hair, who was trying to tickle his knee under the back of a seat.

BONER BROS
Presents

THE SHADMOCK

Starring
Clark Suckdri and Helen Munchem
with
Wendy Lickmouth
Thomas Barebones
Henry Teardown
Christopher Gutwinder

Donald yawned and was in fact on the point of falling asleep, when he was aroused by a crash of background music, and the nudging elbow of the werevamp. On the screen a car was driving down a lonely country road . . .

The Shadmock

A car was driving down a lonely country road.

Such a car could have only belonged to a man who was well endowed with this world's goods and had a subconscious desire to advertise the fact. The car must have been made by Messrs Rolls Royce in one of their off moments, for the paintwork was bright red, the headlamps gleamed with blue chromium plating and a naked brass lady sat on top of the radiator. The interior further proclaimed the affluent and original taste of the owner, for the seats were covered with rich, bright yellow leather, the switchboard was a mass of complicated gadgets and there was a faint aroma of expensive cigar smoke and aftershave lotion.

The man behind the steering wheel was easily recognisable as one of those streamlined wolves who lurk in air-conditioned offices perched on top of shoebox-shaped buildings, and roar their Napoleon-brandy-tainted rage over the chilly depths below. He was a large man, with a beefy, rather brutal face that was lit by a pair of small blue eyes and surmounted by a mass of iron-grey hair. His massive shoulders and heavy, bulky body were encased in an electric-blue suit that looked as if it had been tailored by a slightly mad artist, and all but screamed its defiance at the purple shirt and green tie.

The girl by his side had the blonde, brittle beauty of an expensive doll. Her pale, unlined face invited admiration rather than passion, her soft yellow hair defied anyone to disturb its perfectly arranged curls, and the full, red, but discontented mouth was clearly reserved for eating beautifully prepared dinners and dispensing exclusive kisses. Her green dress and open mink coat was a concession to titillation – and good taste. The bosom promised but did not reveal: the hemline dared but never retreated above mid-thigh. Her long, red-tipped fingers toyed with a diamond ring, as she looked bad-temperedly out at the racing, grey-ribbon stretch of road.

'Why the hell you want to take a place in the sticks, is beyond me. We've got more houses now than we know what to do with.'

The man grunted and switched on the headlights for the first shadows of night were falling across the open countryside.

'Sheridan,' the cool, brittle voice rose sharply, 'I do wish you would answer me sometimes. I'm not one of your junior executives to be ignored or grunted at.'

'Caroline, your body talks, your tongue makes a noise, but you say little that is worth listening to, let alone answering.'

Caroline creased her smooth forehead into an angry frown, and her large, hazel eyes became as chips of fire-tinted glass.

'You are taking me to a dead and alive hole called Wittering . . .'

'Withering,' Sheridan Croxley corrected. 'You may remember I was born there. The son of a cowherd and a kitchen maid. Both of my parents worked at the Grange. Now I have bought it. Do I have to say more?'

'No.' The girl smiled derisively. 'You've got a chip on your shoulder the size of Everest and this is one way of getting rid of it. Lord of the Manor where your old man shovelled cow-shit. I should have known.'

The great head swung round and the little eyes glared at her, but she merely shrugged and deepened her mocking smile.

'You going to hit me now, or wait until you've stopped the car?'

The head jerked back and redirected its cold stare at the road, but Caroline saw the huge, hair-covered hands tighten their grip on the steering wheel.

Darkness had won its daily battle with the dying day when the large car roared between the twin rows of huddled cottages that made up the hamlet of Withering, and continued on under an avenue of trees that terminated where a massive iron gate barred the way. Sheridan hooted the horn twice and presently was rewarded by the sight of a bent figure that emerged very slowly from a stone-walled lodge that stood to the right of the gate. This apparition shuffled into the beam of light cast by the headlamps and Caroline saw the gross outline and the hideous bearded face.

'What an awful looking creature,' she said. 'I sincerely hope you intend getting rid of that.'

'You'll find keeping servants down here is more than a problem – it's well nigh an impossibility. You keep what will stay.' He lowered the offside window and leaned out. 'I'm the new owner. Open the gates and get a move on.'

The man nodded his head and the long, white hair writhed like a nest of bleached snakes; then he opened his mouth to reveal black, toothless gums, in which Caroline could only suppose to be a derisive grin.

'Come on, damn you. Open the gate,' Sheridan roared.

Still nodding, still grinning, the grotesque figure reached out great, clawlike hands, that, in the fierce beam of light, seemed to grow to gigantic proportions – and gripped an upright bar of each gate, before pulling them apart. Then with an abrupt jerk of the powerful wrists it thrust the gates backwards and with a shriek of oil-starved hinges, they crashed against the flanking walls.

'Must have the strength of an elephant,' Sheridan muttered as he eased the car forward. 'One good thing, there's no need to worry about trespassers with him on the front gate.'

Caroline turned her head as they drove past the terrifying figure with its gaping mouth, toothless gums and heavy, bowed shoulders. 'He's got a dampening effect on me too. Honestly, Sheridan, if the rest of the staff are anything like that – that thing – I'm all for going back to town tonight.'

'You'll do no such damn thing,' Sheridan growled. 'If people who work for me do their job, I couldn't give a monkey's curse what they look like.'

They were racing along a tree-lined drive and the terrified eyes of a rabbit glittered momentarily in the headlights, before it scampered into the dense undergrowth. Then the trees slipped behind to be replaced by an overgrown lawn that lay like an uneven carpet before the great house. It had possibly begun life as a farmhouse, but over the centuries extensions had been added, until now it sprawled out as an untidy conglomeration of turrets, crouching chimneys, glimmering windows and weather-beaten brickwork. Sheridan braked the car before a wide porchway, then climbed out on to a gravelled drive and looked up at the house with evident satisfaction.

'What do you think of it?' he asked Caroline who had come round the car to join him.

'There's no lights anywhere,' she complained. 'It looks awfully desolate.'

'Hell, what do you expect. There's only three of 'em in there.

Mother, father and son – but they keep the place spotless. I expect they are in the kitchen at the back.'

He scarcely finished speaking when the massive double doors slowly opened to reveal a brilliantly lit hall and a man dressed in a decent black suit, who respectfully inclined his head as Sheridan Croxley strode forward.

'You were on the ball, Grantley,' he said genially. 'We've only just this minute driven up.'

The man again inclined his head and stood respectfully to one side.

'I have sharp ears, sir.'

Caroline thought that if size were any criterion, his ears should have detected a pin drop in a thunderstorm. They resembled monstrous, tapered wings that stood up on either side of his narrow head and were not enhanced by the thick, black hair which was combed up into a thick pile, thus adding another four or five inches to the man's height. His face was deadly white and the slanted eyes ebony black. When he smiled – a respectful smirk – the unnaturally thin lips parted to uncover great yellow teeth. Although his appearance was repellent, even sinister, he was not unhandsome in a grotesque, nightmarish sort of way.

He gave Caroline one swift glance, then murmured with his husky voice: 'Good evening, madam. May I take the liberty of welcoming you to Withering Grange?'

She could do no more than acknowledge this gracious greeting and was again rewarded by that yellow-toothed, but respectful smirk. When they had entered the large, oak-panelled hall, he clapped his hands and as if by magic, a green baize lined door opened and two persons entered.

'May I,' requested Grantley, 'present my wife, who combines the duties of housekeeper and cook?'

Mrs Grantley had all the attributes that are needed to make a beautiful woman – plus a little extra. She was tall, dark, with splendid brown eyes and a mass of black hair which she wore shoulder length, and her full, mature figure was calculated to excite any man's interest. But it was the little something extra which drew Caroline's wide-eyed attention and forced her to involuntarily cry out. Mrs Grantley was endowed with a full, rich, and very luxurious beard. It began as a drooping moustache and spread out over the pale cheeks and chin, to flow down over the shapely bosom, where it terminated in a few straggling hairs that quivered slightly when their owner spoke.

'I will endeavour to give satisfaction, madam.'

Caroline was incapable of speech and could only stare at the housekeeper's unusual appendage, while unconsciously shaking her head in disbelief.

'Women of our kind are not permitted to shave,' the butler said softly. 'This,' he motioned a young man to step forward, 'is my son, Marvin. He can act as footman when the occasion demands, but is normally employed as odd job man.'

Caroline switched her gaze from father to mother, then to the youth who stood a little in front of them, and instantly it changed to one of unstinted admiration. The expressions – good looking – handsome – flashed across her mind, then were dismissed as being totally inadequate. He was beautiful. There was no other word to describe the perfect, pale features, the wonderful blue eyes, the long, blond hair, the white, even teeth and the muscular, but slim, body. There was nothing feminine in that beautiful face; on the contrary, Caroline was aware of an animal magnetism that made her forget his bizarre parents and the presence of her husband who had been watching her previous discomfort with sardonic amusement.

'I think, Caroline, Mrs Grantley is waiting for your instructions regarding dinner.'

'What!' She tore her gaze away from the beautiful face. 'Oh, yes. Whatever is convenient. I . . .'

'For God's sake!' Sheridan broke in impatiently. 'Not what – but when? I should imagine dinner is almost ready.'

'Oh . . . in about an hour.'

Grantley was the epitome of a perfect butler.

'Would eight o'clock be satisfactory, Madam?'

'Yes . . . that would be fine.'

'Then permit me to show you to your room.'

'Surely,' she overcame her reluctance to address this strange creature, 'you must have some help with the housework. It seems too much for three people. I mean the house is so big.'

Grantley was leading them up the great staircase and answered without turning his head.

'We manage quite well, thank you, madam. It is simply a matter of keeping to a system and my father comes up from the lodge each day to do the heavy work.'

'Your father!' She remembered the awful old man who had opened the front gates and shuddered to think that he would actually enter the house – perhaps even walk up these stairs. 'Surely he's too old . . .'

'He's very strong, madam,' Grantley stated suavely, as he opened a door and stood to one side so that they could enter. 'The blue room, sir. You expressed a preference for this one, I believe.'

'Yes, this will do fine.' Sheridan Croxley walked across the room and then turned and looked round with evident satisfaction. 'Used to be old Sir Harry's room. Used to sleep his after dinner bottle of port off in here, while my old dad was pigging it down in the village.'

'Will that be all, sir?' Grantley enquired.

'We would like a bath,' Sheridan replied.

'Of course, sir. Marvin is running them now. The bathrooms are on the opposite side of the passage.'

He went out and closed the door with respectful quietude and they heard his soft footsteps recede along the passage. Caroline sank down on the bed and mopped her forehead with a lace handkerchief.

'Good heavens, where did you find them?'

'I didn't.' Sheridan removed his jacket and walked to the dressing-table. 'They came with the house. Old Sir Harry Sinclair died some twenty years ago and I gather it has been empty off and on ever since, with this lot acting as caretakers. But I should say they are worth their keep. You can see how the place is kept and Mrs Grantley's cooking has to be sampled to be believed.'

'But she looks like something that has escaped from a fairground,' Caroline protested. 'Did you hear what he said? "Women of our kind are not permitted to shave." Sheridan, we can't have a bearded lady about the place.'

'I see no reason why not,' Sheridan growled. 'She's a good cook and can't help having an – an unusual growth. Don't suppose she enjoys it.'

'But what about him? Grantley, for God's sake! Those ears and that great pile of hair! And that thing on the front gate!'

'Not to mention the young one,' added Sheridan caustically. 'I saw you giving him the once over.'

'Now you're being ridiculous. Although how that pair produced a son like that is beyond me. Sheridan, this place gives me the willies. Let's get out of here.'

'We will. On Monday morning. But not one minute sooner. So have your bath, put on some glad rags and make the best of it.'

He was glaring at her with that cold, baleful stare she knew so well – and she flinched.

'If you say so. But surely we don't have to dress for dinner when there are only the two of us?'

He grinned and Caroline felt the familiar surge of loathing and desire that seemed to originate somewhere in the region of her stomach and set her brain on fire. She trembled and his grin broadened.

'Not now, my little slut. As my old man would have said – we have company coming. The local sky-pilot. Bloody old fool, but he's been here for over forty years and it'll be fun to let him know how the world has changed.'

Caroline felt the blood drain from her face and thwarted passion curdled and became unreasoning rage.

'You bastard! You dirty, bombastic bastard. You haven't an ounce of decent feeling in your entire body.'

He leaned over her and she had a close-up view of the veined cheeks, the pouched eyes and the small, brutal mouth. He playfully slapped her cheek.

'But you wouldn't have me any other way. Would you, little slut?'

She pushed him away and he went laughing into the dressing-room, to emerge a few minutes later wearing a towel dressing-gown and beaming with obvious delight.

'Look at this!' He spread out the skirts of the dressing-gown. 'I found it in the wardrobe. Must have belonged to old Sir Harry. Little did he realise that one day the son of his cowherd would be wearing his dressing-gown.'

'Big deal. If you rummage round, you might find a pair of his old socks.'

She ducked as Sheridan flicked a towel at her, then relaxed when he left the room. Scarcely had the door closed when there was a soft tapping on the panels, then after an interval, it opened and Marvin entered carrying two large suitcases. Caroline felt her heart leap when she again saw that flawless face and sensed the strange magnetism that seemed to radiate from the clear eyes and slim, upright figure. He spoke in a low, beautifully modulated voice.

'Your bath is ready, madam.'

'Thank you . . . Marvin.'

'Where would you like me to put the luggage?'

'Oh,' she managed to laugh, 'on the bed will do.'

She watched him as with effortless ease he laid the heavy cases on the bed, then turned to face her. 'Would you like me to unpack, madam?'

'Eh . . . yes. Unpack my husband's – and lay out his dinner jacket.'

'Very good, madam.'

He worked silently, gracefully, every movement of his long-fingered hands was an act of poetry, and Caroline cursed herself for a fool when she found her legs were trembling.

'What does . . .' It was such an effort to speak clearly, '. . . a good looking boy like you do in a dead and alive hole like this?'

Marvin looked back at her over one shoulder and she had a perfectly ridiculous feeling that he was peering into her soul. That clear, cool glance had ripped aside the silly pretensions, and the ugly sores of warped sensuality, the scars, the blemishes – all were revealed and she was as naked as a sinner on judgement day. He turned his head away and continued to unpack Sheridan's case.

'I read a lot. But mostly I like to work in the garden.'

'Do you really?'

He held up Sheridan's dinner jacket and brushed out an imaginary crease with the back of his hand.

'Yes, madam. I like to make dead things grow.'

Caroline got up and walked slowly towards him and no power on earth could have stopped her laying a hand on his arm. He expressed no surprise at this act of familiarity, or in fact gave any sign that he had noticed. Her undisciplined mind allowed the words to come tripping off her tongue.

'You are very handsome. You must know that.'

He piled two shirts, two vests and a spare pair of pyjamas over one hand, then walked slowly to the tallboy.

'Thank you for the compliment, madam. But I have always understood that I am singularly plain.'

'Who on earth told you that?'

'Those who have real beauty. The beauty that is born of darkness and suffering.'

'You must be a poet. A beautiful, slightly mad poet.'

He closed a drawer, gave one quick glance at Sheridan's dinner jacket and frilled shirt which was laid out on the bed, then backed gracefully to the door.

'You are very gracious, madam. Will that be all?'

'Yes . . . yes, that will be all. For the time being.'

He inclined his head, then turned and quietly left the room.

Caroline went back to her chair and for some reason began to cry.

The Reverend John Barker was a scholar first and a clergyman second. A more bumbling, inarticulate, woolly-minded old man would have been hard to find, but he also had a built-in compass that directed him to the local houses that employed the best cook and kept a distinguished cellar. He rode up to Withering Grange on an ancient female bicycle, and having propped this under the nearest window, removed his trouser clips and pulled the massive bell-handle.

Caroline, eye-riveting in a silver dress that revealed more than it concealed, heard his high-pitched, rather squeaky voice, as he instructed Grantley as to the disposal of his outer garments.

'Hang the coat on a chairback near the kitchen fire, there's a good fellow. And wrap the muffler round one of the hot-water pipes. Delicate chest, you know.'

Caroline advanced into the hall, looking like one of St Anthony's more difficult trials. She smiled sweetly, although the sight of this thin old man, with stooping shoulders and the face of an inquisitive rabbit, did not forecast an entertaining evening, and extended her hand.

'I am Mrs Croxley, you must be . . . ?'

She paused as Sheridan had not bothered to inform her of the expected guest's name, but the clergyman hastened to repair this omission.

'John Barker, dear lady. Barker – canine proclamation – doggy chatter – Fido protest. John – as in – but alas – not divine.'

Caroline said: 'Good Lord!' then hastily composed her features into an expression of polite amusement.

'Both my husband and I are delighted you could come, Mr Barker. Would you care to wash your hands before dinner?'

The Reverend John Barker waved his hand in an impatient gesture.

'Good heavens, no. I had a bath before I came.' He began to wander round the hall, peering at the panelling, fingering the scroll-work. 'Wonderful old place this. Always wanted to see inside, but old Sir Harry never let anyone cross the door mat. I once tried to sneak in the back, but that bearded horror in the kitchen stopped me.'

'Would you care for an aperitif before dinner?' enquired Caroline in a voice which suggested she was not far from desperation. 'Cocktail or something?'

Mr Barker shook his head violently.

'Thank you, no. Rots the guts and ruins the palate. Which way to the dining-room?'

'First door to the left,' said Caroline weakly.

'Right.' He shuffled quickly in the direction indicated and presently Caroline heard his little cries of pleasure as fresh antiquarian delights attracted his attention. He poked his head round the door.

'Dear lady, do you realise that you have a genuine Jacobean sideboard?'

'No.' Her smile was like a faulty neon sign. 'How marvellous.'

'And the dining-table is at least early Georgian.'

'Really!' Caroline cast an anxious glance at the staircase. 'Would you excuse me for a few minutes, Mr Barker?'

'Of course. I want to examine the fireplace. Take your time, dear lady.'

Caroline found Sheridan in his dressing-room where he was adjusting the angle of his bow-tie.

'Sheridan, that clergyman is here. He's mad.'

'Eccentric.'

'Well, whatever he is, I can't control him. He keeps running about examining the furniture.'

'Wait until I jog his memory and let him know who owns it.'

When they entered the dining-room, Mr Barker was seated at the table with a napkin tucked in his shirt collar, and an expectant expression on his face. He beamed at his host and rose quickly to his feet.

'You've dressed, my dear fellow! Upon my soul, I did not realise that people still did that sort of thing. Haven't seen my monkey suit and boiled shirt for years.'

' 'Evening, Barker.' Sheridan held the ecclesiastical hand for a brief second, then released it. 'Glad you could come at such short notice. Sit down. Grantley tells me dinner is ready.'

Indeed, at that moment the butler entered pushing a food trolley, followed by Marvin who assisted his father in piling dishes on to the sideboard. Mr Barker watched the operation with lively interest.

'First class staff you've got here, Mr Croxley. Efficient and un-usual.'

'They seem to know their job,' Sheridan retorted briefly.

Mr Barker raised his voice and addressed Grantley.

'Passed your father by the front gate, Grantley. He seems hale and hearty.'

Grantley watched his son serve each of the diners with iced melon before answering. 'He keeps very well for his age, thank you, sir.'

'Should think he does.' The vicar sampled his melon, then nodded his approval. 'The old chap looks now as he did twenty years ago. Come to think of it – you all do.'

Grantley adjusted the flame under a hotplate and turned his head away so that his face was hidden from the old man's sharp-eyed gaze.

'It is very kind of you to say so, sir.'

'Well, Barker,' Sheridan filled his guest's glass with some fine old claret, 'I don't suppose you ever expected to see me in this house.'

The clergyman sipped his wine, then after reluctantly removing his gaze from Grantley, looked at his host with some astonishment.

'I must confess I had not given the matter any thought. I am sure you and your beautiful lady grace the Grange admirably.'

'But damn it all,' said Sheridan with some heat. 'I told you who I was. My father was George Croxley – the cowherd. I went to the old church school. You used to come every Wednesday morning and put us through the catechism.'

'So I did.' The Reverend Barker smiled indulgently. 'I gave up that pastime years ago. Doubt if I could recite the catechism meself now. 'Fraid I don't remember you. Remember your father though. Used to get drunk every Saturday night.'

'Well, now I'm here,' Sheridan insisted.

'So you are.' The clergyman nodded gently. 'Nothing extraordinary about that. I mean to say, we all sprang from humble origins. Goodness gracious, who would have thought that a species of monkey would take over the kingdom of the world?'

'Yes, but . . .' Sheridan tried to bring the conversation back to a mundane track, but the reverend gentleman was astride a hobby horse that was not easily checked.

'I cannot but help feel that the monkey was not a good choice. Surely one of the cat family would have been much more satisfactory. They have a much less emotional approach to life . . .'

'Grantley,' Sheridan unceremoniously broke into the clergyman's discourse, 'when you have served the first course, you may leave.'

'Very good, sir.'

The tall, oddly featured man and the handsome boy served the roast beef, placed the vegetable dishes in Caroline's vicinity, then silently departed. The Reverend Barker watched the door being slowly closed, then exploded into an excited torrent of words.

'Extraordinary! Fantastic! Unbelievable, but possible. Quite within the realms of possibility. Goodness gracious, yes. Thought so for years, but never dared believe. May I be forgiven for my lack of faith.'

Sheridan glanced at his wife, then screwed his face up into a scowl.

'Don't follow you, Barker. You're not making sense, man.'

'Really!' The long, lined face expressed surprise. 'I would have thought the facts were clear to anyone of normal perception. But of course you are not a student of monstrumology.'

'Say again,' instructed Sheridan caustically.

'Monstrumology. A much neglected line of research which is unfortunately often treated with derision by the uninformed. As I said earlier it is most surprising that the kingdom of the world should have come under the sway of a species of monkey, and there is reason to suppose there were other claimants to the throne. I refer you to Astaste and his *Book of Forbidden Knowledge*, which devotes no less than six chapters to the *Caninus-fulk* and the *Vampr-Monstrum*. Many legends are based on his findings and I have often believed – now I know – that the old people – as they were known to the unlettered peasantry of medieval Europe – did not completely die out. Quite a large number must have continued to exist even to this day.'

'I have never . . .' Sheridan began, but the vicar was leaning back in his chair, his eyes closed and hands folded across his stomach. His voice droned on – and on.

'Conrad von Leininstein, who disappeared mysteriously in 1831, stated categorically that they had started to crossbreed. Vampire to werewolf, ghoul to vampire, then crossbreed to crossbreed, thus producing terrifying hybrids. His illustrations are really most edifying. He also hinted they were moving up into high places, which has often led me to conject about the possibility of my bishop – '

'Look here,' Sheridan roared, 'this has gone quite far enough. You are alarming my wife and unnecessarily irritating me.'

'But, my dear sir,' Mr Barker opened his eyes, 'I am only telling you all this for your own good. If my suspicions are well founded, then you have a shaddy on your front gate, a mock for a butler and a maddie in the kitchen. The first can lick the flesh from your bones, the second blow the skin from your face – if not something far worse – and the third kill or possess with a gaping yawn. They can all infect their victims with a transforming virus.'

Sheridan Croxley did not bother to comment on these allegations, but emptied his wine glass and glared at the ceiling. Caroline decided to ask a question.

'Mr Barker, what is a shaddy and those other things you mentioned?'

Mr Barker sat back and prepared to deliver another lecture.

'A very good question, dear lady. A shaddy is the offspring of a werevam and a weregoo, which in turn have sprung from the union of a vampire and a werewolf – or in some cases a common or churchyard ghoul. Whereas, a maddy is the fruit of a cohabitation – such unions are not of course blessed by mother-church – between a weregoo and vamgoo – thus having ghoul connections on both sides . . .'

'Damnation hell,' Sheridan muttered, but his exasperation appeared to be lost on the clergyman who continued his discourse.

'A mock – most naturally – is the seed of a shaddy and maddy, or in some cases a raddy, who, as will be supposed, has sprung from the loins of a werevam and vamgoo . . .'

'But,' Caroline interrupted, her fear – disbelief, but – heavens above – growing doubts, overcome by a terrible curiosity, 'the young man, the good-looking boy – surely he cannot be a monster?'

The Reverend John Barker sat upright and beamed with ghoulish pleasure. 'But, dear lady, he is, if I might coin a phrase, the cherry on top of the trifle. If my calculations are correct, that young man – if indeed he is young – is the offspring of a mock and a maddy, and therefore is the dreaded, the horrific – shadmock.'

Sheridan lowered his head and sneered at the irritatingly enthusiastic clergyman.

'Surely among this phalanx of monsters, there is not much to choose between one or the other. What with – what was it? – yawning, licking, blowing and heaven knows what, there isn't much left for a milksop boy to do. What is his speciality? Spitting?'

Mr Barker shook his head in sad reproof.

'Do not, I beg of you, treat this matter lightly, my dear sir. The shadmock may be the lowest branch on the monsteral tree, and therefore been denied the more fearsome aspects of his sires – as for example the horns his father hides beneath that piled-up hair – but he has a gift that is said to be the most venomous in the entire family. He whistles.'

'Whistles!' Sheridan repeated.

'Whistles,' said Caroline dreamily.

Mr Barker tried to demonstrate by whistling himself, but a set of ill-fitting false teeth defeated his object.

'Yes, indeed. In none of the works which I have read, is there mention of the style of whistle, or what its immediate effect will be, but all unite in maintaining it is fearful to the extreme. I wonder if I can remember the old rhyming jingle that emphasised this fact.'

And he screwed up his eyes and after some thought, began to recite the following words:

'Fall to your knees and pray out aloud,
When the moon hides her face behind stormy cloud.
Blame not the wind for the midnight shriek,
Or pretend 'tis the floorboard beginning to creak.
Wonder not why your hair stiffly bristles:
Just abandon all hope when the shadmock whistles.'

Caroline screamed softly and Sheridan began to swear very loudly.

Sheridan's rage had not abated when they retired to bed.

'The old fool is as cracked as a fried egg. When I think that a maniac like that climbs up into a pulpit every Sunday and preaches to a lot of simple-minded yokels. I feel like going up the wall myself. Did you ever hear anything like it? Shaddies, mocks and what was it? – shamrocks?'

'Shadmock,' Caroline corrected. 'But, Sheridan, those three do look awful.'

'Ninety-nine per cent of the human race look bloody awful. Now, for heaven's sake, dismiss all this rubbish from your mind and go to sleep. I've come down here for relaxation – not to listen to the prattling of an old madman.'

Sheridan slept. Caroline lay on her back looking up at the ceiling and listening to faraway sounds that were so faint as to be well-nigh indistinguishable, but could not be dismissed as imagination. A long, drawn-out howl, a scream that was choked in mid-note, and once, much nearer, the soft thud of running feet.

It was a long while before Caroline found the courage to climb out of bed and approach the window. That she finally did so was the result of necessity rather than desire. Imagination created terrifying mental pictures of what might be taking place in that moonlit, unkempt garden, and there was a burning need to be reassured that all was well. In fact, when she at last looked out over that expanse of grass-clad earth, and the still, naked trees that stood like giant sentinels beyond, the scene was one of surprising tranquillity. The moon had tinted every tree, bush and blade of grass with silver, and in those places where it was not permitted to stray, slabs of soft shadow lurked like sleeping ghosts waiting for the kiss of sunlight. A large tabby cat wandered out from beneath the trees and when it had reached a spot some twenty yards from the house, sat down and began to lick its fur. Caroline watched the dainty movements; the flickering pink tongue, the raised paw that slid round pointed ears; the grey streaked fur that glittered like polished steel in the cold moonlight. Suddenly the cat froze and became a study in still-life. Head to one side, yellow eyes staring with awful intensity at the glowering trees, one paw still held over erect ear, back arched, tail coiled like a grey, tapered spring. Then it was a blurred streak that sped across the garden, and with it went the tranquillity, the soft, melancholy stillness that reigns in places where animated life has ceased to walk. Fear stalked across the grass and breathed upon the house.

The old man from the front gate – the shaddy – came out from under the trees and shuffled into the centre of the garden. He was carrying a dead sheep over his shoulders, draped round his neck like a monstrous fur collar, and blood trickled down his shirt front in a red, glistening stream that sprinkled the grass with moonbright rubies. He stopped, then turned and Caroline heard a low, rumbling laugh as Grantley stepped out of the shadows bearing a brace of rabbits slung over one arm. The woman at the window whimpered when she saw the small shrivelled heads; all the fur burnt away, the ears crumpled into crisp curls – the teeth blackened stubs. Father and son stood side by side: two hunters home from the chase, each bearing the fruits of his own particular skill – both waiting for the third to put in an appearance.

Marvin came running across the garden, and Caroline caught her breath when she watched the long, graceful strides, the strange, almost animal, beauty of the youthful face and form. A hot wave of desire submerged the fear – the loathing – of the older creatures, making her clutch the window frame, until her fingers were like streaks of frozen snow.

Marvin carried a basket filled with some peculiar white vegetables.

Here surely was a beautiful Abel coming home to a pair of evilvisaged Cains? He held his basket out for their inspection, and the hideous old man laughed – a raucous bellow that savaged Caroline's ears – and Grantley shook his head, so that the piled-up hair was disarranged and two black horns glittered in the moonlight. Then Marvin put his head to one side and his full lips parted – and instantly the laughter sank down to a rumbling gurgle. The elder men – creatures – became as still as stricken trees, and both stared at the handsome youth as though he was a cobra preparing to strike. Marvin jerked his head towards the house; a brief, imperious gesture, and they trotted away like two wild dogs before a thoroughbred stallion.

Caroline returned to the great double bed and after lying still for a few, heart-thudding minutes, reached out and nudged her sleeping husband.

'Sheridan.'

He was dragged up from the slough of sleep. Came awake spluttering, voicing his irritation by a series of snorted words.

'What is it? Wassat matter?'

'Sheridan . . . I can't sleep.'

'What!'

'I can't sleep.'

The morning was clear and cold, with a wind-scoured sky and a frost-bright sun. The naked trees fought with a keen, east wind, and below the iron-hard earth was a graveyard for an army of dead leaves that seethed and rustled as though mourning the green-adorned summer of long ago. But Caroline was watching the old man from the front gate hoover the carpet.

As he worked, his bearded mouth opened and closed, and his red-black tongue darted between the thin lips in a most extraordinary and revolting way. Caroline was reminded of a snake looking for blowflies. When she passed him on her way to the stairs, he looked up and grinned, baring those obscene black gums, and a gurgling sound seeped up from his throat, which Caroline hopefully translated to mean good morning.

Down in the dining-room Sheridan was already seated at the breakfast table, and he greeted his wife's entrance with an irritated scowl.

'You might try to come down to breakfast on time. We haven't a houseful of servants.'

Grantley, who was now his usual dapper self, with black hair piled high, white face a mask of solicitude, eased a chair under her legs and murmured.

'If I might be allowed, sir. We are so delighted that the old house has a master once again, there can be no trouble involved in serving both you and your gracious lady. Only pleasure.'

'Damned decent of you,' Sheridan growled. 'Come to think of it, must have been lonely with no fresh faces all these years. How long have you been here?'

Grantley served devilled kidneys, then poured coffee from a silver pot.

'It must be a trifle over twenty years. I remember the old gentleman – Sir Harold Sinclair – was delighted when we offered our services. Servants are, apparently, loath to stay in this isolated place and our arrival was timely.'

'How did you get on with the old devil?' Sheridan inquired.

'Unfortunately the poor old gentleman met with an accident soon after our installation. Fell over the banisters on his way to the bathroom. My father, who was but a few steps behind at the time, was inconsolable.'

Sheridan said, 'Good God' and Caroline trembled.

Grantley deposited a toast-rack on the table, then added a dish of fresh butter.

'The poor gentleman had been so kind as to make provision for us, prior to his untimely end, so we have been able to stay on at the house which, if I might be so bold, we have come to love.'

'Damned pleased you do,' Sheridan grunted. 'Your wife is an excellent cook, the place is run to perfection. I could wish the garden were in better shape – but then, I suppose you can't be expected to do everything.'

'I am of the opinion, sir, that unbridled nature serves the house more adequately than mutilated grass and tortured plants. Which, regrettably, reminds me of a melancholy item of news it is my sad duty to impart.'

'Sad news!' Sheridan paused, a fork holding a morsel of kidney half way to his mouth. 'What is it?'

'The reverend gentleman, sir. Your guest of yesterday evening. He, like my late employer – met with a fatal accident. It appears that he was cycling past Devil's Point – a steep incline, which to my mind is inadequately fenced – and due possibly to a fainting fit or some other mishap, fell over and broke his back.'

'Good God!' Sheridan dropped his fork and Caroline slid down in her chair. 'Broke his back?'

'Yes, sir. Between the second and third vertebrae.'

Sheridan took up his knife and fork and quickly recovered from the shocking news.

'The old fool was a mad old windbag, but still, I'm sorry he came to a sticky end.'

'He was, I believe, a knowledgeable gentleman,' remarked Grantley urbanely. 'And knowledge, when widely broadcast, can be disconcerting. Even – under some circumstances – dangerous.'

Caroline felt sick with terror. She knew, with the same certainty that would have been hers had she witnessed the terrible act, that Mr Barker had been murdered. Or did one associate murder with these creatures? Could a lion, or any wild beast, commit murder? She would have screamed, yelled out the unthinkable truth, had not Marvin entered the room carrying a plate of bread and butter.

For a heart-stopping moment his eyes met hers and instantly Caroline became as a condemned gourmet who is looking forward to his last breakfast, and refuses to think about the grim ceremony that must follow. Terror was now a delicious excitement that blended with her deep-rooted masochistic urge and became almost unendurable pain-pleasure. He leaned over the table and her fevered gaze was rivetted on his smooth, round wrist. Sheridan looked up and grinned.

'Heard about what happened to our guest of last night, lad?'

The beautiful head nodded. 'Yes, sir. Most regrettable.'

Sheridan's grin broadened. 'Well, he won't call you a mock again.'

Marvin straightened up and smiled gently.

'With respect, sir. A shadmock. My father is a mock.'

Caroline giggled when she saw the look of amazement spread over her husband's face and the spark of anger that made his little eyes gleam.

'I'm inclined to think that old Barker was not the only one

with a screw loose. Perhaps all of you have been here too long. A change of scenery would be beneficial.'

Grantley's voice was so gentle, so reasonable.

'I venture to suggest, sir – that would not be convenient.'

Sheridan Croxley flung his napkin aside and rose so violently his chair went over. Marvin calmly pulled it upright, then stood to one side and waited for the storm to break. Sheridan's face turned to an interesting shade of purple and his voice rose to a full-throated roar that had made many senior executives tremble.

'Not convenient! Damn your blasted insolence. You may think you're indispensable, but this is not the only house I own. This place is only a weekend retreat – a whim – of which I may soon tire. So, guard your tongue.'

Grantley appeared to be in no way put out by this tirade, but merely inclined his head, then motioned Marvin to remove the plates.

'I greatly regret if my words have given offence. I am well aware that your stay must, of necessity, be of short duration.'

Sheridan's anger was further incensed by this roundabout apology and without saying another word, he strode abruptly from the room. Caroline seemed to have become glued to her chair. She had only eyes for Marvin, ears that had an insatiable hunger for the sound of his voice and hands that wanted to touch, rip – fondle.

'You must not mind my husband. He has alternating moods.'

The words were addressed to Marvin, but it was Grantley who gave her a quick glance, and it seemed that the respectful mask was slipping. There was a hint of contempt in his eyes.

'Gentlemen have their little ways. More coffee, madam?'

She had lifted the cup to her lips when there was the sound of approaching footsteps, the door was flung open and Sheridan was back, roaring his anger.

'Grantley, not a telephone in the house works.'

'That is correct, sir. They have not worked for over twenty years.'

'What!' The tycoon shook his head in disbelief. 'Why then in God's name haven't they been repaired?'

Grantley raised an eyebrow and permitted himself a pale smile.

'It was never considered needful, sir.'

'Never considered . . . !' Caroline thought for a moment that her husband was about to suffer the – on her part – long desired heart attack. 'What sort of world have you damned people been living in? I am beginning to believe that that poor old fool was right. You are monsters . . . half baked . . . addled brained monsters.'

Grantley did not reply to this accusation, but stood with bowed head, rather like a larch tree, bending before a particularly violent wind. Sheridan regained a measure of self-control.

'Well, I'd better drive down to the village and telephone from there.'

Grantley coughed. A gentle, apologetic clearing of the throat.

'I regret to say, sir – that will not be possible.'

Sheridan swung round and glared at the dark figure.

'Indeed! Why not?'

'Because – with respect, sir – we could not permit it.'

The old man – the shaddy – moved into one doorway; his mouth was open, his long arms hung limply, but the stubby fingers were curved into menacing claws. At the same time the door leading to the back regions opened and Mrs Grantley, her beard quivering with frightful anticipation, entered and took up a position beside her husband.

Sheridan Croxley turned his head from left to right, then bellowed his rage and defiance.

'What the hell is going on here? I warn you, if that ugly old brute doesn't get out of my way, I'll knock him down.'

Grantley shook his head as though he deplored this aggressive statement, then said softly: 'I can promise, he will not lay a hand on you, sir.'

Sheridan slowly approached the heavy, grotesque figure, and when he was within striking distance, shot out his massive fist, straight for the gaping mouth. Grandfather-Shaddy did not so much as flinch. His mouth opened even wider until his face was split in half by a great gaping, gum-lined hole – then the black tongue twisted and became a long, vicious whiplash, that flicked the threatening fist – then quickly withdrew. The mouth closed with a resounding snap and the shaddy began to chew with every sign of intense satisfaction. Sheridan roared with pain, then stepped back and stared at the raw gash that ran across his knuckles and up the back of his hand. In one place the bare bone glimmered softly like red-tinted ivory. The shaddy swallowed and growled some unintelligible words. Grantley translated.

'My father wishes to compliment you on your flesh, sir. He says it's very tasty.'

With a roar of rage, Sheridan flung himself at the taunting figure; leaped across the intervening space with outstretched hands, motivated by an overwhelming urge to kill. Grantley tilted his head back and made a kind of subdued rumbling sound. Then when Sheridan's eyes came level with his own, he opened his mouth and – blew. It was not by any means a hard blow. A mere puff that might have extinguished a candle flame, but its effect on the big man was electrifying. He screamed and clasped shaking hands to his eyes, trying to claw away the burning agony that had come from a tainted breath. The voice of Grantley had not lost one iota of its respectful quality, as it spoke comforting words.

'Your discomfort is only temporary, sir. Nothing in the least to worry about.'

Gradually Sheridan ceased to dance from one foot to the other; the time came when he was able to lower his hands and look, with red-rimmed eyes, at his tormentor.

'What the hell are you? In the name of sanity – what – who are you?'

Grantley parted his lips in a mirthless smile and looked thoughtfully over his victim's right shoulder. Caroline was watching Marvin. The handsome one . . . the dream-lover . . . the walker of the darkways . . . He was leaning against the wall staring aimlessly at the open door and it seemed as though nothing could ever disturb the quiet serenity of that beautiful face, or bring a flash of passion to the clear blue eyes. Then Grantley answered.

'We are you, sir, as you would be – without your clothes.' Then his expression changed and he became once again the attentive, even, solicitous butler. 'May I suggest, sir, that you go to your room and lie down. This has been an upsetting experience for you. If you wish, my father can accompany you.'

'I'll see you damned,' Sheridan roared. 'Somehow, be you madmen, animals or monsters, I'll smash you. If you were wise you'd kill me.'

They all shook their heads. 'We couldn't do that, sir,' Grantley explained. 'We need you.'

Sheridan rushed from the room and the sound of his heavy footsteps could be heard ascending the stairs. Caroline remained in her chair and watched Marvin who had now resumed his duties and was clearing the table. Once he threw her a smile-tinted glance and she was so happy she almost cried.

Sheridan barricaded himself in their bedroom.

Grantley and his father were polishing the dining-room furniture – the former with effortless ease, the latter with much gumbaring glee – and Caroline was following Marvin round the house to a plot of cultivated ground.

The shadmock – the designation was now firmly rooted in her mind – was carrying a spade and hoe and did not, despite an occasional plaintive whimper, acknowledge her presence, or bother to turn his head when she stumbled over a lump of concealed masonry and measured her length on the ground.

The cultivated plot was about twenty feet square and stood out from its unkept surroundings like a sheet of clear water in an arid desert. It had been lovingly fashioned and meticulously tended and presented neat rows of piled earth that curved gracefully down to rounded valleys. Marvin laid the hoe and spade down, then removed his jacket and rolled up his shirt sleeves. Caroline watched him like a puppy waiting for a kind word – or at least an encouraging whistle – and when it was not forthcoming, dared to make her presence known by timidly touching his arm.

'I want to help. Please let me help.'

He smiled politely. A mere matter of parted lips, creasing of mouth, but she was as grateful as Lazarus for a sip of water.

'You are very kind, madam. If you would care to hoe the furrows, I would be greatly obliged. But, please do not tire yourself.'

She seized the hoe – an instrument that to date she had only seen in an ironmonger's window – and began to worry the loose earth that lay between the mounds. Marvin watched her with evident anxiety.

'Be careful of the young shoots, madam. They are just germinating and a moment's carelessness could be fatal.'

'I'll be careful.' She was so happy that he was at last talking to her, but fearful that this frail contact might wither away before it had time to grow. 'I didn't know anything grew at this time of year.'

'My plants are all perennials, madam.'

Caroline peered at the nearest mound and saw for the first time, little white shoots that were just beginning to peek coyly above the black earth. White, seemingly soft, they could have been sprouting tulip plants or maybe baby leeks.

'What are they?' she asked.

'Corpoties, madam.'

'What on earth are they? A vegetable?'

He smiled at her childish ignorance and shook his head.

'Not quite, madam. I suppose one could say they are a kind of meat-and-veg plant. They need a lot of careful attention. I use bone-manure in the early stages, then water them at regular intervals with a blood mixture. But of course the initial chopping up of the seed specimens is most important. If one chops too small, the result is a stringy and entirely inedible result. Too large,' he shrugged and Caroline was delighted to see his face was alight with boyish enthusiasm, 'means a soggy and flavourless plant. Are you keen on gardening, madam?'

'Absolutely,' Caroline exclaimed. 'Please go on, I could listen to you for hours.'

Now his smile was wonderful to behold. All the icy reserve had gone and he was bubbling over with the joy of a stamp collector who has discovered an educated postman.

'I say, I'm so glad. You see, Father and Mother, and of course Grandfather, are all hunters. They have no appreciation of the intense satisfaction that comes from planting, then reaping the fruits of the earth. Sometimes I become quite irritated with them and worry most awfully in case I lose my temper and do something dreadful. But, dash it all, the earth is so generous. You get so much more from it than you put in.'

'You're so right,' Caroline agreed gushingly, grabbing his nearest arm between her two hands. 'I expect you've got green fingers.'

He frowned and she trembled. Had she said the wrong thing?

'No I haven't. Only the long dead have green fingers. The ripe dead – the ready-for-planting dead.'

Her hands dropped from his arm and she shook her head in token denial, while her brain screamed its fear and grief. Because of his face, his beautiful exterior, she had been thinking of him as a normal, if rather shy boy, who could be transformed into a passionate lover. But now she knew he was just as much – perhaps more – a monster as his hideous elders, but – and this was the real horror – it did not make the slightest difference to her feelings towards him. His boyish enthusiasm would not be denied.

'There have been three sets of new owners during the past fifteen years, but they were not all *just right*. They did not always keep and ripen in the way that is so important. And Father and Grandad are so rotten. They keep on about the essence which keeps us strong, and how the specimens must be drained, and no one will listen to me . . . and only give me the rubbish . . . the old, the sick . . . the ones that are almost dry . . .'

At last Caroline reached the frontier where she moved out of the shadows and met reality face to face. She turned and ran back to the house and Marvin's young voice called after her.

'Please don't go. I can't bear it when people go away, it makes me angry . . . y . . . y . . . y . . .'

The last word ended in a kind of drawn out whistle. Not a full-lipped whistle, just a suggestion of liquid vowels; a hint of what might follow. Caroline ran even faster.

Sheridan, at first, would not let her in. He shouted from behind the barricaded door: 'You're on their side. Don't try to tell me any different. I saw you mooning over the young one and you did nothing to stop them. Nothing at all.'

'Please, Sheridan. Let me in. We've got to help each other. My God, if you only knew.'

'May I be of service, madam?'

She stifled a scream as the soft voice spoke behind her – and there was Grantley, grave of face, respectful of demeanour, standing a few feet away.

'The door . . .' She shrank back against the wall and allowed the first words that came to mind, to come tripping off her tongue. 'The door . . . it's stuck.'

'Kindly permit me, madam.'

He placed one large hand on the left panel and after pausing for a moment, suddenly pushed. The door flew back and there was a resounding crash as a wardrobe went hurling back against the side wall. Caroline saw Sheridan sitting on the bed, his face a white mask of abject fear. Grantley bowed.

'Will you forgive the intrusion, sir. But I have to inform you that Mrs Grantley will be yawning in half an hour. I trust that this will be convenient.'

Sheridan made a noise that was half way between a scream and a shout and Grantley bowed again.

'Thank you, sir. I am obliged.'

He departed, closing the door behind him and from somewhere along the landing they heard a muted growl – a low, impatient sound that could have been menacing or enquiring. Caroline ran to her husband and clasped his arm.

'We must try to get away. Sheridan, listen to me, I am sane at this moment, but, God help me, if I see Marvin again, I will be helpless. Please do something.'

He shook her off and all but snarled his rage-fear, looking so much like one of *them*, Caroline covered her eyes and sank down on the bed. Her husband watched her for a few minutes, then his lips curled up into a sneer and he beat his fists on to the bedside cabinet.

'I won't run. Do you hear me? I won't run from a set of degenerate madmen. I haven't got where I am by running. The entire set-up is one gigantic swindle. Grantley is not the first man to spit fire – acid – and the old man, not the last who will attach a length of wire to his tongue. Haven't you ever been to a fairground, for God's sake? But I won't be caught a second time. Once bitten . . .'

Caroline raised her head and screamed at him.

'Stop fooling yourself. They are monsters. MONSTERS. A different species – throwbacks – creatures we all know exist, but dare not think about. Try to remember and stop pretending you are not afraid. Remember the face in the crowd: the room you accidentally entered: the howl you heard in the night: the thing that peeped round the corner – all the memories the mind chose to forget. Now – if you dare – say you do not believe.'

He sat down beside her and was suddenly a tired, middle aged man, who had forgotten how to relax.

'Perhaps you're right. I wouldn't know. I have met so many

monsters, I'd never be able to distinguish one from the other. But
if what you say is true, what is the point of running? They must be
everywhere. A vast freemasonry of tooth and claw, fur and fang.
There can be no escape.'

As they sat together and watched the morning grow old, there
was peace between them for the first time in four years. Despair
flattened the hills of contention, filled in the pits of derision and
left free the plains of tolerance.

'I can't help myself,' she whispered. 'He . . . you know who I
mean . . . has something that calls to me.'

They did not speak again until a quiet knock on the door brought
horror back and a muffled cry to Caroline's lips. The door opened
and Grantley entered.

'Beg pardon, sir – madam. But Mrs Grantley is ready to yawn.'

Sheridan Croxley climbed to his feet and after one quick glance
at the bearded face that looked over the butler's shoulder, backed
to the window.

'I warn you,' he said quietly, 'I will defend myself.'

'That would not be wise,' said Grantley suavely. 'We have no
wish to cause you discomfort and in any case resistance is useless.
Please try to understand, sir, we only wish to help you. Fulfil your
potential.'

Mrs Grantley came into the room and never had she looked
so grotesque. She walked with a strange stiff-legged gait; her eyes
glittered and did not move, but stared at the, by now, terrified
man with the cold intensity of a venomous snake. She strutted
towards him and he made no move to defend himself, but became
as still as a hypnotised rabbit; lower lip sagging, eyes bulging and
face so white the erupted veins stood out like red streaks in polished marble. Then they were standing face to face, shoulders to
shoulders, hips to hips, and they could have been lovers about to
embrace. Then the maddy yawned.

Her mouth opened until the lower jaw hid her neck and the
upper lip curled up over the nose, so that her mouth was one
gaping cavern where discoloured teeth glimmered like two rows
of weather-stained tombstones. A yawn – a shuddering rumble –
began somewhere behind her heaving bosom, then rose up and
became a body shaking roar. Her shoulders quivered, her buttocks

and legs jerked, her arms flailed like wind tossed branches, but her head remained still. Then the yawning roar died. Was cut off as though a hidden switch had been pulled and at once all movement ceased. Both figures became as rigid statues. Croxley a study in frozen terror. The Maddy an awful automaton that is preparing to carry out a scheduled programme. Then she suddenly leaned forward and pressed her gaping mouth to that of Sheridan Croxley. Caroline heard the hiss of expelled breath and Sheridan gave one mighty shudder, before falling back, senseless against the wall. Mrs Grantley picked him up as though he were a child and laid his limp body on the bed.

The butler gave a little sigh of satisfaction.

'Pray do not distress yourself, madam. Mr Croxley's period of unconsciousness will be of short duration. When he is himself again, you will soon find a great change in his character. My wife has erased what is commonly called the soul and the gentleman will be able to develop his natural attributes without the hindrance of a conscience.'

They both looked thoughtfully at Caroline who screamed once, thereby causing Grantley to shake his head in sad reproof.

'There is no need for alarm, madam. We have no intention of – how shall I put it? – desouling you. This is not our normal practice. But Mr Croxley can be of great service to us – if I may be allowed to make such a bold statement. We have long wished for a representative in the upper strata of the business world. When the gentleman has fully matured – and I would remind you, madam, that he has been licked by a Shaddy, blown on by a Mock and yawned upon by a Maddy – he will indeed be one of us and advance our interests to everyone's satisfaction. We may even put him up for parliament. It would be nice to have one of our number in the cabinet. We have several on the back benches, but that is not quite the same thing.'

'What . . . what do you intend to do with me?' Caroline asked.

Grantley smiled and adjusted his bow tie.

'It is not always wise to ask leading questions, madam. Suffice to say, you will not be wasted.'

They went out and Caroline was left to await the waking of her desouled husband.

The sun was setting when Sheridan stirred, then sat up and looked round the room with a slightly puzzled expression. Caroline could not see any alteration in his appearance, although there was a certain bleakness in the eyes that usually meant he was about to erupt into a fit of bad temper.

'What the hell happened?' he asked.

'Don't you remember?'

'I wouldn't ask if I remembered. We were sitting here frightened about something. And, oh yes, Grantley came in with that wife of his. Rather attractive in an odd sort of way.'

'That . . . that thing . . . attractive!'

'I wouldn't expect another woman to agree. Now get out of here. I feel strange and probably another sleep will do me good.'

'But, Sheridan,' Caroline pleaded, 'this is no time for us to be parted. That . . . woman yawned on you and . . .' Sheridan was staring at her and there was a baleful gleam in his eyes that reminded her of a vicious dog that has cornered an intruder and is now seriously considering attack. When she moved the cold, watchful stare followed her and soon an unreasoning flood of fear made her run to the door and go stumbling down the stairs.

Marvin was in the dining-room and looked up when Caroline entered and although he appeared to be pleased to see her, his first words were those of reproach.

'Why did you run away? I thought that I had at last found someone who liked gardening. I was so disappointed and almost became angry. And no one must make me angry.'

Despite her fear, the awful knowledge, Caroline again came under the influence of that strange, animal charm, and suddenly he was a tree standing alone in a desert of madness. She ran to him and grabbed one limp hand and held it to her face.

'I am so frightened. Please help me.'

He looked surprised – even alarmed.

'Why, madam? I am not angry.'

'Please don't call me madam. I am afraid of your father – and the others. They have done something dreadful to my husband.'

He nodded – almost cheerfully.

'I expect they have desouled him. Now he will be one of us and feel much better. Why, do you want to be desouled?'

'No.' She shook her head violently and tried to bury her face in his shirt front, but he moved away.

'Just as well. I have never known a woman to be desouled. Father usually drains them and I plant what is left in the garden. Women make good corpoties. I expect that is what will happen to you.'

'Nooo.' She screamed her protest and tried to shake him in a frenzy of horror, but he was like a deeply rooted tree, or a rock that has its foundations deep down in the earth, for he did not move. 'You must not let them touch me. Please . . . please protect me and I'll do anything you say. Anything at all.'

He considered this proposal for some time. Then he put his head on to one side and asked: 'Anything at all? Even help me all day in the garden?'

'Yes. I will . . . I will.'

'Help me plant the little bits and pieces? Do the thinning out? Transplant? Water? Chop-up? Mince? Prepare the mixture?'

'Yes. Yes . . . oh God . . . yes.'

He nodded his approval

'That is very good. You have made me very happy.'

'Then you will protect me from them?'

The beautiful blue and so innocent eyes looked straight into hers.

'If they try to drain you, I will become angry.'

'Yes . . . but will you protect me?'

He frowned and Caroline flinched.

'I have already promised. I will become angry.'

He turned and walked away with that kind of hurt and resentful expression that one might expect to find on the face of a boy scout whose word of honour has been doubted. Caroline felt like a mouse who has taken refuge in a mousetrap from a herd of ill-intentioned cats. She sank down on to a chair and closed her eyes and instantly a crazy network of words spread across her brain. 'Drain . . . desoul . . . mock . . . shaddy . . . mock . . . shadmock . . . lick . . . yawn . . . blow . . . whistle . . .' The voice of the lately departed Mr Barker came back as a haunting whisper.

Wonder not why your hair stiffly bristles.
Just abandon all hope when the shadmock whistles.

Caroline giggled and pursed her lips and tried an experimental whistle. What was there so terrible about whistling. But – and now she could not suppress a shudder – who would have thought there could have been anything extraordinary about licking, yawning or, for that matter, blowing.

'What the hell are you doing?'

Her eyes snapped open and there was Sheridan standing by the door, his eyes cold mirrors of contempt. Already she could detect the subtle change. His face had that bleached, deathlike whiteness that was characteristic of *them*. A stubble of black beard darkened his chin, and it might have been the result of a fevered imagination, but were there not two little bumps rearing up through his hair?

She said: 'I am waiting . . . For dinner . . . or something.'

He grunted – or was it a growl? – then turned and went out through the door which led to the servants' quarters. About twenty minutes later Grantley entered pushing a food trolley, and Caroline at once noticed a trifling alteration in his appearance. His hair was no longer piled-up to form a raven crest over his head, but was neatly combed around his pointed ears and parted in the centre. The two, gleaming ebony horns did not – if one could only view them dispassionately – seem out of place. They added an almost noble aspect to his long face, and drew attention to his rather well-shaped skull. But Caroline could not help screaming and clutching clenched fists to her mouth. Grantley ignored or did not notice her distress, and after depositing a number of covered dishes and a single plate on the table, bowed most respectfully.

'Mr Croxley presents his compliments, madam, and instructed me to inform you that he will be dining in the kitchen. He feels he should now be among his peers.'

Caroline did not comment, but continued to stare at the horns which were causing her deep concern. Grantley gave one educated glance at the table, then walked with unruffled dignity back to the door. There he paused and coughed apologetically.

'There is one little matter. Will it be convenient for madam to be drained at eight o'clock?'

Caroline made a strange noise that terminated with the single word – drained! Grantley appeared to accept this sound to mean acquiescence, and inclined his head.

'I am deeply obliged, madam. I must apologise for this unseemly haste, but I find we are rather short of essential fluid and madam's contribution will be greatly appreciated.'

Caroline groaned and slid from her chair and then rolled over on to the floor. She was not aware that Grantley came back into the room and without too much effort replaced her unconscious body back into its former position. By pushing the chair tight against the table, he was able to ensure that such an unfortunate mishap would not occur again.

There is absolutely no doubt that mocks – apart from a few distressing weaknesses – make excellent domestic servants.

The shaddy, and the maddy came for her at eight o'clock.

Two bearded faces, two pairs of powerful hands, two muscle-corded backs; they lifted Caroline from her chair and carried her out of the dining-room and down a long passage. The prospect of imminent death is a great reviver, and she was wide awake when they entered the long, sparsely furnished room.

Sparsely furnished! A long table, a large galvanised iron bath, two plastic buckets, two carving knives, one saw and a roll of rubber tubing. Grantley was wearing a butcher's apron.

'If madam will lie down,' he bowed in the direction of the table, 'we will proceed.'

Caroline struggled, kicked, screamed and did all in her power to break free from those iron-strong hands, but it was hopeless. Grantley looked on with an expression of shocked surprise.

'It is to be regretted that madam cannot see her way clear to co-operation.'

She was being dragged closer to the table, with its straps and headclamp, and when she jerked her head round, there was Sheridan standing by the window, tall, bulky, looking more like *them* by the minute, with lust gleaming in his eyes. He chuckled – a low, growling laugh – and rubbed his hands together with fiendish delight.

Caroline swung her head from side to side, but nowhere was there a sign of the protector, the beautiful one, the innocent with the fatal whistle. Her scream took on words.

'Marvin, help me! Marvin . . .'

She was on the table and the two bearded monsters were preparing to strap her down, when the door opened – and he was
there. Blue eyes wide with alarm, full-lipped mouth slightly open,
his blond hair tousled as though he had lately risen from a virginal
bed. He said nothing, but looked enquiringly at his father.

Grantley frowned. 'This does not concern you. When she has
been drained, you may plant what remains.'

'I want her to help me in the garden,' the soft voice said.

The mock deepened his frown and shook his head angrily.

'You cannot always have what you want. There are others to
consider. Her essence must be drained and stored, so that we may
all be nourished during the winter months. You really must grow
up and face your responsibilities.'

'I want her to help in the garden,' Marvin repeated.

'Marvin,' the Maddy was trying the mother approach, 'be a
good boy. We let you have that stockbroker to play with before he
was drained, and we did not interfere when you pulled the legs off
that property speculator, even though he was useless for our purpose afterwards. But now the time has come for us to take a stand.
There is no point in licking or yawning the humwoman, she has
no monsteral qualities. She must therefore be drained, minced and
planted. Then – if you are a good boy – you will be able to harvest
the corpoties next spring.'

Marvin opened and closed his hands, while his entire body
became rigid. When he spoke his voice was very low – almost a
growl.

'Let . . . her go.'

Before Grantley or either of the other monsters could speak,
Sheridan lurched forward, his great hands balled up into fists, his
little eyes like tiny pits of blue fire.

'See here,' he was spitting the words out, 'it's all decided. All
cut and dried. I gather I'm not completely one of you lot, until,' he
jerked his head in the direction of Caroline, 'she has had the chop.
I'm hungry, pretty boy. Hungry for more money, more power, and
when I'm hungry, I smash anyone that gets in my way. So go and
play in your garden, unless you want to get hurt.'

Marvin's eyes were wide open and they gleamed with cold contempt. At the same time he looked so young and helpless, standing

there before the bulky, powerful figure of Sheridan Croxley. Then he said softly: 'A peasant should learn to guard his tongue.'

Sheridan's fist caught the boy squarely under the chin and lifted him off the floor, before sending him hurling across the room and crashing against the closed door. The door trembled, the Maddy shrieked, the Shaddy roared and the Mock – Grantley – voiced his objections.

'In Satan's name, you should not have done that, newly acquired brother. Now he will be angry.'

'I'm angry,' Sheridan retorted. 'Bloody angry.'

'Yes,' Grantley was watching his son with growing concern, 'but the anger of a fly cannot be compared with the rage of a lion.'

'A fly!'

'Quiet.' Grantley waited until Marvin had regained his feet and stood upright against the door. 'Now, son, control. Our newly acquired brother will be disciplined for this act, you may have no doubt about that. So don't get angry, please practise some self-control. He alone was to blame, so there's no need to make us all suffer . . .'

Marvin took a deep breath, if that can describe the rumbling intake of air; the unnatural expanding of the chest, or the dilated cheeks which bulged like white-walled tyres. Grantley hesitated for only a moment, then turned and made for the solitary window, where he arrived a bad third, his father and wife having been similarly motivated.

The lower sash had been raised – not before all the glass panes had been broken in the frantic struggle – and grandfather Shaddy had his head and shoulders out over the sill, when the whistle began.

Caroline had watched the eyes dilate, the head go back, the hands slowly turn, revealing the smooth, hairless backs, the fingers stiff and widely spread; the pink tongue coiled back until it resembled a tightly wound spring. Then the whistle. It was born somewhere deep down in the stomach and gradually rose up until it erupted from the throat as a single note of shrill sound.

Just abandon all hope when the shadmock whistles.

In the midst of her terror, Caroline thought: 'It's not so bad. After all, what can a whistle do?' Then quickly changed her mind when the sound rose to a higher pitch.

A whistle – a shriek – a sound that went higher and higher until it reached a pitch that seemed to make the walls tremble and broke the remaining fragments of glass in the window. Then from the shadmock's mouth appeared a pencil-thin streak of light. It shot across the room and struck Sheridan in the base of the throat.

The big man screamed and for a moment clawed the air with convulsing fingers, before he crashed down across the table, his head hanging limply over the edge. Blood seeped from his open mouth and formed a pool on the floor.

The shadmock advanced slowly forward and the whistling sound rose to an even higher pitch, while the beam of light became a pulsating, white-whiplash that flicked across the conglomeration of bodies that were jammed in the window frame. Marvin moved his head from side to side and the three bodies jerked, quivered, bellowed and screamed. Only that of Sheridan remained still.

It was then that Caroline realised that the door was unguarded. She crept towards it like a mouse in a den of fighting wild-cats, and hardly daring to breathe, eased her way out into the passage.

The front door was not locked.

Caroline ran desperately down the drive. Running under trees that shook their naked branches as though in sinister merriment; stumbling over pot-holes, bowed down by the horrible fear that rode on her shoulders.

She staggered round a bend and there were the front gates, mercifully unguarded. The iron barrier that partitioned the world of everyday activity that men call sanity, from the bizarre realm of the unacceptable. She ran by instinct, not daring to think, prepared for disaster to strike at every step.

The gates were locked. A thick iron chain was wound several times round the rusty bars and this was secured by a massive pad-lock. The rough ironwork rasped her soft palms, when in a frenzy of despair, she shook the gates and cried out her hopeless appeal.

'Help me . . . help me.'

Barely had the sound of her voice died away when running footsteps came crashing through the undergrowth and Marvin emerged from beneath the trees. Beautiful as Adonis, graceful as a golden snake, he came to her, and at once the fear, the urgent need for escape, was submerged under a blanket of slavish desire. His voice was gentle, but reproachful.

'Why did you run away? I was not angry with *you*.'

'I was frightened.'

He began to lead her back up the drive, talking all the while, like any enthusiast who has found a kindred soul to share his burning interest.

'There's no need to be frightened. My parents have decided to let me have my own way. They always do in the end. Now you can help me in the garden. Help me prepare your husband for planting. Will you do that?'

'Yes . . . yes, Marvin.'

'Cut him up and watch him grow ripe?'

'Yes, Marvin.'

'And you won't make me angry will you?'

'No, Marvin.'

'I expect I'll be angry with you sometimes. I just can't help myself. But I'll be awfully sorry afterwards. That should be a great comfort for you. I'm always sorry afterwards. Always . . . afterwards.'

They disappeared round the bend in the drive and for a while peace reigned among the slumbering trees and the rolling hills beyond. Then a colony of rooks rose up with much flapping of wings and raucous cries and became black, wheeling shadows against the clouded sky.

Monster Club Interlude: 4

The film ended amid a murmur of appreciation which terminated with an outburst of applause, in which Donald's companions most enthusiastically took part. When the lights came up the ghoul leaned forward and addressed the entire row.

'Gentlemen, I trust you will join with me in rendering a vote of thanks to our entertainment committee for securing permission to screen this film. Here we had the ingredients I mentioned earlier. Monsters and humans, with bad triumphant and a miserable ending. One cannot – indeed should not – ask for more.'

Everyone murmured 'hear, hear', and the werevamp added his unstinted praise. 'I feel uplifted. There is no other word for it. I must confess there was a bad moment when I thought the wench was going to escape. Thank hell that the gate was locked. Which only bears out the maxim: "When inattention comes in through the window, dinner flies out of the gate".'

Eramus nudged Donald in the ribs. 'Have you ever eaten corpoties?'

Donald shook his head violently and tried not to look as sick as he felt. 'No . . . no, I do not think they would agree with me.'

Eramus smacked his lips. 'You don't know what you've missed. As you know, usually I can't keep solids down, but give me a plate of boiled corpoties, served up with red gravy, and I'm as happy as a ghoul in a mortuary. Begging your pardon, sir.'

'That's all right,' the ghoul waved his hand and smiled indulgently. 'Rather crudely put, but I get your point. Personally, I prefer them baked. Baked corpoties and churchyard bouillon go down very well. Hullo, what's going on now?'

While he had been speaking an extremely handsome, grey-haired vampire had mounted the stage and raised his hands for silence. As the murmur of subdued conversation died away, Eramus again nudged Donald.

'Lintom Busotsky the vampire film-producer. He is this year's club chairman. Has turned out some epics in his time.'

'Hush,' the ghoul admonished. 'Kindly remember the words of Dark John the ghoul philosopher: "The small should be silent when the great speak".'

Lintom Busotsky spoke with a pronounced transatlantic accent.

'Fellow members, I guess you haven't come here to listen to me spout a lotta crap. But tonight, folks, we gotta special treat for you and I thought I oughta say a few words as a kinda intro-duc-tion. Folks, friends, sit back for a second feature.'

A wave of pleasurable excitement ran over the audience and Eramus rubbed his hands in joyful anticipation.

'Gee,' he said, thus paying tribute to his distinguished chairman, 'a second feature! Two films in one night and it won't cost us a drop.'

'Please do be quiet,' the ghoul warned. 'I happen to know Lintom is very touchy about being interrupted. Do you want your blood ration cut again?'

'Tonight,' the chairman went on, 'I've de-cided to show one of my earlier movies which I made during my red period. It tells the story of one of our sadly ne-glected brothers – in fact – I'm gonna to be so bold as to say – our most neglected brother. I refer to the one and only, the inimitable, the stu-pen-dous, the comer-up-from-down-under, the . . . wait for it, folks – the Fly-by-Night. Known, I am giv-en to under-stand, affec-tionately to all you bad people as Old Night-Basher.'

A roar of laughter – or what passed for laughter in the club – greeted this sally and the ghoul shook his head in wonderment.

'What a sense of humour he has! Genius and dourness so often go together.'

The vampire-producer again raised his hand for silence and the sound of merriment died abruptly.

'I have been criticised because this film has a happy ending for the humes . . .'

A groan of protest greeted this announcement and the club chairman waited with ill-concealed impatience until it had died down, before continuing.

'We-ll, almost happy. But, folks, ain't that life? We monsters are always getting the rough end of the stick and always will, I guess, until the Black One – may his shadow never grow less – comes into his own.'

The ghoul muttered, 'Bmen,' and several members made an X
sign.

'The Fly-by-Night,' Lintom went on, 'is a kinda associate member of our dis-ting-uished or-gan-isation, but he is no less welcome
for all that. He came up from down-under, but he's here to stay
and I'd sure like to pay trib-ute to those that I see among the audience.'

Several Fly-by-Nights stood up and flapped their wings and there
was a thunderous round of applause. The chairman-vampire-film-
producer clapped his hands, then wiped his mouth with a black-
edged handkerchief.

'We-ll, I guess that's all I have to say. Sit back, enjoy the movie
and behave yourself in the back row.'

Donald thought this was very sound advice, because the little
vamgoo was making unmistakable advances to the vampire usherette, a course of action which did not appear to meet with her
approval, if her menacing fangs were any criterion. But the club
chairman vacated the stage, the lights dimmed, the red curtains
parted and the screen erupted into a blaze of technicoloured life.
Donald found he was looking at a mass of billowing clouds, while
a disembodied voice was thundering out the following narration:

The Fly-by-Night

Let it be known that there is the earth and all things that do breathe, eat and walk thereon.

Then there is the underearth and all things that do not breathe, eat or walk, but most certainly exist. They have no flesh, but have substance: they neither spin nor toil, but find much to do: they speak not, but communicate. Their natural habitat is the lower regions of that uncharted country men call Hades, and since time began, they have crawled, slithered, or flown between the dark, fire-tipped mountains that border mist-filled valleys.

But there are those which over countless ages have evolved and become aware. With knowledge comes desire, and after desire comes determination, and after determination comes action. They wormed their way up through the dark tunnels which spiral around the place where lost souls mourn the passing of life, and came at last to the plane of the air-breathers. To some the light was not good and they either perished, or took to haunting the dwelling places of shadows, or ventured forth only when the sky was masked by night clouds. But some adapted, merged into their surroundings and learned to imitate the appetites of man. Such a one was named by the wise men of old as The Flucht-Daemon: but the common people drew upon their own limited vocabulary and called it: The Fly-by-Night.

The cottage stood on the edge of a great forest and to a person of vivid imagination it appeared to have crawled out from the shelter of giant trees and was now tentatively tasting the sunlight. A small garden was bordered by a white picket fence, and within its confines neat rows of cabbages, feathery carrots and sturdy potato plants presented a green, patchwork carpet that trembled under the caress of the morning breeze.

Long ago the cottage had been the dwelling place of a woodcutter, and before that a charcoal burner, but now it was occupied by Newton C. Hatfield and his daughter, Celia. Newton was a novelist of some repute: Celia was a would-be actress, who, when resting, tried to follow in her father's literary footsteps. The third occupant was a black cat who answered to the name of Tobias: a mighty hunter before the Lord, who brought live fieldmice home, then watched with an expression of profound surprise when Celia jumped up on to a chair and gave a pretty performance of feminine alarm. On such occasions Newton would corner the mouse, take it out to the edge of the forest, and there release it.

'Damn nonsense,' he growled. 'Frightened of a creature that will fit into the palm of your hand.'

'But it might run up my legs,' Celia protested.

'What the hell would it want to run up your legs for?' her father enquired. 'It hasn't got the morals of some of those types you go about with.'

'You are a disgusting old man.'

'Disgusting I may be, old never.'

One day Tobias brought home a bird.

It was a fine healthy starling that was in no way hurt, for Tobias treated his victims gently, being content to take joy in the hunt, then sit back and wait for the applause. The bird, once released, flew round the room and made a futile attempt to force its way through the window panes. Celia was full of concern and hampered her father's efforts to capture it by clutching his arm and exhorting him to be careful – don't hurt it – poor little thing, and other compassionate ejaculations. Newton finally netted it with a looped bath towel, then released it out of the front door and watched the black streak as it sped for the nearest tree.

'Women!' he shook his head with deep concern. 'I will never understand you. You go up the wall when a tiny mouse stirs a paw in your direction, but go all ga-ga when a bloody great bird goes flapping round the place. Do you realise if that had got entangled in your hair, you would have had something to scream about?'

'But . . . but it was only a poor little bird.'

'And what about that ferocious tiger we've got sitting under the table?'

Celia bent down and tickled Tobias's ears, an action which earned his full approval.

'He was only acting according to his nature.'

Newton made straight for his typewriter.

'I give up.'

Two days later Tobias brought home something that was not a bird or a mouse.

They found it when they came home one evening after a visit to town. It was crawling over the carpet and made a strange twittering sound when they entered the room. Newton swore and glared at Tobias, who was crouched in one corner and watching his capture with intense interest. Celia ran forward with a cry of concern.

'Oh, poor little thing.'

Newton grabbed his daughter's arm and pulled her back.

'Hold it. Before you go into raptures, I should first of all find out what it is.'

'It's some kind of bird.'

'Is it?' Newton bent forward and examined the creature carefully. 'Well, I've never seen a bird that looked like that. Look for yourself.'

The creature – before it unleashed its tail – was about six inches long, and had a pair of black leathery wings that assisted it to crawl over the carpet. But when the tail suddenly uncoiled, and it appeared to have been tucked away between the minute hind legs, another three inches was added to its length. Newton went out into the hall and returned with a thick walking stick.

'You're not going to hurt it?' Celia exclaimed.

'Oh, for heaven's sake.' He brushed her to one side, then inserting the point of the stick under one wing, flipped the creature over on to its back. 'Now, have you ever seen anything like that?'

A tiny, black fur-covered body, which terminated in bent hind legs: a narrow little white and completely hairless face that was lit by a pair of exquisite blue eyes, and surmounted with a mop of shining black hair. The tiny teeth were white and pointed, the ears tapered, the red lips were full and parted. Newton had the impression it was grinning at him.

'Isn't it sweet?' Celia said.

'Sweet!' Newton's bellow of rage made the creature look up, and its lips slowly closed. 'Sweet! That is the most horrible thing I've ever seen.'

'Oh, it's not. I should think it's some kind of bat.'

'Ah!' Newton nodded grimly. 'A mouse. A flying mouse.'

'Yes, I know, but it's not the same. Oh, look at his eyes!' Celia bent forward and assumed a winsome smile. 'He's not a nasty old mouse, is he then? He's a little dinkom-diddens. Yes, he is . . . he's a little dinkom-diddens . . .'

'For heaven's sake, stop it. How the hell you can make noises at a . . . a monstrosity like that is beyond me. Let me get a shovel and I'll put it outside somewhere. Preferably as far from the house as possible.'

Celia made a cry of protest and the creature blinked its blue eyes and seemed to look upon her with approval.

'How can you be so heartless? It's probably hurt, otherwise it would be flying about. We must look after it until it's well. As it was our cat that injured it, that's the least we can do.'

'Then let the cat look after it,' Newton suggested.

Celia ignored this trite remark and busied herself in lining a plastic clothes-basket with one of Newton's woollen vests, an act of vandalism that roused his freely expressed wrath. Then she gingerly picked the creature up and laid it in this home-made nest. A second later and she was wringing her hands.

'Gosh, but it's cold. It's like ice. Do you think we ought to put a hot water bottle . . . ?'

'No, I don't,' Newton roared. 'I can't understand how you were able to touch it. You do realise, it might have bitten you?'

'Nonsense. It looks so happy and content I wouldn't mind betting it was someone's pet.'

Newton shut himself in the back room he used as a study, and Celia, still consoling the creature with comforting words, carried the basket into the kitchen and deposited it near the fire. But what disturbed her was the fact it refused to accept any form of nourishment. She tried bread and milk, some of Tobias's cat food, a plate of cold lamb, some rice pudding left over from yesterday, and finally a quarter of a pound of smoked ham that had been purchased for Newton's tea – all to no avail. The creature ignored all offerings, but continued to stare up at Celia with possibly greater approval than before. Neither did it appear to want to sleep, but lay on Newton's woollen vest and watched its protector as she moved round the kitchen, and even sometimes peered over the basket when she moved out of sight.

'I'm awfully worried,' she informed Newton at bedtime. 'It hasn't eaten a thing and is wide awake. Do you think I ought to take it to a vet?'

'Wouldn't be a bad idea,' Newton nodded. 'A vet could put it to sleep in no time at all.'

'You are a cruel, unfeeling beast.'

'Perhaps I am. But that thing gives me the willies.'

It was three o'clock in the morning when she entered his room. 'Dad, wake up. It's gone.'

He sat up, turned on the bedside light, then blinked.

'What! Who's gone?'

'It has. I went downstairs to see if it was all right, and the back door was open and it's gone.'

'Good.'

'But, Dad, listen. Don't go back to sleep. Who unlocked the back door?'

'That's a point.' He sat up and scratched his head. 'You can't have locked it.'

'But I did, and I remember the little thing sat up and watched me. Honestly, would I go to bed and leave the back door wide open?'

Newton yawned. 'Well, you're not suggesting that little horror is capable of manipulating a ruddy great rim lock, then turning the door handle? Though now I come to think of it . . .'

'I don't know what to suggest. All I know is, the door is open and the sweet little thing has gone.'

'Well,' Newton pounded his pillow. 'Shut the door, lock it, and go back to bed.'

'Suppose it wants to come in again?'

'It will be a very disappointed little horror.'

Celia departed with much shaking of her head and Newton grinned as he heard her calling from the back door: 'Come boy . . . come . . . come.' The answer she received was an expectant cry from Tobias, who assumed he was due for an early morning snack. Presently she remounted the stairs and Newton gave a sigh of relief when he heard her door shut.

Next morning she smiled sweetly at her father over the break-fast table and said: 'He's come back.'

Newton reached for the marmalade pot. 'Has he! Who?'

'The little thing. There he was, perched on top of my wardrobe when I woke this morning.'

'Indeed! How did he . . . it get in?'

'Through my window. I left it open.'

There was a silence of some three minute duration, then Newton began to frown.

'Look, I've been half serious about all this up to now, but I've been thinking. There's something – I don't know – something un-natural about that damned thing. After all, we don't know what it is, or where it came from. I'm of the opinion it escaped from a zoo or some private menagerie. Perhaps we ought to report . . .'

'No.' Celia got up, her eyes blazing. 'It's not doing you any harm. If it did escape from some zoo, I'm glad, and I'll be damned if I'll see you, or anyone else take it back again.'

'Now, see here,' Newton pushed his chair back. 'Don't use that tone to me. I'm not one of your pansy boy friends. This happens to be my house, and if I say that miniature horror goes – it goes.'

'And I'm telling you – it won't. I'm not a kid for you to order about.'

They were interrupted by the sound of flapping wings; the grad-ually increasing rustle of disturbed air, and the winged creature flew into the kitchen, glided round the ceiling and finally settled on the table. There it sat with folded wings and looked at the two antagonists with gleaming eyes. Newton's anger drained away and was replaced by a feeling of utmost dread. There was no disre-garding the look of intense pleasure on the minute face. The head was turning from side to side, the eyes raking each face as though to absorb the maximum satisfaction from the flushed features, while the tapered ears were pricked so as not to lose a fragment of angered sound. Newton put his thoughts into words.

'The damned thing is getting a kick out of us having a row.'

'Don't be so silly.'

'For Pete's sake, look at it. It's licking its lips. Just as though it had just eaten a good meal.'

'It's pleased to see us.'

Newton laughed like a man who is not amused.

'You can say that again. There's something weird about this.'

He stopped short, let the sentence trail off into oblivion and kept his eyes on the grimacing creature. There was no avoiding the fact, it was unique. Moreover, the tiny face, the slender form, and above all, the exquisite blue eyes, were indescribably beautiful. He wondered why he had not realised this before. It was an evil beauty, combining the repellent fascination of a venomous snake, and the sinuous charm of an infant beast of prey, but there was beauty. Or to be more accurate, an extreme prettiness. He felt a sudden, a ridiculous urge – a well nigh overwhelming need, to stroke its head – to take it on to his lap and tickle its ears. He turned abruptly away and snapped: 'Do what you like, but keep it out of my sight.'

During the next few days it became apparent that something was missing from their normal relationship. Gone was the slightly mocking, affectionate comradeship, that at times, though neither suspected, bordered on the flirtatious. Now there was politeness, words were marshalled with care, before being uttered. They were like two people walking through a gunpowder factory, knowing that a wrongly placed foot could cause a spark. Newton appeared to have forgotten about the existence of the creature, and Celia was careful never to mention it. Nevertheless he was acutely alive to its continued presence in the house. Several times, when the kitchen door was open he heard the strange twittering sound, and once, the rustle of air as it flew up the stairs. There was a terrible urge to go out and watch that slow, graceful flight; feast his eyes on the evil, pretty little face. But he continued to sit resolutely behind his typewriter, vainly trying to make his fingers co-operate with his brain. But the brain was not at all prepared to manufacture sentences, play with plots, create fictional drama, when the bizarre was in his own house. He decided to break through the barrier of suspicion and doubt which had come into being during the past few days.

'I'm going back to town,' he announced one morning at breakfast. 'I've finished work on the rough draft and I'd like my agent's advice before I go any further.'

Celia said, 'Oh!' and poured a fresh cup of coffee.

'What are your plans?' he enquired with a carefully casual air. 'Would you like to drive up with me?'

'No thanks. I'll stay on for a bit.'

He felt a surge of irritation that threatened to sweep aside his carefully erected defence: words bubbled to the surface of his mind and demanded release. But for a while he retained control.

'By yourself? It will be a bit lonely.'

She shrugged and picked up a newspaper.

'I'll be all right.'

Irritation blunted its sharp edge against his self-control and became a blast of anger.

'Don't be so damned silly. How the hell can you stay down here by yourself?'

'Easy. I'll lock the door and stop anyone coming in.'

'Look,' he slammed his cup down. 'This place is meant to be a place where we get our breath back. We've been down here three weeks, and I think it's about time both of us got back into circulation. Haven't you got any work coming up?'

She shrugged again. 'So so.'

'What is that supposed to mean?'

'I intend to stay on.'

'Why?' He shouted and sensed the flutter of wings, but the door was shut and his anger was clamouring for outlet. 'You've never wanted to before. If you had someone with you I would understand. Wait a minute . . . I've got it . . . you've got some man coming down. Just waiting until I'm out of the way.'

'If I were, it's no business of yours.' Her eyes were now blazing pools of hate. She was shouting, betraying signs of coarseness, that shocked him, even while it reinforced his anger. 'I don't have to ask your permission before I take a man to bed. If I invite an army down here it's no damn business of yours. It's about time you remembered you're my father, not my husband . . .'

His hand swung out and struck her left cheek with such violence, she went hurling against the closed door. The door trembled, and from beyond came an excited twittering, and the pulsating thud of wings on wood that strangely kept in time with his furious heart-beat. Lying there on the floor she swore at him, using words he was not aware until that moment, she even knew, and a lingering spark of reason made him spin round and run from the room. He flung open the front door, and ran blindly to his car, anger warring

with a submerged sense of intense danger. It was not until the car
was roaring down the main road, he realised what that danger had
been. In that moment of mad rage, when the thing had beaten
the door with its wings, he – Newton C. Hatfield, had been but a
heartbeat away from murdering his daughter.

Newton spent the remainder of the day in the town flat.

He tried not to think, but thoughts scurried across his brain
like marauding rats. Since the death of his wife some seven years
before, the relationship between him and Celia had been one
of almost perfect concord. Whatever disagreements they might
have had were without rancour and soon forgotten. But now, on
two occasions, there had been undiluted hate, and he had struck
her too. The only conclusion was, either they were both going
mad or that horrible little monster was, in some inexplicable way,
responsible. He remembered the look of joyful lust when they
had quarrelled, and the sound of beating wings as it tried to force
its way through the door. But what was it? His imagination tried
to explain an animal – but was it an animal? – that could stir up
the basic instincts, and then – he dared to face the implication –
draw strength from the resulting storm. Now, safe in the heart of
London, the idea was fantastic, it scarcely merited consideration,
but every argument that he presented to refute it was destroyed
by the facts as he remembered them. He now went a little farther
down the path of forbidden knowledge. If – whatever the thing
was – drew strength from the black silt that lies at the very bottom
of human nature, then it surely followed, he and Celia had been
– feeding it. And, as everyone should know, the end result of feeding is *growth*. Having given this conclusion his full consideration,
Newton tore downstairs, jumped into his car and drove back the
way he had come.

Newton stopped the car and looked down upon the cottage and
the great army of trees that stood in the background. The moon
lit up the countryside and made every object stand out as though
it were a figure freshly painted on a canvas. He was struck by the
stillness; the complete absence of sound, and it seemed to his by
now fevered imagination, that he had somehow strayed into a

plane that was either a little above, or some way below that of normal existence. There was a dreamlike quality about the scene laid out before him: the motionless trees, the solitary cottage with its gleaming windows, that resembled four watching eyes, and the grey ribbon that was the road, which looked as if it had never known the tread of solid foot, or the hum of revolving car wheel. But suddenly, as though in mockery of his fanciful supposition, there was movement. The right hand casement – Celia's bedroom – opened, and a black shape slowly emerged into the moonlight. It perched on the window sill for a full minute, then opening black wings, rose gracefully into the air. Newton felt the horror slide down into his stomach like a lump of black ice. The flying creature circled the cottage, then began to flap slowly towards the forest, but before it was lost in a sea of shadow, the moon highlighted it for an awful moment, so that every feature stood out in stark relief. They were all perfectly recognisable: the narrow head, with its pointed ears and mane of black hair, the slender body, the wide spread wings, but there was a terrible difference. It had *grown*. At least three feet from wing-tip to wing-tip, and possibly thirty inches from crown of head to rear, and the tail was coiled up between the hind legs. Newton made a sound that was midway between a shout and a scream, as he pressed the self-starter, then drove swiftly down the hill, and screeched to a halt before the front door.

The hall was empty, save for the lingering ghosts of sated fear: the living-room was a deserted battlefield, where overturned furniture lay like the dead of a defeated army: on the stairs he found a piece of torn dress, and three steps up, a discarded shoe. Celia's bedroom door was open, and beyond was the gaping window, with a tattered nylon curtain hanging limply like the wedding veil of a violated bride. She was lying across the bed, the clothes ripped from her body, deep scratches disfiguring her face and white skin. When Newton, crying like a child who has come to understand the meaning of darkness for the first time, leaned over her, she opened her eyes and murmured sleepily: 'It is growing up.'

They argued long into the night. Newton shouted, threatened, walked out several times, but he always came back. Finally he begged.

'Come away. You can't . . . no one can stay in this place. Please listen to me.'

The angry scratches were fading from her face and arms, and that in itself was a matter of fearful concern. But worse was Celia's smile, her cool refusal to discuss what had happened, and her emphatically stated intention not to leave the cottage.

'You go,' she said. 'We don't want you. You're much too goody-goody.'

'For heaven's sake,' he stared at her with alarmed eyes. 'What have you become, girl?'

For a moment she looked wistful, almost sad, then she smiled. 'I thought I knew what I was. Now . . .' She shrugged. 'Now I know I was wrong.'

'That thing,' he jerked his head towards the window, 'it is beast, more, it's evil.'

'Don't play with words.' She moved to the window and stood looking up at the moon bright sky. 'It is the seed from which we sprang. As the coal is to the fire, so that is to man. What is evil anyway? Don't you realise it is the anagram of live?'

'It is also the anagram for vile,' he retorted. 'You . . . you are sick. Please believe me, you must come away now. Don't even wait to pack a bag. Just jump in the car and we'll be off.'

Her smile was scornful and suddenly he was afraid of his daughter.

'You haven't got the message yet, have you? Don't you realise wherever we go, it will follow us? There is a bond that can never be broken.'

'Tell me,' he pleaded. 'What the hell is – It?'

She shook her head. 'It is so hard to explain, and I can't communicate very clearly – yet. There's no voice in our sense of the word. It talks to me in my head. But I have been promised power. Unlimited success. To someone who has always been on the losing end, that's really something. I suppose a few centuries ago I would have been burnt at the stake.'

And she began to laugh as the moonlight turned her hair to silver-gold, and it seemed to the horrified father that he was listening to the laughing child of long ago.

*

During the days that followed Newton watched his daughter with terror inflamed anxiety, and never did he dare ask the question that haunted his waking and sleeping life. Where was it?

Whenever he ventured into the kitchen, it was not there. Or in the living-room. He had not the courage to go out at night and watch Celia's bedroom window, and no sound now came to disturb the long, dark hours, but he knew it was still nearby. Tobias no longer brought his prey home, but seemed content to sit by the window, curiously alert to every sound, and apparently watching something or someone that was not visible to Newton's eyes.

Celia appeared to have forgotten that there had ever been cause for friction between them, and treated her father to the old bantering good humour that disturbed him more than the former bad temper. She had revealed to him a face that had undergone a terrible change, and now the veil had been resumed, he could only guess at what further deterioration had taken place. But he began to listen and watch for any clues as to the creature's whereabouts and habits. One evening he was rewarded.

'I left my handbag upstairs,' Celia exclaimed.

'I'm going up,' Newton waited for the angry refusal. 'Would you like me to fetch it?'

She smiled sweetly. 'Thank you. You're a pet.'

Her bedroom was bathed in moonlight, the window was open and he detected a faint, musty aroma. Two of his questions were answered. The thing spent the day in Celia's bedroom, and it flew by night.

Next day what could have been further information came from another source. Celia left him alone in the house, and an hour later returned with a bundle of newspapers and magazines. Newton for want of something better to do, for his work was sadly neglected these days, seized a copy of the *Daily Mail* and began to skim through it. The possible information was on page four. A little paragraph in the right hand bottom corner of the page.

MYSTERIOUS BIRD

Several eye witnesses have reported seeing a strange and very large bird in the vicinity of Clavering in Kent. Descriptions vary from: 'a batlike creature with pointed ears and a vast wing span', to, 'something resembling a giant crow'.

Reliable sources think it likely this is some form of freak bat, particularly as it is only reported to have been seen at night.

The other item had possibly no connection with the thing that flew by night at all, but it still afforded Newton some further disquiet.

RISING CRIME WAVE IN KENT

There has been an unexpected outbreak of crimes against persons in Kent during the past few days. Several cases of robbery with violence, rape and one attempted murder have come to the attention of the police. All have been committed by people who have, up to now, led seemingly blameless lives.

Chief-Superintendent Hargraves of the Kent Constabulary, said in a statement last night: 'Television and films depicting violence have much to answer for . . .'

Newton put down the newspaper and forgot that there was a subject he must not mention.

'Celia, for God's sake, where . . . ?'

She turned on him savagely: 'Shut up. Don't . . . don't . . .'

She broke off suddenly, then quickly regained control.

'Don't ask questions that I cannot answer.'

Well aware that another outburst of mutual anger might mean the flutter of wings, Newton lapsed into silence. But a terrible resolution came slowly into being.

He allowed weeks to pass while the resolution grew into awful maturity, and during that time living with constant fear became a natural state of existence. It was then he realised that hell could not be such a dreadful place, because in time, the damned soul would get used to it. Cold dread entered his bed and became a sleeping partner: nagging anxiety robbed him of appetite: black terror came out of the past and pointed a skeleton finger towards the future. But at the same time his brain, well trained in the art of manufacturing plots, creating problems that must be solved, devised a plan that was based on cool reason.

The thing – whatever its original state – was solid: there must be a form of flesh, which coated a framework of some matter that was akin to bone. Therefore it followed the creature – now a title, an easily recognisable name, began to frequently cross his crowded brain – Fly-by-Night – could be destroyed. Perhaps it would quickly recover from wounds, it might well be beyond his strength to inflict any kind of damage, but there was an element that no solid creature could resist. Fire. The resolution mated with the plan and became an operation.

So that his precious stock of courage should not be reduced by sights and sounds, he deliberately did not look out of the window once the sun had set, and he plugged his ears with cotton wool after retiring to bed. Then, when the moon had begun to wane, he went into purposeful action.

Eight sleeping pills powdered and mixed with cocoa made a near lethal drink, but the situation demanded drastic measures. He watched Celia sip from the earthenware mug, then trembled when she put it down with freely expressed disgust.

'Horrible!' She wiped her mouth, then glared at him with sudden suspicion. 'What the hell did you put in it?'

He got up and moved towards her, grimly determined that nothing should delay or impede his great plan.

'Drink it,' he growled and she shrank back, for he was now like any animal that has been driven into a corner. 'Drink it.'

'No,' she shook her head wildly. 'No, I'll not let you do . . .'

'Damn you, drink it.'

He grabbed her and made brutal by his great rage, flung the slender form on to the sofa, where it lay with staring eyes and gaping mouth. Then Newton took up the mug. He gripped her lower jaw with one hand, while he poured the liquid down her throat with the other. Then he stepped back and waited.

'You fool.' She was ugly now; her face twisted up into a mask of hate, her brown-smirched mouth spitting out words. He knew if he had not killed her body, he had at least slain any regard she might still have retained for him. But it was not important – not now. 'You can't fight him. Whatever you do, he can't lose. Get that into your sanctimonious head. You cannot possibly win.'

'I can try,' he said softly. 'My soul would be damned if I did not try.'

'Your soul!' She laughed. A loud, harsh sound that crashed across the room, and went echoing round the house. 'What makes you think you've got a soul? A speck of awareness: an atom of intelligence, which will never withstand the shock of death. Immortality is only for the brave.'

Still he waited, and presently he saw her eyelids droop, while her tongue released words that had drifted from a mist-shrouded brain.

'My love flies in on the night wind . . . his breath is fear . . . he speaks with the voice of desire . . .'

The voice trailed off, the words died, Celia slept and Newton was now free to prepare for the coming battle.

From the kitchen dresser he produced a gimlet, screwdriver and a bag of three inch screws. He then went upstairs and entered Celia's bedroom, where he sought for fresh signs of the creature's tenancy. They were not hard to find. On the floor by the right hand side of the bed, was a thick eiderdown and a pillow. On the dressing-table stood a bowl of greyish water, and of all things, a razor and a tube of shaving cream. Somehow, this commonplace evidence of personal hygiene seemed both horrifying and obscene. The thought of that creature (and oh, my God, how it must have grown) scraping the bristles from its face, made Newton feel sick. And hard on the trail of that discovery came another – it was imitating the habits of man. Blindly perhaps, for no other reason than this was one of the customs of the air-breathers.

The casement window was wide open, and beyond the moon looked down on sleeping countryside. Newton closed it, then setting to work with his gimlet he drilled holes in window and frame, before inserting his screws. When he had finished the room was sealed up and only by breaking the glass would the creature enter. As an afterthought, inspired more by hope than judgement, he drew a large red cross with Celia's lipstick, on each windowpane. It took him three hours to screw up every window in the cottage, and during all that time he kept looking up at the steel blue sky.

Locking both the back and front doors, he went over to the

small garden shed, and there prepared the fire-trap. It was simple and he hoped, effective. A mixture of paraffin, creosote and petrol was sprinkled over walls, a pile of dead wood, and placed in cans, bucket and a small barrel. After making a torch from a length of thick wood, and padding one end with paraffin soaked rags, he sat down on the garden seat and waited.

The night was so beautiful: the sky was at peace and was a perfect setting for the crystal moon and the cold star-diamonds that spread out into infinity. He had a ridiculous feeling that he was the focal point for a billion eyes; a miserable biological specimen that was under a mighty multi-galaxy microscope, and was now being watched to see how he would react in the coming battle.

Tobias came ambling across the garden and rubbed his body against Newton's legs. He picked the cat up and deposited it on his lap, where it purred loudly, then settled down for a short sleep. Newton grinned ruefully when he remembered that Tobias was the innocent reason for him sitting here in the small hours, with his daughter drugged in a locked house, and the garden shed full of inflammable material waiting for a match.

The first pale fingers of dawn were clawing the eastern sky, when Newton stiffened and then gently lowered Tobias to the ground. A large black shape was slowly flying out from the shadows cast by the trees. It circled the house and as the monstrous shape passed overhead, Newton gasped when he realised the extent to which it had grown. Even allowing for the bent hind legs, it must be all of five feet tall, and what was even more alarming, the wing span was almost as wide. Gripping the unlighted torch in his right hand, Newton edged his way round the house, being careful to keep well within the shadow, and watched the creature's flight with fearful anxiety. What would be its reaction when it realised that the house was sealed up? There was always the possibility that it might break the glass and once inside, his plan would be frustrated.

After circling the house three times, the winged shape sank down and glided towards Celia's window, where it hovered, while the wings flapped with intense rapidity. The ensuing shriek made Newton cringe against the wall, for it was a cry of baffled rage; an almost frantic scream of disbelief. Two long thin arms emerged from behind the pounding wings, and a pair of taloned hands pawed the moonbright windowpanes, where the red crosses gleamed like blood streaks.

The shriek was terminated by a hoarse cry, and the creature, as though it had been electrocuted, fell heavily to the ground. There it crouched while, the wings half folded, it examined its hands, while twittering with pain or rage. Then it hopped up and down and blew on the extended claws like a schoolboy who has been caned. Newton dared to move a few paces nearer, still hugging the wall, but when he came to the corner of the house, the protecting shadow abruptly terminated and one more step would have brought him out into the full moonlight.

He stepped back and the heel of his shoe clicked against the wall. Instantly the creature became still: changed from a hopping monstrosity to a black frozen statue. Suddenly the head jerked round and Newton was staring at the sinister, pretty face, the exquisite blue eyes and the outstretched claws. He knew it could see him, but there was a completely silly thought, that if he kept perfectly still, it would forget all about him. The clawlike feet moved apart and it was bounding towards him like a giant winged-bullfrog. The hind legs acted as springs, the half-folded wings as stabilisers, and doubtless behind the blue eyes lurked something that did service for a brain. Newton for a while forgot his plan, ignored the dictates of reason that stated now was the time to make a stand, instead, he surrendered to a blast of pure terror, turned on his heel and ran.

From little horrors, mighty monsters grow. Such was the impromptu thought that went with him as he ran. If only he had crushed the little thing that Tobias had brought home, now he would not have been running from something that leaped like a frog and twittered like an overgrown sparrow. A flapping sound told him the Fly-by-Night had taken to the air and the attack would come from above. His foot became entangled with a root and he went sprawling on the ground, where he lay waiting for the end. A minute, perhaps more passed, then he ventured to look up. The creature was flying in rapidly decreasing circles, and it was in obvious distress. It made a strangled cry, then dropped a few feet, rather like an aeroplane that has hit an air pocket, and it took Newton some while before he realised the reason. The first golden spears from the rising sun were gliding across the clear sky. At

once fear receded before a wave of new hope: the Fly-by-Night
was a thing of darkness, it did not like light. It would be ridiculous
to suppose that, like the legendary vampire, this monster would
disintegrate with the rising sun, but it was uncomfortable; had a
problem that could only be solved by finding shelter in a very short
time. The house was sealed up, on the other hand the garden shed
was waiting – its door wide open. Newton fumbled in his pocket,
found his cigarette-lighter, then lit the torch.

The Fly-by-Night came down for a bumpy landing. It dropped
the last two feet and rolled over, while emitting a series of hoarse
shrieks that made the newly awakened birds in the nearest trees rise
up on fluttering wings. It regained an upright position and began
to leap towards the house, presumably still instinctively regarding this as a natural place of protection. Newton ran forward, and
with courage he did not suspect until that moment he possessed,
stood in its path waving his flaming torch, while moving slowly
forward.

The Fly-by-Night, confronted in mid-leap by what it most feared,
fell over, and Newton took advantage of the situation by thrusting
his torch direct into the grimacing face. An ear-splitting shriek and
it was flapping, creeping, lurching across the ground, oblivious of
the growing light of day, fired only by the need to escape from the
searing flames. Newton guided his quarry into the desired path by
waving the torch to left and right, until the open shed door was in
the creature's line of vision. It managed to fly the last few yards,
a kind of flapping run; then it disappeared through the opening,
and Newton, his courage by now dangerously low, flung the torch
on to the pile of oil soaked wood, and closed the door. He hastily
fastened the padlock, then ran towards the house.

There was first a roar, then an explosion, and when he looked
back the shed was one gigantic flame. Such a fire would have glad-
dened the heart of an arsonist; it crackled, sizzled, spat out little
gobbets of spluttering flame, and reached upwards, as though to
lick the stars, with yellow and blue edged tongues of flame. The
roof fell in, the walls collapsed, and presently flame gave way to
grey-black smoke and it was all over. When Newton at length
walked slowly over to the smouldering ruins there was nothing to
see but grey ash, charred wood and a few pieces of twisted iron.

Then he broke down and cried.

It was late afternoon before Celia awoke. She did not speak until her father had prepared a cup of sweetened tea and a few slices of hot buttered toast, then she asked: 'What have you done with – with him?'

'Don't talk about it now,' he pleaded. 'Wait until you are more yourself.'

She smiled. 'I will never be more myself than I am now. What have you done with him?'

'I,' he paused, then for better or worse, announced boldly, 'I burnt It. I burnt it in the garden shed.'

Celia daintily sipped her tea, then put the cup down. She nibbled the toast and after waiting until her mouth was empty, said simply, 'I see.'

He was at first puzzled, then encouraged by her calm acceptance of the news. Hope came to him.

'It's all over now,' he said. 'That creature is utterly destroyed and can never influence you again. Now we will begin to forget.'

She took another bite of toast and shook her head.

'No we won't.'

He knelt down by her chair and took her disengaged hand in his.

'Darling, you must try to understand. The creature has gone – burnt to a cinder – nothing remains.'

She finished her slice of toast, wiped a butter smeared mouth on the back of her hand. Then she smiled again.

'Yes it does.'

'Celia, dear, please listen . . .'

She giggled and tilted his chin with the tips of her cool fingers.

'You listen, daddikins. They will grow very fast and very big.'

He brushed her hand to one side, then stood up.

'What will?'

Laughter clogged her throat, made her eyes water, but somehow the words came bubbling out.

'His . . . his children. The ones I'm going to have any minute now.'

Epilogue

The curtains closed, the lights came up and all the monsters made a dash for the entrance in an effort to beat the first stirring chords of the 'Monsters' Anthem'. Once back in the restaurant, Donald was escorted back to their table, where Eramus and Manfred eased him gently, but firmly, into a chair.

'Really,' he protested. 'I must think about getting home. This has been an awfully jolly evening, but, well, all good things must come to an end.'

Vampire looked at werevamp and Eramus spoke for both.

'Never known a chap so keen on going home. Honestly, Guv, don't you like a bit of social life?'

'Oh, yes,' Donald hastened to erase this slur on his sociability. 'I love parties and going to the pictures and being told stories – and of course meeting unusual . . . people.'

'Well then,' Eramus was about to remonstrate further, but the ghoul tapped on the table with his tearing knife and rose, with great dignity to his feet.

'Gentlemen – fellow members, I wish to crave your indulgence while I make a little speech. I am – possibly quite wrongly – of the opinion that our guest feels somewhat uncomfortable in this – and let there be no false modesty – distinguished company.'

Some monsters said, 'Ah!' and others said, 'Oh!' and all looked very superior and complacent. The ghoul again tapped on the table.

'I am going one step further. I dare to suggest he may even feel inferior to us, the favoured minority. For, gentlemen, is it not an indisputable fact that the minority always rank over the majority?'

Manfred said, 'True. He has a point.' Everyone else nodded gravely, with the exception of Donald who was beginning to feel like a bricklayer who has strayed into the smoking room of the Junior Carlton.

'But,' the ghoul raised a grisly forefinger and wagged it pontifically. 'Has not the time come for us to reverse our mode of thinking? Having weighed the pros and cons, having sifted the evidence, listened, watched, eavesdropped, read and finally understood, I have come to the conclusion that we have no right to feel superior to the human race.'

This announcement was greeted by a storm of protest from every part of the restaurant. One weregoo of fanatical aspect was heard to shout, 'Blasphemy,' and one elderly vampire lady loudly expressed her opinion that the ghoul should be boiled in oil. But that personage appeared to be unmoved by the upheaval his words caused and calmly waited for order to be restored. At length he was once again able to make his voice heard.

'Friends, I am grieved beyond words that it is necessary to face you with this unpalatable truth. But let us list our gifts and measure our achievements, then weigh them in the scales against those of the despised humes. We sup, hunt, tear, lick, yawn and on occasion whistle. With what result?'

A giant vampire rose and bellowed his answer.

'I drained one hundred humes last year. What hume can dare boast of doing that?'

'And I,' a raddy hastened to advertise his record, 'licked over two hundred and fifty.'

'And I yawned over one hundred and ninety times,' a maddy stated.

'Blew on three hundred,' announced a mock proudly.

'I whistled over one thousand times,' a shadmock said with becoming modesty and pretended not to hear the gasp of admiration that greeted his claim. Then the ghoul dropped his thunderbolt.

'In the past sixty years the humes have exterminated one hundred and fifty million of their own kind. No effort has been spared to reach this astronomical figure and the methods used must demand our unstinted admiration. The humes began with many serious disadvantages, but these they overcame with wonderful ingenuity. Not having claw, fang or a whistle worth talking about, they invented guns, tanks, aeroplanes, bombs, poisonous gas, extermination camps, swords, daggers, bayonets, booby-traps, atomic bombs, flying missiles, submarines, warships, aircraft-carriers, and motor-cars. They have also perfected a process for spreading a lethal disease on any part of the planet.

'During their short history they have subjected other humes to death by burning, hanging, decapitation, electrocution, strangulation, shooting, drowning, racking, crushing, disembowelling and other methods too revolting for the delicate stomachs of this assembly.'

The ghoul ran out of words and breath and the remainder of the club members of protests. Donald found he was becoming the focal point of growing admiration.

'I was not aware that you were so talented,' the werevamp said, staring at the guest with profound astonishment.

Donald blushed, he was essentially a modest young man.

'I didn't like to boast,' he said.

It was then that the chairman, the great Lintom Busotsky himself, rose and flashed his fangs in an engaging smile.

'Folks . . . friends . . . I guess we are all grateful to brother ghoul for the en-lightening and edi-fying dis-course which it has been our privi-lege to hear. I am there-fore going to as-ske you to fill your glasses and join me in drinking a toast to one whose blood will enrich, whose deeds are without parallel and whose bad in-tentions promise so much for the future.'

Glasses were filled with whatever beverage suited that individual member's need or taste, then the august chairman turned to Donald and raised his glass.

'Folks . . . I give you the most stu-pen-dous, the most outstanding, the gift-ed, the most dia-bolical, the bloodiest, the most murderous, the great-est monster of us all. MAN.'

A host of hairy, fanged, scaled, blanched and evil countenances were turned towards Donald and a veritable chorus of voices, screamed, roared, hissed, squeaked or simply shouted the one, profane word. 'MAN!'

When the glasses were empty, they were thrown against the nearest wall, although one or two found a lesser target as a bellow of rage from an injured werevamp testified. Then the chairman spoke again.

'Folks, I would like to propose that we herewith el-ect the said monman a member of this dis-ting-uished community.'

The ghoul rose and cleared his throat. 'Mr Chairman, I would like to second that proposal.'

'All those in favour please sig-ni-fy in the usual way.'

A unanimous chorus of 'Ayes' announced that Donald McCloud had been elected to the most exclusive club in the world. The ghoul gravely shook his hand, the werevamp slapped his shoulder, Eramus poked him in the ribs and a pretty vampire kissed his cheeks and would have doubtlessly expressed her pleasure in more biting terms had she not been pulled away in the nick of time. Then there was a united demand for a speech and Donald was hoisted to his feet and made to face an expectant audience. Being unaccustomed to public speaking his offering was brief and hesitant.

'I would like . . . to thank you all . . . for the . . . for the great honour you have . . . done . . . done . . . me. And I would like to say . . . that I will do my best . . . to be a monster . . . you will be proud of.'

He sat down amid roof-raising cheers and accepted a triple Bloody Mary which Eramus thrust into his hand.

Presently the tumult died away, everyone returned to their tables, but there remained an atmosphere of expectancy. Donald's immediate companions, after the initial round of congratulations, remained curiously silent and were careful to keep their glances on their empty glasses. At length the ghoul spoke.

'Well, my dear fellow, now you are a full member. How excited you must be.'

'Yes,' replied Donald who had by now downed his triple Bloody Mary and felt quite excited. 'Ab . . . absolutely marvellous.'

'I am so pleased,' the ghoul murmured. 'I hate to bring up such a mercenary matter in the midst of this jollification, but I expect you would like to pay your dues. Get them off your . . . eh . . . chest, so to speak.'

'Dues!'

'Yes. There's the membership subscription, which is always a bit stiff the first year. Then, it's traditional for a new member to push the boat out on his first evening in the club. I should imagine that you would not wish to go against tradition.'

'No . . . no, of course not. How much do I owe?'

The ghoul beckoned to a nearby waiter who came forward carrying an excessively long bill-pad.

'How much is tonight's little do going to cost my friend, Markus?'

The waiter consulted his pad.

'Three rounds of mixed drinks, repast for eight, eight cinema tickets, cover charge and ten per cent for service. That will be two-o-two, sir.'

The ghoul frowned and then tried to look distressed.

'Then there's your subscription – that's another ten. 'Fraid, my dear fellow, you'll have to shell out three-o-two.'

Donald reached for his wallet, while expelling his breath in a vast sigh of relief. 'Is that all? Three pound and tuppence? I call that very reasonable.'

The ghoul looked very embarrassed and chose his words with care.

'I feel you haven't quite understood, my dear chap. We do not deal with hume currency here. Your total bill comes to three gallons and two pints.'

'Three gallons . . . two pints! Of what?'

They all answered together.

'BLOOD.'

'Of course,' the ghoul did his best to soften the blow. 'You will not be expected to pay it all at once. Dash it all, we're not blood-suckers – at least not in the allegorical sense. And in any case, you'd never be able to deliver. No, I would say two pints down, and the rest on . . . well . . . the never-never.'

Donald allowed himself some little time for serious thought, then he decided on prompt and very swift action. In fact he got as far as the front foyer, before he was tripped up by the vampire receptionist. They dragged him back to the table amid a storm of boos and derisive cat-calls. The ghoul looked shocked and hurt.

'A bilker,' he shook his head sadly. 'Who would have thought it? A blessed bilker.'

Then a vampire wearing a chef's hat and a white overall, came up from the kitchen, carrying the largest and longest syringe that Donald had ever seen. It took one weregoo, one werevamp, one werewolf and Eramus to hold him down while they drew off the first pint.

RONALD HENRY GLYNN CHETWYND-HAYES was born in Isleworth, west London, in 1919. He grew up a film fan, and in between working odd jobs appeared as an extra in several pictures, including *A Yank at Oxford* (1938), which starred Lionel Barrymore, Vivien Leigh, and Maureen O'Sullivan, and *Goodbye, Mr. Chips* (1939). He oerved during the Second World War, and after demobilization returned to London and worked in furniture sales. He sold his first short story in 1953, and his first novel, a science fiction tale, *The Man from the Bomb*, was published in 1959. He went on to write some 200 short stories and a dozen novels and also edited anthologies, including twelve volumes of the *Fontana Book of Great Ghost Stories*. Known as 'Britain's Prince of Chill', Chetwynd-Hayes developed a reputation and a large fan base for his old-fashioned ghost stories and his tongue-in-cheek monster tales. Though Chetwynd-Hayes's works were not always huge sellers, his books were always in high demand with library patrons, and he was consistently among Britain's top earners of public lending rights. In 1989, he received the Horror Writers of America's lifetime achievement award and also won an award from the British Fantasy Society for contributions to the genre. He died in 2001.

ABOUT THE COVER

The cover painting by John Bolton was originally used as the cover art for a 1980 comic book based on the screenplay of the film adaptation. The comic was used as a promotional item to generate interest in the film; only about 1000 copies were printed, and they are highly collectible today. The Publisher is grateful to John Bolton for permission to reproduce his art, and to Liliana Bolton for providing a digital reproduction of the painting.

MORE CLASSIC HORROR FROM VALANCOURT BOOKS

M.G. Lewis
THE MONK
Introduction by Stephen King

'A black engine of sex and the supernatural that changed the genre – and the novel itself – forever.' *Stephen King*

Michael McDowell
THE AMULET
Introduction by Poppy Z. Brite

'[O]ne of the best writers of horror in this or any other country.' *Peter Straub*
'The finest writer of paperback originals in America today.' *Stephen King*

Basil Copper
THE GREAT WHITE SPACE
and NECROPOLIS
Introductions by Stephen Jones

'The best writer in the genre since H.P. Lovecraft.' *L.A. Herald-Examiner*
'In the same class as M.R. James and Algernon Blackwood.' *Michael and Mollie Hardwick*

Gerald Kersh
NIGHTSHADE AND DAMNATIONS
Introduction by Harlan Ellison

'Horrific in the extreme.' *Penguin Encyclopedia of Horror & the Supernatural*
'Kersh has a strange, perverted sense of genius. And how he can write.' *Virginia Kirkus*

Thomas Hinde
THE DAY THE CALL CAME
Introduction by Ramsey Campbell

'[A] sunlit nightmare of a book.' Robert Baldick, *Daily Telegraph*
'[Will] bring forth nightmares in broad daylight.' Irving Wardle, *The Observer*

STEPHEN GILBERT

RATMAN'S NOTEBOOKS

Introduction by Kim Newman

'A magnificently malignant horror story.' *Kirkus Reviews*
'Horrific, grisly and truly frightening . . . a masterpiece of terror.' *Washington Star*

SIR CHARLES BIRKIN

THE SMELL OF EVIL

Introduction by John Llewellyn Probert

'If you are at all sensitive, leave him well alone.' *Hugh Lamb*
'Few writers of horror today approach the standards of Birkin.' *Ulster Star*

JOHN BLACKBURN

BURY HIM DARKLY

Introduction by Greg Gbur

'John Blackburn is today's master of horror.' *Times Literary Supplement*
'The best British novelist in his field.' *Penguin Encyclopedia of Horror & the Supernatural*

CHARLES BEAUMONT

THE HUNGER AND OTHER STORIES

Introduction by Bernice M. Murphy

'Belongs on any shelf of the best contemporary weird tales.' *Chicago Tribune*
'Charles Beaumont was a genius . . . and one hell of a storyteller.' *Dean R. Koontz*

STEPHEN GREGORY

THE CORMORANT

Introduction by the Author

'Gregory writes with the hypnotic power of Poe.' *Publishers Weekly*
'A first-class terror story that would have made Edgar Allan Poe proud.' *New York Times*

FOR A COMPLETE LIST OF TITLES, VISIT US AT VALANCOURTBOOKS.COM

Lightning Source UK Ltd.
Milton Keynes UK
UKHW040952041221
395073UK00002B/225